“I find it ha[illegible] n’t have had a [illegible].”

“Many proposal[illegible] young men hav[illegible] impulsively after our first meeting. Once they realized I possessed strong ambitions, as well as a porcelain complexion, their ardor quickly cooled.”

He shook his head. “Hard to believe, Miss Baldwin.”

“If God wants otherwise, I trust he’ll send the right man into my life, one who will see my heart.”

Stewart’s voice took on an unexpected fervor. “Perhaps he did. Are you sure you’d recognize him even if he stood in front of you?”

Anna took a hard look at the man in front of her. She’d warned him about flirting with her on the ship, but this was a more serious tone. Had his flirting concealed something deeper? “Mr. Hastings, are you suggesting you’re the man God has sent for me to marry?”

Books by Debbie Kaufman

Love Inspired Historical

The Doctor's Mission
Journey of Hope

DEBBIE KAUFMAN

As a child growing up in Kentucky, Debbie Kaufman never heeded her mother's advice to get her nose out of a book—except when it was time to have adventures outside the written pages. Adventures like running a rural airport, working as a small-town journalist, teaching school and traveling to China to establish an adoption program, just to name a few. Of course, all these things were accomplished with a book in one hand.

While still searching for her next big adventure, Debbie enjoys creating action-packed historical romances on the written page for others to experience. Debbie currently lives in Georgia and enjoys spending time with her husband, their four children, three grandchildren and two dogs. She supplements her reading habit with the occasional crochet project, baking and visits to her favorite coffee shop, where she is often found writing her next book.

Journey of Hope

DEBBIE KAUFMAN

HARLEQUIN® LOVE INSPIRED® HISTOR

Recycling programs for this product may not exist in your area.

ISBN-13: 978-0-373-82998-9

JOURNEY OF HOPE

For where your treasure is,
there will your heart be also.
—*Matthew* 6:21

To Caroline, who put me on this missionary-writing path in the first place. Darling girl, your strength and beauty of spirit always leave me in awe.

To Dave, Dan and Emily, whose presence in my life is a constant blessing.

To my darling husband, who makes it all possible with his unconditional love.

To the Ladies of the Lake: Susan, Sandy, Sia and others. Your support is invaluable, your friendship a true treasure.

Chapter One

Monrovia, Liberia
September 1920

When the annals of desperation were written, Stewart Hastings figured his name would have its own chapter. What was it going to take to acquire a competent guide into the Liberian jungle? Clearly his visit to this harbor-side tavern was another complete waste of time.

Six days to interview a promising list of a dozen names, and yet not a willing guide among them. The wages Stewart had offered the previous candidates should have been enough, but the joke was on him. Apparently he was the only man foolish enough to take big money for an expedition into cannibal territory.

He put his sterling on the wooden bar for the meal he'd just eaten, stepped outside and headed off to meet the final name on his list of potential guides. From his understanding of the street layout, his destination wasn't far from the boardinghouse where he had rented a room.

The cool ocean breeze off the promontory invigorated him, providing momentary relief from the overheated barroom, whose smells of whiskey, palm oil and humanity had left him with a throb behind his right temple. The relief quickly faded as he walked the moonlit turf-covered streets. Whoever said tropical countries didn't get cold had never been to Monrovia on a September night. After the daily rains let up, the temperature drop had him jamming his hands into his pockets and hunching his shoulders against the chill.

He couldn't have come all the way to Africa only to lose his best hope of securing his and his ailing mother's future. With little more than a day before his ship departed, the outlook was bleak. Exploring for minable geological deposits in a little-mapped jungle area was difficult enough, but add in cannibals and subtract a guide and the task became downright impossible.

His dead father's drunken rants echoed in his memory. Maybe the son of a dockworker would never be more than a scholarship boy trying to shake off the stench of the slums. With no family name to propel him to success, failure was always a strong possibility. This time it wasn't an option he could allow.

He had to persist. His mother's heart doctor was right. Even without the results from that newfangled electrocardiograph machine, the signs were all there, no matter how she tried to hide them. She reached for her digitalis more frequently, became short of breath working in her garden. Spending her days scrubbing the floors of the rich was a ticket to an early grave. She needed the rest and diet the doctor prescribed. Stewart had promised her a better life the day they buried his father. Now that she was ill, he couldn't fail in that promise.

He had to find a guide and meet his deadline. His hard-won degree from Harvard would mean nothing to his financial future if chaperoned by a reputation for failure.

He crossed Broad Street. Moonlight mocked the darkened light poles lining the avenue. Another confirmation of the government's financial crisis, one his employer hoped would drive down prices for the Putu Mountains area mining concession they planned to make an offer on.

Clouds rolled across the moon, forcing him to temper his stride or risk a misstep. A figure came toward him in the dark. His hand reflexively moved to the knife at his side and then relaxed as the figure grew closer. A lone Liberian woman with a sleeping baby strapped to her back, hurrying along the otherwise deserted streets. A tiny prick hit his heart as he watched the child's head gently bobbing with the mother's swaying pace until the pair was out of sight. He'd always wanted a large family, but without a wife, that would never happen. Even if he was ever deluded enough to believe in love again, what woman would have him once she'd seen the scars the Great War had left?

A piercing high-pitched scream rent the night and then abruptly cut off.

The woman with the baby? Wrong direction. Every instinct the military had honed in him rushed to the forefront.

There. The sound came from the cross street just ahead. Near his boardinghouse. He moved quickly, keeping to the deepest shadows as he assessed the situation.

Two native men with a woman struggling between them. She held a thick book, clutching the volume as if it was written in gold.

Robbery? Why won't the woman give it up? It's only a book. Hardly worth her life.

These two miscreants left him no choice but to intervene. Attacking a woman, no less. His frustration boiled to the top. The man he was to interview might not wait, but Stewart couldn't walk away.

He looked for any others hiding in the wings as he pulled the blade from its leather scabbard. Only the two. He banished fleeting thoughts of the consequences for pulling a knife on Liberian citizens. No one attacked a helpless woman in front of him without repercussion, not since the first time he was big enough to stand up to his father.

Stewart closed in without signaling his presence. She dropped her book and… *Oh, that had to hurt.* Bet they hadn't expected her to fight back. He stifled a laugh when one assailant grabbed his foot, hopping and howling. An umbrella tip made an effective weapon. Silently he applauded her while continuing to move forward. The little lady was a feisty one, he'd give her that.

The other native pressed something white up to her face. Moonlight blazed out as the clouds retreated. A handkerchief fluttered to the ground when the attacker loosed his grip on her face and each man grabbed an arm. The woman sagged and Stewart's anger rose. What had they done to her?

One of her attackers looked up before Stewart got close enough to disable him. The man froze, his eyes glued to the cold steel in Stewart's hand.

Stewart dropped his voice to a chilling softness. "Let the woman go, and I'll allow you to live." Whether they spoke Liberian English or a local dialect, his tone said the same thing in any language.

The two men exchanged a quick glance, not loosening their hold on the woman. *Not smart.* At six foot three, Stewart had them each by a good nine inches of height. More when you added in the six inches of steel in his hand.

The one on his right tensed. *Always a mistake to telegraph your intentions.* Stewart stepped in and punched him with his free hand. The man flew backward, releasing the woman's arm as he fell. The other attacker grabbed her closer and pulled his own knife. His cohort picked himself up off the ground.

These two weren't giving up. He'd hoped the sight of an armed man would have put them to flight. His options dwindled. He couldn't risk the woman's safety in a knife fight.

He watched for any signal of their next move. Both assailants stood wide-eyed, uncertainty growing in their eyes. Ha! Probably hadn't expected any interference.

A door squeaked to his left. The attacking duo glanced toward the sound and froze. Stewart risked a quick look. A tiny female figure walked out the front door of the boardinghouse where he'd rented a room. Momma Elliott shook her finger at the two, loudly threatening them in another language.

Stewart braced himself. *How to protect two women?*

But no attack came. Both men took one look at the wizened little black woman with her head wrapped in blue country cloth and a righteous fervor of scolding on her tongue and they promptly dropped their victim and ran.

Stewart lunged for the falling woman, grabbing an arm and hoisting her up. He barely managed to keep her head from hitting the ground where her book had fallen. Momma Elliott marched out after the fleeing men with a warrior's air about her. If he'd had a platoon of women that brave at the front, they'd have routed the Germans much sooner.

Once the miscreants were out of sight, she turned her attention to Stewart, schooling him with her impatient tone. "Well, what are you standing there for, Mr. Hastings? Are you going to bring her inside or not?" She picked up the book and umbrella, turned and walked back through the doorway.

With the unconscious woman in his arms, he followed the warrior grandma. The young woman he carried was a feather's worth of weight. Her hat bobbed precariously, a casualty of the confrontation. Her hair had escaped its confines. Silken strands brushed his left hand.

She smelled like cinnamon, but with every gentle exhale came a sickly sweet odor.

Chloroform?

His stomach roiled at the buried memory. The last time he'd inhaled that odor, his own life hung in the balance. Chloroform explained everything he'd seen: the white cloth and her loss of consciousness when clearly she was more a fighter than a fainter. Where would two natives in a primitive country get such a dangerous chemical? Chloroform was too elaborate for a simple robbery. Something else, then. Kidnapping?

He stepped into the entryway. His boots sounded thunderous on the polished floors. No Momma Elliott. From deep in the house he heard her sharp, urgent tones. A young native boy dressed as if he'd come from a Sunday meeting blurred right past him and out the door before Stewart could speak.

The parlor to his left appeared unoccupied, and it came equipped with the answer to the problem in his arms—a davenport.

He gently placed his slight burden on the rosy velvet-covered couch. He felt for the hat pin where he'd seen his mother reach a thousand times and removed the young woman's dangling straw creation. He found a small pillow for her comfort and then turned up the oil lamp on the table beside her. The light revealed the mahogany color of her errant hair and its cascading waves. Her pale skin seemed almost translucent, her dark lashes a smudge on the porcelain complexion. When he considered her small-boned frame, his anger at the men who'd attacked her stirred anew.

What if she became sick from the medicine? Chloroform had a deadly reputation even in trained hands. He'd relax once she woke up. Maybe Momma Elliott had gone to get smelling salts. That was what the hospital nurse had used when his former fiancée had fainted at the sight of his mustard-gas burns. Worked like a charm. Maybe too well. Julianne had sputtered, averted her eyes and left as soon as she'd recovered.

He'd received her engagement regrets by messenger later the same day. Somehow he'd failed her by returning less than the whole man she'd watched ship off to war. His shirts would hide the damage, but she couldn't face seeing those scars for the rest of her life.

He told himself he was well rid of her if that was the measure of her character. He'd let a pretty face and protestations that love could overcome their class differences override his better judgment. He'd let his guard down.

He wouldn't make that mistake again.

Stewart shrugged off the memory and moved closer to check the woman on the davenport. No evident sign of distress from the drug. A familiarity nagged at him.

Julianne. This woman with her stunning beauty reminded him of Julianne. Both women were small-boned and had a similar hair color. This one had higher cheekbones, a daintier nose, generous lips and, on closer observation, a small faded scar on her left cheek. Unlike his mustard burns, her little imperfection added appeal, keeping her from being too perfect. Still, if she and Julianne had ever met, Julianne would have taken to her bed, mirror in hand, and fretted for a week at being eclipsed.

"Come on," he said softly. "Wake up. Fret, complain, anything—just wake up." What color would those eyes be? If only she would open them.

Spry steps in the hall broke his study.

Momma Elliott entered the room with a basin of water and a rag in her hand. She eyed the unconscious woman and looked around as if expecting to see someone else in the room. She must have heard him talking. She knelt beside the sofa, dampened her cloth and folded it into a compress. "You did well, Mr. Hastings, to grab her up from those scoundrels. Gradoo has always been a disappointment to his mother. But to hurt a woman…a foreign woman… He'll be lucky to avoid a hanging if the magistrate's in the wrong mood."

"You recognized those ruffians?"

"One of them. Taught him in Sunday school as a young lad. Obviously didn't take his Bible to heart. Didn't recognize the other Kru man with him. But birds of a feather…"

"No wonder they ran, seeing as you're able to identify them. Is she going to be all right? I think they gave her chloroform."

Momma Elliott seemed to weigh his words. "Now, that is surely a strange thing. Where would those two get something like chloroform? Good thing this one is tougher than she appears. I nursed her through the malaria when she first arrived from Connecticut. Still, for caution's sake, I've asked for the doctor to come around."

He nodded toward the unconscious woman. "Does she live nearby?"

"No, Miss Baldwin is rooming with me for a few days.

She's attending a mission conference. They're installing the new bishop from the States. Only something big like that would bring her out of the jungle."

"She lives in the jungle?"

"Of course. Miss Baldwin is a missionary spreading the Gospel to one of the interior tribes."

Stewart couldn't hold back the proverbial jaw drop. He'd saved a missionary who lived in the jungle. His mother's voice and all her notions of God's plans flooded his mind. Easy to see why she believed such things. He could almost believe it now. Almost. But rational thought reasserted itself. Missionary or not, no one would send a single woman anywhere near where he needed to go. Every time he'd been specific about his destination, grown men paled and refused. Or they laughed outright.

"Something wrong, young man?"

"Sorry, ma'am. Just thinking." Might as well ask. "You don't happen to know what tribal area she, uh, missions in, do you?"

Her head cocked at the sound of footsteps on the porch. "You can ask her all about it once she wakes. Wait here. Keep an eye on her while I greet the doctor." She headed for the front door.

Now he was grasping desperation by the throat. Asking Miss Baldwin would be a waste of time. To a lone woman, working in the interior probably meant a little ways outside the city.

Oh, no. A waste of time… Time. He groaned and checked his watch. As soon as Momma Elliott came back with the doctor, he'd have to leave. He hoped the man he was to interview had waited.

A soft rustle caught his attention. He looked and got his answer. Brown. Lovely deep brown eyes opened and blinked. She blinked again and the unfocused look began to fade from her eyes. When she tried to sit up, his reverie broke. "Miss, uh, Baldwin. Please don't move. Just lay still. Momma Elliott will be right back."

Her focus flitted around, taking in her surroundings before stopping to look at his face. For one short moment the room lost all its air as he fell into the depths of her serene gaze. How could she wake so calm after what she'd just been through?

She whispered.

He tilted his head downward. "I'm sorry. I couldn't hear you."

She whispered again.

He shook his head and apologized, bending to catch her words. "Do you need something?"

Her soft voice quavered. "Nothing. You…you asked…"

"Asked?"

She tried again. "You…asked…where."

"Where? Oh. You heard me talking to Momma Elliott."

She nodded and whispered again. "Putu. Near the Putu Mountains. I work with the Pahn."

His limbs turned to marble. The answer to his dilemma had been dumped literally into his arms. Or had it? Unease snaked its way into his thoughts just as Momma Elliott and a redheaded woman with a medical bag, waddling with the weight of the child she carried in her rounded belly, bustled into the room. A woman doctor? And her patient another woman who couldn't protect herself in the relative safety of the city, yet lived among cannibals? What kind of country was this?

He gave a nod to Momma Elliott and headed for the front door. Even if he missed his meeting, he didn't regret his actions. Not when a woman had been in danger. But he sincerely hoped the guide wasn't too impatient and he would agree to the job. Otherwise Stewart would be trying to talk the woman he'd saved into saving him. Not good since the last time he'd placed his future in the hands of a beautiful woman, it disappeared in a cloud of mustard gas.

Anna Baldwin awakened to bright morning sunshine streaming in through her bedroom window, Dr. Mary Mayweather attending at her side and two sure conclusions about her life: God was looking out for her, as evidenced by last night's providential rescue, and He wouldn't have called her to the mission field without providing for her. True, last night was a trial of some magnitude. Being attacked, chloroformed and almost kidnapped made the news she'd received at the conference pale in comparison. At least she was still alive to serve another day, something she had failed to thank her blue-eyed rescuer for making possible.

Now she had to find a way to stay beyond the short weeks her limited funds left her. But first she had to reason with Dr. Mary. The good doctor wanted Anna to lounge in bed. Clearly a woman so heavy with child should be following her own orders. Anna rebuked herself for such an uncharitable thought about her dear friend. She was grateful that missionaries like Dr. Mary and her pastor husband had taken her under their tutelage when she'd first arrived. Still, they'd trusted her to God's care when they'd helped establish her post with the Pahn, so being overprotective now about a random attack on city streets seemed a contradiction in that trust.

No, she needed to be out of bed so she could begin the process of looking for a new source of funding. This foggy-brained feeling from the drug would pass.

Dr. Mary sat on the edge of Anna's bed. "Anna, did

you hear me? Three days' rest, minimum. Chloroform can be hard on the heart."

"Three days? My ship leaves for Garraway tomorrow morning, Dr. Mary. And I can't count on the Elder-Dempster Company refunding my fare." Anna stifled a rising panic. "Even if they change my ticket, I have no money for the additional change fees."

"Not to worry. I'll ask my William to talk to them. Most steamship lines bend their rules to accommodate God's work. Missionaries are lucrative business for them. If there is a fee, I'm sure we can appeal to the bishop for discretionary funds."

Hot tears built a pool behind Anna's eyes. She fought them back and spoke once she trusted her voice. "Is it really all about money? Even here as a missionary? No, an ex-missionary. I'm losing my posting over money. The bishop has already drawn on his discretionary funds to keep me here a little longer while I seek a new source of support."

Dr. Mary tilted her head. "Well, that explains a lot. When you left the mission conference in such a hurry last night, I feared something was wrong. What happened to the support money your church promised?"

"They fell on hard times. It's a small congregation, but they scraped and saved to help me get here. Their monthly pledge after my parents blocked all access to the trust my grandmother left me was a godsend." Anna picked at a stray thread on her bedcovers. "Originally, I planned to fund my support myself. The trust included a monthly allowance from the interest. As long as I was frugal, that money would have been most of what I needed to stay here."

"You never told me your parents so actively opposed you."

Anna shuddered. "Because it does no good to dwell on their past actions. Having a missionary daughter went against all their social ambitions. They wanted me to marry someone handpicked for his social and financial standing. Blocking my trust was only one of the ways they dealt with my refusal. My only consolation is that the entire trust comes under my control once I marry or turn thirty-five, whichever comes first."

"But eight years is a long time to wait when you're in need now. Maybe like my father did, they'll come around eventually. If you do end up having to return home, surely the time apart will have softened their hearts."

Anna shuddered, remembering. "You don't know my parents." She reached out and gripped Dr. Mary's arm. "And other than my facility with languages, I have no useful skills for employment. Returning home is one problem, but I have to get back to the Pahn. How can I live with myself if I can't get the tuition to send Taba to the boarding school at Newaka? I promised him. You know what will happen to a twelve-year-old convert if I can't get him out of the clutches of the devilmen. Once they get him into the sequestered Poro school..."

Dr. Mary paled. "He won't be coming back out."

Anna looked at Dr. Mary, waiting for some answer. After a moment Dr. Mary spoke in a low, serious tone. "I can't tell you what God is going to do in your life or Taba's right now. I can only remind you of how seconds before the Pahn chief was about to succeed in his plan to kill me, God proved He does work all things to the good. Whatever happens, don't forget that fact. William and I are living testaments to God's sovereignty in all things."

Anna was humbled remembering the story of how Dr. Mary and her husband, Pastor William Mayweather, had narrowly avoided death at the hands of the cannibal tribe. "I believe, but I counted on Bishop Michaels to advance Taba's tuition money. Before the board's overhaul of financial policies, my request would have been no problem. Bishop Michaels is clearly sympathetic, but the new rules leave no room for any debt. He's done what he can so I can return to the village temporarily and try to secure Taba's safety."

"Anna, does Taba's family hold any status or wealth in the village?"

"No, which is why I was counting on my funds to help with tuition. I already made arrangements with Karl and Hannah Jansen when I passed through Newaka. They promised to keep him for two years if I can come up with the money for one."

Dr. Mary absently rubbed her swollen belly. "The Jansens would be ideal, but even they can only stretch their sterling so far. Why not send Taba to Nynabo with us? We can manage."

"You're too close. Nana Mala proved that when he stormed your compound with armed warriors. The devilmen have enough reach that Taba wouldn't be safe if he stayed with you."

"Point taken. What about asking Bishop Michaels to let you use your return-ticket funds while you seek other means of support?"

Anna shook her head and the room spun. "No. You know the rules—no service under the Mission Board's policies unless your return fare is banked against the day you leave the mission field."

Dr. Mary stood. "Continue to pray, Anna. God has a plan for this boy's life and yours. Sometimes God provides in ways we don't expect. Look at last night. God provided a rescuer when you needed one." She grinned at Anna. "A tall, strong one at that."

Anna felt the heat rise in her cheeks. "Dr. Mary!"

"What? I still have high hopes for you to find a fellow laborer in the mission field."

"And you think you'll help me find one by trying to play matchmaker with a total stranger? You don't give up, do you? Not everyone can find a man like your William. Finding a husband isn't a priority for me, and I don't think our Heavenly Father would send me a mate by way of a robbery attempt." She snorted. "Sounds like one of my father's poorly thought-out schemes. Never mind the consequences to me, because the end of things always justified the cost, especially since he wasn't the one paying it."

Dr. Mary took her medical bag from the nightstand. "I guess it is a little far-fetched. God often requires sacrifice of us, but He has our best interests at heart. Pray and ask what He would have you do. Three days of bed rest should give you ample time to come to a conclusion."

With no extra funds, missing the ship would curtail most of Anna's options. She had to be on the SS *Boma* when it left in the morning. She hadn't been this desperate since she'd escaped to the ship that carried her to Liberia, thwarting her parents' plans to marry her off to the odious Dr. Reginald Hightower. Even without God's call to the mission field, she couldn't have married a man who'd made it clear that her "excess" of religion was unacceptable in his social circles.

God had provided a means for her then, so she had to believe that He would supply the means for Taba's safety now. She respected Dr. Mary, but she would be on that ship.

As if she'd read her thoughts, Dr. Mary added, "Anna, I see that look. I'll go to the bishop if necessary. Don't you even think about sailing tomorrow. Missionaries who live long enough to serve past their first bout of malaria are too scarce here. He may have just arrived in Liberia, but even the bishop knows not to take chances with your health."

Anna weighed her options. The bishop could prevent her from ever returning to the Pahn if he so chose. She'd have to get him on her side before staging a rebellion against Dr. Mary's orders. "Fine, I'll stay abed."

"Three days, Anna."

Dr. Mary knew her too well. Anna couldn't promise that so she changed the subject. "You know, being a doctor doesn't make you right about everything. Take matchmaking, for example. I still can't believe you'd even suggest that being rescued by a blue-eyed, blond, Viking-like warrior type is a basis for an enduring, godly marriage."

Dr. Mary laughed. "Blue eyes, huh? So you did notice him before he left."

Anna's cheeks heated to an alarming degree. A thundering rap on the bedroom door saved her from any reply.

Dr. Mary opened the door. "Just a moment, Bishop."

Anna reached for the wrapper at the foot of her bed. Dr. Mary admitted a concerned-looking Bishop Michaels, the fringe of white hair on his head standing straight out all around like a demented halo.

Anna fanned her cheeks and forced her facial muscles into a pleasant smile. The bishop. If she couldn't have his blessing to get on the ship tomorrow, how was she going to tell him she now needed more money just to return to an unfunded posting? This might be the proverbial last straw. She was at a loss as to how to spin it into gold.

Dr. Mary said, "Anna, I'll send Momma Elliott right up with some nice broth. Send word if you need me again. Bishop, I'll see you at meeting tonight." She left the door open.

The bishop stood, hat in hand, sincerity to the forefront. "My dear Miss Baldwin. I have been ever so worried about you and not ceased to pray since I heard the terrible news. We all have. Are you all right? Have they caught your attackers?"

"No, the magistrates have no word about the two men. They left an hour ago with promises to keep looking. But I'm fine, Bishop. Only frustrated to be idle when so little time remains to me in Liberia."

The bishop's cheery countenance brightened further. "And yet, even in this trying situation, God has made a way. I have found the answer to all your problems, and he's waiting in the hallway." He stepped outside the room.

Anna's nerves sounded an alarm. The answer to all her problems? Her father's favorite phrase, the one that always preceded disaster in her life, now straight from the lips of Bishop Michaels. She shuddered and fought against the memories. *No, this is not my father, but my spiritual authority. The bishop, a man who steeps his life in prayer and seeks God's Will. Wait, did the bishop say "he"?*

Two decidedly male voices in the hall, one the bishop's. The sound of the other scratched at her memory. Finally the bishop walked back in, followed by a familiar-looking man, cap in hand, who ducked his blond head to step through the doorway. His crisp, white, high-collared shirt, jodhpurs and polished boots presented a striking picture. When his chin lifted as he cleared the doorway, she caught sight of his squared-off jaw and a patrician nose that didn't quite follow its original lines. She couldn't help but smile at the sight of him. "Oh, it's you! I never got the chance to thank you last night. You saved me from those men. Thank you."

He grinned and humor sparked in his memorable blue eyes. "You were doing a pretty good job of fighting them off when I showed up. I think you'd have had them if it weren't for the chloroform." Her rescuer looked expectantly at the bishop standing next to him.

"Miss Anna Baldwin," the bishop said, "let me formally introduce you to Mr. Stewart Hastings, a mining engineer with the American Mining Corporation. He and I just finished a long talk in the parlor. I believe it was God's providence Mr. Hastings came along when he did. Had he not come to Monrovia on his current assignment…well, I shudder to think what would have happened to you last night."

Her rescuer brushed off the compliment. "You give me too much credit, sir. Momma Elliott actually scared the miscreants off. I just held them at bay till she came on the scene."

Was that a wink?

The bishop shook his head. "You're too modest, sir." He turned to address Anna. "Now that we're all acquainted, we can get on with the plan." The bishop rocked onto the balls of his feet, eager to impart his idea.

Anna asked. "The plan?"

"Yes, my dear. I found a way to solve all our problems. Rather, I should say God has provided."

There was that phrase again. Tacking on that it was God's provision still left her uneasy. And Mr. Hastings studiously looking everywhere but at her?

The bishop's eyes twinkled. "I haven't told Mr. Hastings, but while hearing his tale, the solution for both of you became obvious. It's clear you two are a match made in Heaven."

Anna almost came out of her sickbed. Was everyone in creation trying to marry her off?

Shock rendered Stewart mute. Had the kindly bishop been out in the brutal Liberian sun too long? Except it was only midmorning. By the look on Anna's face, she harbored similar questions.

Bishop Michaels prattled on. "Mr. Hastings saved you, Miss Baldwin, and now you can save each other."

Stewart ground his teeth to hold back a rebuttal. Was this some evangelical approach to win his soul? If so, the bishop had another think coming. God already had ample opportunity to show up in the trenches of the Great War.

Stewart found his voice. "Sir, even if I were a praying man, which I'm not, I'm not sure I would understand the course of this conversation."

The bishop gave him a patient look. "Didn't you just explain to me in the parlor how you exhausted your other possibilities and were in need of a guide to the interior while you explore for mineral deposits? In the Pahn territory and surrounding area? I believe you named a generous figure for the service you need."

"I did, but..."

The bishop waved his hand. "Miss Baldwin here is in immediate need of an income and you are in need of a guide. Ergo, you two are a match made in Heaven."

Stewart caught sight of Anna's eyes widening in shock and disbelief. They must be mirroring his own. He hadn't taken Bishop Michaels for an escapee from Bedlam when they'd first met. A match made in Heaven? "Bishop Michaels, Miss Baldwin told me last night that she works with the Pahn. But, with no offense intended to her, I need a guide, not a wife."

The choking sounds coming from Miss Baldwin were

alarming. Both men looked at her with concern. The bishop asked her, "Are you all right, my dear? Do you need water?"

She shook her head violently and managed to croak a response. "Not even to save my place here in Africa would I—"

The bishop broke in. "No, no. You both mistake me." He turned back to Stewart. "I'm proposing a business agreement, one that will effectively save Miss Baldwin from having to make an untimely return home to Connecticut from the mission field.

"With the budget you mentioned, she can take you to the village and secure a relationship for you with the chief. Then she can afford to stay among the Pahn people another three months while she searches for longer-term funding. Along with the government permission your company already obtained for exploration, you, in turn, will have one of the only outsiders acceptable to the chief to vouch for you and your mining enterprise. God has provided for your needs, too."

Anna protested, "Bishop, with all respect, Nana Mala is one of the most warlike and unpredictable chiefs in the interior. Government permission will only provoke him. We might lose any further chance to win souls in this village over mixing man's business with God's, especially since Mr. Hastings has already proclaimed himself an unbeliever. I cannot see… Oh, Mr. Hastings, I meant no slight."

"None taken." Being categorized as an unbeliever might be awkward in her view, but not in his. At least she had the sense to see how unworkable this plan really was, even if her reasons were different from his. He'd thought he was coming to discuss a guide, not hire Miss Baldwin.

The bishop's jovial tone sobered. "Sometimes we need others, my dear, to see what's best for us. I believe this situation will serve the Gospel by keeping one of my most fervent missionaries in a tribe that, if reached for Christ, could turn the tide in many surrounding villages. I'm sure you can manage the distinction between business needs and the Gospel." He gave a fatherly smile. "Unless, of course, you have another financial solution, one God revealed since our conversation last night?"

She didn't say anything at first, but Stewart could see the gears of thought turning. She nodded.

Was she really considering this? Was it money that swayed her? As for the bishop, had he lost his mind? But manners dictated Stewart not declare the sentiment aloud. "Bishop Michaels, I cannot see how your suggestion could possibly work. Look at her." Stewart pointed. "She's clearly incapacitated. I only wanted information on finding a guide. The last thing I need is a *female* missionary slowing me down on the trail."

Anna glared. For a missionary she sure could give a look that would peel paint off a battleship.

Stewart ignored her and continued, "Besides, she's an unmarried woman. Even if I had no objection, you can't tell me you missionaries would send the two of us into the jungle alone."

The bishop was not dissuaded. "Of course not. She'll need someone to travel with her on board ship for her recovery and the proprieties of ship life. I met the perfect candidate last night at a late supper hosted in my honor. She and her husband are returning to their coffee plantation outside of Harper. Then, once in the jungle, you'll be surrounded by your caravan. Last night's incident notwithstanding, most Liberian men are quite protective of missionary women, as those who have served alone have found in the past. I think you'll see that the caravan itself is more than sufficient as a chaperone."

Every obstacle Stewart could think to raise was steamrollered flat by the bishop's growing enthusiasm. He continued unhampered, "Besides, Mr. Hastings, even I know that being guided into the area isn't enough. Not if you want to come back safely. You need Miss Baldwin."

If he wanted to come back safely? He'd survived the Germans. Miss Baldwin had barely survived Monrovia. How could the bishop even suggest…?

The bishop must have taken Stewart's silent ruminations for acceptance. "Now, if you'll excuse me, I need to secure this companion for Miss Baldwin in the little time left before you two depart. Sir, if you will deposit half the funds with the Mission Board's secretary, then you can make the rest of your arrangements directly with Miss Baldwin for the balance upon completion."

For such a well-rounded man, the bishop was quick on his feet. Stewart stared at the now-empty doorway. What had just happened? He'd been waltzed right into another situation where a beautiful woman would be making arrangements for his life. He had a deadline; dragging a woman along through the jungle would only slow him down. No, if he was to fail, he'd rather it be on his own terms and not the result of a woman's whims, as before, or her innate physical frailties.

"I'm sorry, Miss Baldwin, but despite what the bishop thinks, there is no way this arrangement will work. Nothing personal, but I simply wanted the name of a guide and felt sure you could steer me to one, since you must use one yourself. I'm in haste and can't possibly consider taking the extra time that bringing a woman along would entail, no matter how valuable the bishop believes your contribution would be. If you could see fit to give me the name of someone willing to go there, I will send a letter of explanation to the bishop later today and be on my way."

Her answer was delayed by the arrival of Momma Elliott with the promised bowl of broth. She placed it at the bedside and went to sit in a corner rocker. "Don't mind me. I'll just wait over here so the two of you can finish your conversation."

Anna smiled at Momma Elliott, and then her voice, both gentle and authoritative, insisted, "Mr. Hastings, I'm afraid you do not understand the gravity of the situation, especially where the chief's reaction to you being in his territory is concerned. The danger is greater than you realize."

The sincerity of her tone carried through. She believed him to be in danger.

"I served in the trenches of the Great War. I feel confident I can handle the danger of jungle travel. The government has offered the territory's mineral rights for sale. Certainly we wish to have good local relations, but ultimately the chief has no authority over these plans." He softened his tone. "I do not wish to disappoint you, Miss Baldwin. I understand how much you need the money, so if you could just direct me to one of the guides you missionaries use, I'd be willing to pay you for the information." He hated the distress shadowing those lovely brown eyes, but there was nothing else he could do for her.

Her pale cheeks flushed at the implication. Delicate hands punctuated her frustration as she spoke. "Yes, I need the money, but that's not why I cannot let you go in there without me. Since the recent attempts of government troops to implement the infamous Hut Tax, Nana Mala views all outsiders with suspicion of working on the government's behalf. He will not welcome you, even if you could find another guide. Which, by the way, you won't."

He got it. She wasn't sharing her guides. "I appreciate the warning." He turned to follow the bishop's path out the door. Now what? He had no one else to interview. Should he board the ship and hope to find one farther down the coast? Every step toward the doorway felt like one step closer to failure, and failure, where his mother's future was concerned, wasn't an option.

Her soft voice stopped him. "Apparently my warning wasn't strong enough. For your own sake…"

"Dear lady, I don't wish my continued refusal of your services to humiliate you. I am sorry for your situation. I'm also well acquainted with desperation born of financial need. I would help you if I could. However, if you aren't willing to share the names of your resources, I shall simply have to proceed without them. My deadline demands it. But I'm not one to hold a grudge, so I sincerely hope we can both conduct a civil relationship together once you reach the village after me."

She expelled a deep breath. "Of course, Mr. Hastings. In fact, I'm quite certain civility will not be an issue between us."

"Good." He tipped his head and smiled at her agreement. "Then I'll see you in the village when you arrive." He nodded to Momma Elliott, who shook her head with ill-concealed amusement.

He didn't clear the door frame before Anna's words froze his limbs in place. "Probably not, Mr. Hastings.

Should you arrive without me to intervene with the chief on your behalf, it's more than likely that you will be killed on thc spot."

Chapter Two

Stewart leaned against the forward-deck rail and watched as Miss Baldwin's companion, Mrs. Dowdy, helped her into the deck chair and tucked the blankets around her. Two days out to sea and her color was vastly improved. The multihued scarf around her head, protecting against the ship's headwind, added appeal to that exotic face.

Not that he was interested. Just a little haunted by the first time he'd gazed into her eyes. Chalk that up to concern for her well-being after saving her. Rescuing her had engendered a protective feeling. He'd shake it off.

Maybe her personal watchdog would leave Anna's side as she'd done yesterday and give them a chance to talk. After hearing Anna out about the chief's murderous proclivities, and realizing exactly why he needed her specifically, preparations to make the next morning's sailing had been his entire focus. He hadn't counted on Anna's chaperone circumventing most of his attempts at conversation since they'd boarded. He never should have told Mrs. Dowdy that he wasn't a churchgoing man when she'd asked, but lying was his father's style, not his. The price of his honesty included glacial stares and less-than-subtle hints that Mrs. Dowdy found him unworthy to associate with Anna.

Fortunately, Mrs. Dowdy wouldn't be with them in the jungle. For now he'd have to watch for his moment. A lot of details needed to be worked out, and he had questions about the area and the people. He'd known there were risks. The Pahn tribe had a past reputation as cannibals, but he'd expected that government backing would protect him, or even that the stories had been exaggerated. Obviously there was a lot American Mining hadn't known when they'd given him this assignment. He couldn't afford any more surprises.

And there was his opening. Ten minutes after seeing her charge settled, she wandered off to one of the covered decks to play a couple rubbers of bridge. Finally his only firsthand source of information was alone, looking bright-eyed and a little bored.

He headed for the empty chair beside her. Besides information gathering, he hoped to find a way to make his expectations clear. He needed her to facilitate his explorations with the tribes along the way and vouch for him with the Pahn chief. But she must leave the decision making to him, her employer. That much had to be clear first. The last time he'd experienced confusion in the chain of command, men had died in the trenches beside him.

Stewart swerved around a group of passengers starting up a jump-rope game and crossed over to the starboard seating area. Anna glanced up at his approach and then cut her eyes back to the book in her lap. A hint she didn't feel like socializing? Or just shyness? The irony of hiring a woman he knew so little about to protect him from a cannibal's wrath struck him hard.

"May we speak, Miss Baldwin?"

She gestured to the adjacent deck chair. "Certainly. Please, have a seat."

He settled himself in and stretched his long legs out in front, crossing his ankles. "How are you feeling today?"

A little sparkle lit those soft brown eyes. "Better than Mrs. Dowdy would have me believe. I'm afraid Dr. Mayweather's permission for me to travel came with instructions my companion has interpreted very strictly."

"In my experience, you can never be too careful with chloroform." He waved off a steward bringing him a blanket.

"Yes, but who would have thought I would encounter chloroform-wielding bandits in Monrovia? Seems I'm safer in the jungle than on the capital's streets."

"I, too, find that odd. I trust the magistrates managed to apprehend the two men and get to the bottom of it?"

She shook her head. "No, but they believe I was targeted because I was thought to be a wealthy American. If they'd known I was a missionary, they probably would have picked a different victim. The magistrate searched, but Gradoo and his cohort were nowhere to be found. The officers that came around seemed happy to hear I was leaving. Either they feared word of what happened getting out, or they believed my departure solved their problem."

"Until the next woman is their victim."

"Exactly my concern."

Perfect opening. He had to get this religious difference out of the way so business could proceed. "I can do nothing for that concern, but perhaps I could alleviate one of your others."

Curiosity sparked her gaze as she inclined herself in his direction. "And what concern would that be?"

His thoughts scattered in response to her intense

focus. He snapped them back to attention, but his plan for a casual conversation opener, making light of the differences in their beliefs, suddenly seemed inappropriate.

He tried a different tack. "Back at Momma Elliott's you mentioned to the bishop your concern that my presence as both an unbeliever and someone with business interests might compromise your objectives with the Gospel. I want to reassure you that I have no intention of compromising your work there. I was raised by a churchgoing mother and fully understand what most religious folks consider acceptable behavior. I will be a model of missionary decorum, just without the preaching."

She put one hand to her heart. "Thank you, Mr. Hastings. Just knowing that you understand the importance puts my concern to rest. I've worked hard to gain the trust of the chief and the parents who have entrusted their children to my teaching. If anything were to jeopardize that…"

"You teach?"

A soft smile played on her lips. "Yes. There are sixteen children in my school, and they are all such darlings. I miss them terribly."

His expression must have given away his surprise.

She looked at him, merriment lighting up her face. "What did you think? Let me guess. You thought I walked around with my Bible open all day long praying and preaching."

"Ah, you got me. I did think something like that. Bet you get that a lot."

She reached over and her delicate hand patted his arm. "Don't worry. Most people have no notion what a missionary's life is actually like."

The easy familiarity threw him, but he wished she hadn't tucked her hands back under her blanket so quickly. "I would be one of them. But I did wonder about the danger for a lone woman, though. How does your family feel about your teaching in the wilds of the jungle?"

She stiffened. "My family has no idea what I do here. We don't communicate."

She'd chosen to bring her beliefs halfway around the world, but not to communicate with her own family? Proof, besides learning she was a teacher, he really didn't know who he'd hired.

She studied his face. "I see by the shock and disapproval on your face that my answer is not what you expected. Tell me, Mr. Hastings, do you come from a close family?"

He cleared his throat to buy time as he contemplated how to answer. "I meant no disrespect. Your answer surprised me. I maintain a close relationship with my mother. My father is a different story. He died in an accident on the wharf where he worked when I was seventeen."

"I'm so sorry. Must have been hard losing him at such an age."

A hollow pit opened up in his stomach at her gentle condolence, and the truth poured out with no further provocation. "The difficult part was before his death. My father's life revolved around the bottle. When he was drunk, he was violent. He had been drinking the day of the accident." He listened to himself with amazement. He never talked about his past. It was those eyes and their long, sooty lashes drawing him in with every glance.

She adjusted her blanket and folded her hands together on top. "I am sorry for your loss. But perhaps you understand, then, that there are reasons family members might not remain close."

"Yes, I can. I can also appreciate that you must be quite a force in the classroom, Miss Baldwin. You schooled me right out of disapproval and led me to a better conclusion effortlessly." He omitted the part of how she'd also managed to avoid talking about herself.

The color in her cheeks heightened at the compliment. "Seeing the truth for ourselves is always more effective, don't you think? We all need a reminder at times that there is usually more to the story than first meets the eye."

He leaned forward in the deck chair, resolved to return to his original business. "Indeed. I've found that to be true with this job. A former commander taught me never to go into a situation without a good reconnaissance, and yet I now see I've walked into this one blindfolded by a very incomplete story. Since my stateside sources were so poorly informed, I not only wish to discuss our travel plans, but the people and their customs. Consider me your willing pupil."

She tucked in windblown tresses and smiled broadly. "I would be happy to discuss my plans and local customs, but I doubt I'll be much help with your mining concerns. I know nothing about prospecting for gold or other minerals. Perhaps I can question the villagers to help you locate what you seek."

"That would be useful. But before we go much further, I must clarify whose plans we're following. You said your plans."

Her eyes widened. "I trust I didn't misspeak?"

"No, but I while I appreciate the experience you bring to this job, I want to clarify that all final decisions about this journey must run through me."

Confusion settled over her features. "Mr. Hastings,

are you saying you hired me to be your guide, but you don't trust my judgment?"

Sounded harsh when he heard it out loud. Maybe he should have soft-pedaled this a little more. "I'm sure you understand the jungle from a missionary point of view, Miss Baldwin. But I have been tasked with prospecting a large territory in a short amount of time. If I meet my assigned deadline, the bonus is significant. I have important plans for that money, plans I cannot risk. So I hope you can understand why I prefer not to leave a business success or failure in the hands of a…uh…a female missionary."

Rather than taking offense, she laughed aloud, a melodious sound whose absence once she stopped made the ship seem empty.

"I take it I've said something quite humorous, Miss Baldwin. Enlighten me so I can do it again. Laughter agrees with you."

Her smile lingered when she said, "You may need less instruction in local customs than I thought. You will fit in easily with the social structure here in Liberia. Only a Liberian man would not have tried to be so polite about not having a woman in charge."

She waved off his protest. "For your first lesson, you should understand that there are rarely women in leadership. The Pahn, like most of the peoples here, are a male-dominated society with strict expectations of the roles each gender can play."

"Sounds like they'll respond better to a man leading then."

She nodded and smiled.

Was she really this agreeable? Was she humoring him? "How do the local people handle you as a single woman, then?"

"Most are initially curious, but later decide that the white bush is different from their world."

"The white bush?"

"Their term for our world. Their world is the bush. Of course, the reality of both worlds is that women rarely own much power in either."

He snorted. She hadn't seen how quickly his future father-in-law had responded to Julianne's demands to sever business ties with him. "Maybe not in the eyes of the law, but you have to admit women still wield a lot of power in men's lives."

"Not here. In Liberia, a woman can be purchased with a bridal price, pawned later if her husband is in financial difficulties and even loaned to visiting male guests as a substitute wife."

Chastened, he said, "I had no idea. Sounds barbaric, almost slavelike."

"Exactly. But this is their culture, not ours."

"I suppose, as a missionary, you hope to change those practices?"

Surprisingly, she shook her head. Both hands now animated her conversation. "While many missionaries in this modern age still seek to change a people's customs, things like how they dress, their social structures, I prefer to focus on bringing God's Word and allow Him to make the changes He sees fit. Immodest dress may make me uncomfortable, but God did not call me to convert someone's wardrobe, only their hearts."

It was his turn to laugh aloud. "You, Miss Baldwin, are an enlightened woman. If not for this God business, I think I would find you quite the enjoyable dinner companion."

The corners of her lips twitched upward. "Let me have a turn at being direct, Mr. Hastings. I will serve many roles on the trail, some of which may not endear me to you as a dinner companion or otherwise. While I have no problem with your general authority and running most decisions through you, I must point out my experience here is not to be taken lightly and there will be times I have to act without your input. I apologize beforehand if that upsets you." She smiled fully, as if to soften the blow.

A sour note gripped his stomach at the memory of a similar attitude, one he'd seen throughout his engagement. If Anna was anything like Julianne, this missionary woman would start small and before he knew it, take over. Precisely one of the reasons he hadn't wanted a woman in this role. They knew all the polite maneuverings to get their way. She thought she'd make critical decisions on this trip?

Not on his nickel, she wouldn't.

But there'd be time enough on the trail to clear up who was in charge. With no other guide and his budgeted funds already contracted through the bishop, Stewart had no choice but to make this relationship work. His mother's future depended on it.

Stewart's face clouded over with myriad emotions, none of them terribly happy and all of them giving Anna concern. He was her only hope for the additional time she needed to try to obtain tuition money for Taba. She had to make this work. If Stewart couldn't handle the idea that her in-country experience might occasionally trump his plan to be in charge, there would be a lot of uncomfortable days on the trail. The jungle's dangers wouldn't wait on constant consultation. He needed to understand the impracticality of running every decision through him. A few days on the trail might accomplish what this conversation couldn't.

Anna caught rapid movement in her side vision. Mrs. Dowdy was making a beeline toward Stewart. "Don't look now, Mr. Hastings, but my companion must not have been able to come up with a foursome for bridge. I think she means to evict you from her chair."

"We're hardly finished conversing. I still have questions for you about what we'll encounter along the way."

Anna laughed. "You're in luck for the moment—looks like she got waylaid by her husband. Perhaps we could talk later in the Grand Saloon after the rains start."

"I don't suppose there is something I could do to better her opinion of me aside from a sudden profession of faith? Mrs. Dowdy's protection of you seems to have leaped beyond the normal bounds and straight into battle mode where I'm concerned."

Anna shook her head. "I'm sorry. I'd hoped you hadn't noticed. Once you told her you weren't a churchgoing man, she decided you'd be a corrupting influence for a missionary."

Piercing blue eyes plumbed her depths. "Do you think that, Miss Baldwin?"

"No, Mr. Hastings. My faith has not so poor a foundation that another's unbelief might sway me to discard what I hold so dear and true. If Mrs. Dowdy knew what it took for me to come to Liberia in the first place, she might not be so concerned." Anna reached out and patted his arm again. "I'll have a talk with her. She means well."

Anna broke off her gaze just as Mrs. Dowdy left her husband and covered the last of the distance between them. Her disapproval arrived before she did.

Stewart vacated the chair, tipped his hat and took his leave. Anna kept her laughter in check. Mrs. Dowdy was indeed in battle mode. But how funny to see a short, dumpling-shaped woman order a towering grown man around without a single word. Maybe Anna should take lessons from her to employ on the journey.

Mrs. Dowdy took the deck blanket the steward hurriedly provided and placed an order for hot tea for both of them. "I don't know what the bishop was thinking. Sending off a young woman with some gold miner into the interior."

"Mining engineer, not gold miner."

"Humph. Whatever he is, nothing good will come of it. Mark my words."

Anna's reply, that the money for her service would save a child's life and keep Anna spreading the Gospel, died on her lips as the woman launched into another tirade, this time about her husband's shortcomings. Experience thus far told Anna she need only nod. She'd have to find a later moment to talk with Mrs. Dowdy about Stewart. Anna's eyelids grew heavy when there was no sign of the wifely complaints winding down. She didn't want to be rude, but the hot tea had made her sleepy. Maybe the chloroform had affected her more than she'd realized. Would Mrs. Dowdy notice if she dozed?

A raucous shout woke Anna and she looked around, alarm spreading through her. Mrs. Dowdy was nowhere in sight, but Anna located the source of the noise.

A crowd on the port side was cheering Stewart on. He was jumping rope.

An apple-cheeked matron Anna recognized from last night's activities in the Grand Saloon and the woman's twenty-year-old daughter were the turners. They stood red-faced and determined, a rope end in each gloved hand, swinging the double-Dutch pattern. The crowd chanted the count as the numbers climbed. Anna rose from her deck chair and walked over to get a closer look, her legs a little wobbly at first.

She edged to the side of a dozen or so watchers. A gentleman next to her, Wilson, an exporter who'd been seated across from her at dinner, leaned toward her and said, "Really something, isn't it? He's top-drawer to take the girl's dare. He just beat her challenge."

Stewart caught sight of her and grinned. He took the Ascot cap clenched in his hands and tossed it right at her to hold, all without missing the rhythm of the ropes. Blond waves of hair went up and down, landing just below his eyebrows before each jump. His white Arrow shirt whipped back in the sea breeze, revealing a muscular composition. The easy grin he now directed at the obviously besotted younger rope-turner marked him as a heartbreaker.

Dr. Mary was right. He cut quite the handsome figure. But she was wrong to think there was any potential in Anna's rescuer being a future husband and help in the mission field. Not only wasn't he a believer, but she'd escaped a controlling father already.

Despite an effortless appearance, Stewart's face took on a sheen as he progressed. At a count of two hundred and fifty, he jumped out and bowed, to the obvious dismay of his audience.

He walked toward Anna and held out a hand for his cap. Wilson grabbed his hand first and shook hard. "I say, you won't mind if I try to best your score, will you?" Breathless, Stewart nodded his head and Wilson declared himself the next competitor. Other men abandoned their deck games and lined up to "beat the record."

Stewart settled his cap on his head. "I guess I started something. They're determined to best me. Say, would you like a turn? I can shoulder all those men aside if you so desire. Think of it as an apology for deserting you earlier in such a cowardly fashion when your companion arrived on the scene."

"No apology needed, thank you. You know what they say about discretion and valor. And I'll skip the rope-jumping for now."

"Ah, come on. Or does the missionary code forbid fun?"

Should she confess her lack of exposure to children's games? No, a smart man like Stewart Hastings would only ask more questions about her childhood than she cared to answer. "Of course not. Missionaries can jump rope and have fun. It's just not an activity I feel up to today."

A roar went up and they both turned to see. Wilson was out. Another quickly took his place.

"You really did start something there. You must have been a real ringleader as a boy," Anna declared.

He shook his head. "Mostly, I never learned how to turn down a dare. Got me in lots of trouble in my youth. Wait…what was I thinking?" He slapped his head. "Of course you can't jump. Mrs. Dowdy would have my hide for endangering your health at the mere suggestion."

She laughed. "I'm hardly an invalid. I…" The wind shifted and a sudden swell rocked her balance. Her legs, shaky from the imposed rest, followed the list of the ship and dropped her right into Stewart's muscular arms.

"Caught you."

Anna's cheeks grew hot. He appeared in no hurry to let her go. She caught the faint scent of bay rum. No man had ever held her so close.

Or made her feel so safe.

This man…

Stop that. What are you thinking? Lord, give me strength to deal with this unexpected temptation of the flesh.

Anna righted herself and pulled away. "So sorry."

There was that easy grin again. "I'm not. Remind me to thank the captain later for dumping a pretty girl right into my arms."

She had to shut down this obvious flirtation. And quickly, before she endangered her witness for God. She forced a polite distance into her words. "No need. It won't happen again. I don't wish to be rude, but I'm afraid I also have certain requirements for our trip together. I must insist we keep our relationship strictly as a business arrangement or this will never work. Now, if you'll excuse me, I have a few letters to finish so I can post them from our next port. I believe I'll retire to the Ladies' Saloon."

His posture straightened and all his lighthearted bantered became a distant memory, lost in a most serious tone. "I apologize for any impropriety, Miss Baldwin. I was attempting to make light of an awkward situation."

Anna nodded and walked down the passageway, relieved to escape. Had she done Mrs. Dowdy a disservice to have thought her too overprotective? Anna preferred not to use such rigid formality as a barrier, but they had a long journey ahead and if this flirtation was the result of only a small space of time spent together, what other choice did she have? Something about Stewart Hastings stirred errant and misplaced feelings in her. No doubt his romantic appeal sprang from his dramatic rescue and the trauma of the event. No man had ever put aside his own concerns to step in for her in any situation. Quite the opposite, in fact. Her needs had never mattered.

She reached her cabin and retrieved her writing supplies and her Bible before heading to the saloon. Studying God's Word would surely conquer any stray thoughts of the handsome yet unsuitable Stewart Hastings.

Stewart would never understand women. And definitely not religious women. For a moment she seemed like any normal girl. A pretty one, too. The rigidness of her departing posture conveyed a valuable lesson. He'd lost himself in a moment of fun, forgotten his job, his worries for his mother and even the fact that the young woman he'd tossed his hat to wasn't someone he could pass the time with, flirting harmlessly. No, Anna wasn't the frivolous type. Her beliefs had carried her away from societal trappings that most women in their mid-twenties lived for and straight into the heart of the jungle to proselytize others. Religion would always rule the day with her, a belief system unsullied by the realities of war. He respected the strength of her convictions, even if they were misguided.

He walked to the ship's rail and looked out on the Atlantic. Driven by the wind, small whitecaps peeked out of the deep sapphire sea and hid themselves again. He took a moment to settle back into the reality of his situation. He'd come halfway around the world after losing his fiancée and the life their marriage promised, taken this job out of financial desperation and now managed to offend the one woman who could possibly help him salvage his circumstances.

He'd lost the love of the first woman and a partnership in a prestigious firm because he'd failed in the trenches, ending up scarred for life. Now his momentary lapse might cost him the help of Anna, and he'd fail again at the cost of his mother's future.

In truth, if there was a missionary rule book, jumping rope might be allowed, but flirting would probably take on the nature of a commandment, as in *Thou Shalt Not.* And that was exactly what he'd done. Flirted with a missionary.

Get ahold of yourself, man. Nothing good can come of flirting with her anyway. She has to be a means to an end. Nothing more. Beauty can't be such a distraction this time. Making the same mistake twice would be foolish.

He should apologize and get on with the business at hand. She'd taken true offense at his actions; otherwise why remove herself to a ladies-only area? Usually she took in the air on deck until lunch or the rains, whichever came first. Once the rains forced everyone off the uncovered decks, she and Mrs. Dowdy joined the gathering in the Grand Saloon for polite conversations, games and music.

He heaved a sigh and mentally constructed his apology. This job was too valuable to endanger over a small, unplanned attraction. Even if religion wasn't a barrier, his hidden scars stood between him and any woman. After all, Julianne had been the epitome of devotion to religion in her own way. She ran every important women's church committee possible. Julianne proved that not even a strong religious leaning could overcome the natural revulsion from such a hideous sight. No, he needed to remember that love and marriage weren't ever going to be in his future anyway and stick to business only from now on.

Resolved, he headed back to join the deck activities. He'd noticed the setup for tossing the rope rings was currently in disuse. If he found a few competitors, perhaps playing a game of quoits would help pass the time.

Anything was better than remembering he had no real future, especially not with someone like her.

The early-morning sun had cleared no more than half the horizon by the time Anna stole up on deck, Bible in hand. Mrs. Dowdy lay below, sound asleep. Anna had dressed by the small amount of morning light coming through the port window, fearing to turn on the electric lighting lest she wake her companion. She no longer needed care. Any more hovering and she'd go mad. And with Stewart in doubt about letting her do the job without his constant supervision, a reputation as an invalid would never do. It was enough of a handicap to have a face that made men forget she also had a brain.

A few crewmen nodded their good-mornings and went about their business, casting glances her way when they thought she wasn't looking. She took a moment and buttoned the jacket of her traveling dress. The thin fabric of her shirtwaist offered little protection against the strong wind on deck. Black smoke from the ship's stack trailed behind at a sharp angle. She made her way to the wooden deck chairs. If the headwind kept up, it would be an unpleasant transfer when they reached Garraway later today. Just the thought of the mammy chair rocking while it was winched down to the ocean's level was unsettling. Getting onto the waiting surfboats transporting them to the beach would be a challenge. She wouldn't rest easy until her shoes sank into the sand.

The jungle she could handle. She'd climb a million downed trees and wade through as many swamps as it took, but the memory of her first mammy-chair ride, missing her footing and her sodden skirts dragging her downward into the sea, left her with a healthy fear of the ocean. There were no words in all of the languages she spoke to express the horror of that experience.

She looked toward the port side. The not-too-distant shore still boasted an empty beach lined with dense foliage. Garraway hid from sight, but couldn't be far. Patience to reach her destination eluded her as she settled herself into the deck chair and tucked in a blanket.

What if the rice harvest came earlier than she expected and the devilmen started the school before she arrived? The rains weren't due to end for several weeks, but she wouldn't rest until she returned and saw Taba with her own eyes. She fingered the pages of the Bible in her lap but worry for his safety left her too distracted to read. After a few moments she closed both the book and her eyes to pray for the grace to trust that this business arrangement she'd entered into would be only the first of God's provisions for her and Taba's lives.

"Good morning, Miss Baldwin." Stewart dropped down in the chair beside her. "Have you been out here long?"

Her heart raced from the startle. "Oh, goodness. You scared me."

"I'm sorry, had you nodded off?"

"No, I was praying. I like to spend time in prayer and reading while I'm waiting for the breakfast gong to sound."

"Are you hungry? I can go find a steward to get something for you." Concern etched his face.

There it was, the kid-glove treatment. Too much in the jungle depended on him being willing to defer to her, not to coddle her, especially since he'd already made his position on her authority clear. She'd have to work to change his opinion if she expected this trip to go smoothly.

"No, thank you. I prefer to wait until they're serving and eat with everyone else." Authoritative, healthy, strong—any of those would have been the better impression to make. Instead she'd sounded curt, almost rude.

He raised one eyebrow. "Am I being deliberately handed the cold and frosty?"

"Sorry, that came out more harshly than I'd intended. I don't like to be fussed over. I'm recovered and fully able to take care of myself." Now she just sounded formal and stilted.

He answered with a grin. "Yes, ma'am. I'll make a note of it. No coddling the missionary lady." He rose from the chair. "You look like you'd rather be alone. I'll push off, but perhaps we could talk on the promenade after breakfast if you can get free of Mrs. Dowdy."

"Wait."

He sat back down.

She heaved a sigh. "I'm a little grumpy today and taking it out on you. I apologize. I often suspect all the scriptures about the tongue were written personally for me."

"Feeling a little punk is usually a good sign of recovery. Or so they told me when I used to bite the nurses' heads off."

"You're being generous. Thank you. So what put you in the hospital?"

He looked like a trapped animal. What had she said wrong?

He rallied. "Just one of the many courtesies of the Great War. Nothing you'd want to hear about before breakfast."

Anna watched the pulse in his jaw. More like something too painful to discuss that he kept hidden behind that smile. Her stomach rumble changed her focus at the familiar throaty resound of the breakfast gong. Anna shoved the blanket back. "Speaking of breakfast. Shall we head for dining?"

He reached out and took her hand to help her up. The gloves she wore were little protection from the heat of his touch or the sudden intensity in his voice. "Not until I speak to you about something. Now. Before I lose my nerve."

Oh, no. She thought she'd settled this yesterday. The last time a man looked that earnest she'd been forced to turn down his unwanted proposal of marriage. Twice. Surely all his flirting didn't actually mean something. Every muscle in her body tensed in anticipation of pending disaster.

"I owe you an apology. I was out of line yesterday with my attentions. I didn't mean any offense. Flirting is an old habit I've yet to break myself from doing."

She relaxed and allowed herself to breathe. "None taken. Apology accepted."

"Good. To paraphrase Mr. Shakespeare, I don't want to get off on the wrong foot. This is strictly a business arrangement and you're my guide."

"Of course. Business."

His relief was palpable. "Good, we understand each other." He let go of her hand.

"Most certainly." She should clarify her whole position while she had the chance. "Of course, to avoid any other possible misunderstandings between us, I need to emphasize that the business of the Gospel is a constant with me and not something I intend to set aside during our journey."

His brow furrowed. "Are you saying you intend to convert me?"

Wind tugged at her scarf and she reached one hand to hold it secure. "I wouldn't be doing my job if I didn't share the Gospel with those I encounter, yourself included. But my main point is for you to understand that if there is a choice between God's work and yours, the Gospel takes first priority for me. I'll do the job you require, but I'll not allow anything to compromise my higher mission."

His gaze grew somber. "I think your standards are clear. But I would rest easier knowing you don't intend to try to make another disciple out of me. You'll have better luck with the local population."

"Ah, now I'm being given the cold and frosty."

"Apparently we both have our sticking points. How about you don't try to convert me and I won't flirt with you. Truce?" He extended his hand, this time for a shake.

Anna shook it firmly. "I'll agree, provided you feel free to rescind your part of the agreement at any time you wish to know more about God. Better to clear the air now, since the jungle trek can be stressful enough. We may have to rely on each other in some very trying situations."

"Having survived the trenches during the war, I'm sure I can handle anything your jungle has for me."

His nonchalance urged her to further explanation. "Despite your military experience, you're in for something quite different here—days on end of narrow, root-ridden paths, climbing over downed trees, wading through waist-deep water and dealing with the sometimes deadly wildlife."

His grin returned. "You make the journey sound so appealing, but you left out the constant daily soakings from the rains. Not trying to get me to turn back, are you?"

Her misgivings must be more obvious than she'd

thought. "No, I'm very grateful for the opportunity to fund my mission work."

"Well, don't worry about me. I think I can manage." He offered her his elbow.

She placed her hand in the crook of his arm and headed to breakfast. "I'm sure you can. You appear very…able."

"It can't be too bad if a little bit of a thing like you can handle it."

She laughed at his implication. "Maybe not. But don't let that overriding confidence build up too far. When we get off the boat at Garraway this afternoon, you'll find the trek to get to our first stop at Newaka a bit misleading as to the difficulty that lies beyond."

He halted abruptly just inside the companionway and turned to face her, freeing her hand from the crook of his arm. "Garraway? No, we are disembarking farther down the coast at Harper. I informed the second steward of the mistake when he asked about the different destinations on our tickets. He noticed that our luggage and equipment were both stored under my name in the hold."

Dismay snatched the core of her being. Oh, no. They hadn't even left the ship and his need to take charge was causing problems. Why was it that every woman she'd met tried to marry her off and all the men—her father, her former fiancé—had to be in charge? No, maybe she was overreacting. Stewart didn't understand the basic geography of the country. "Mr. Hastings, I wish you had consulted me first. I could have told you that departing from Garraway is the most direct route to the village." Now to soften the blow by allowing him a semblance of control. "Shall I inform the second steward of the need to unload our supplies at this stop or would you prefer to be in charge of that?"

His voice repeated her patient tone. "I would have consulted with you. But, if you recall, yesterday we were interrupted by Mrs. Dowdy. Later you took to your cabin. I looked for a chance to discuss the details at dinner, but felt it improper to come directly to your cabin when I didn't see you in the evening."

He was too polite to say so, but between her self-imposed seclusion and her overzealous chaperone, he'd been left without all the information he needed to make the right decisions. At least he'd made an effort. "No matter. This is easily remedied. I'll speak to the steward and meet you at breakfast."

She turned to go. A hand at her elbow stopped her.

"I'm afraid you don't understand. Harper is exactly where we need to disembark. The territory I must cover extends from the Putu Mountains near the Pahn village and well to the east. The mountains near the Pahn village will be my focus, but getting an overview of the entire area, prospecting and collecting samples as we go, those are all necessary objectives."

Icy shards coated her stomach. This job meant the ability to save Taba and to have a provision for her to stay in the country while she sought more funding. The security of having all these needs met had been as much of an illusion as her father's love. The journey Stewart proposed was far lengthier than she'd expected and over unfamiliar terrain. If there were significant delays, this plan could put her arriving after the Poro school started.

"Mr. Hastings, this was not my understanding of our agreement. I fully expected to depart this ship at Garraway today, hire my usual porters and travel to the mission post at Newaka just before first light in the morning. From there, on to the Pahn. I have my own obligations at my mission post."

"I'm sorry, Miss Baldwin. We need to go up the Cavalla River and stop south of the first set of rapids. We'll go overland to the west until we reach the outer edge of the prescribed mining concession area. Then we'll slow our pace if I find areas with any real mining potential. This itinerary meets the company's requirements and was planned with them before I left the States. I've mapped the whole thing out. Your bishop raised no issue with this when we discussed it in the parlor."

"The bishop is as new to this country as you are, Mr. Hastings. He can't be expected to understand the challenge your itinerary poses or the later implications of taking that route once we reach the Pahn."

"Maybe not, but I understand the implications of not being thorough and doing my job. I studied all the available maps. This is the best route for my needs. I'm sorry for the confusion, but we have until Harper to discuss any other details so we are both in agreement after this."

In her experience a man wrapped up in his own needs responded best to reason, never to emotion. If she'd learned nothing else from her father, this was one certain truth. "Do you have any idea how rudimentary and incomplete maps of the interior are? Rough approximations from a handful of explorers. Hardly accurate. Being unfamiliar with the terrain in those areas, I have to warn you that this could add unnecessary weeks to your travel time, especially with the rains still upon us. You are better off concentrating on your main objective and then journeying to the east if your deadline allows."

"I recognize how little of this country has been mapped. I had not recognized that the terms of your employment would be such an issue, Miss Baldwin."

He stood there without malice, just the natural confidence of a man used to being obeyed.

The buried frustrations of her lifetime made their way to the surface. Was there no end to men with plans designed around their own needs who must have their way? This delay…

Hold your tongue, Anna. Don't... Lord, help me here.

"Mr. Hastings, this plan extends my service time in such a fashion that I must protest. I must get back to my village post. My needs have not been considered in your decision at all."

He looked dumbfounded, but she had to stand firm now or lose any chance to redeem this situation. Panic over Taba rode on her words and made them stronger than she intended. "Simply put, this was not our agreement."

Stewart took a slight step back, revising his estimate of the overall passivity of the missionary temperament. Then he remembered how she'd wielded her umbrella before her two attackers got the better of her.

Not their agreement? Was she trying to back out? He'd never thought to question her integrity before hiring her. Perhaps with her missionary background she knew little of how the business world worked.

"Miss Baldwin, I paid half the money down for you to guide me to the Pahn village, help me secure a working relationship with the chief and to do so in a timely manner so I can meet my deadline. The balance upon completion."

An alarming red flush crept up her neckline and threatened to engulf her countenance. What had he done so horribly wrong? He must be explaining things incorrectly. "I did consider your needs, Miss Baldwin. A significant part of our journey will be on the Cavalla River." He caught himself from rubbing his shirt-covered scars, a habit that only surfaced under stress. "Riding in canoes will be much less taxing for your delicate frame."

She took a deep breath and exhaled. Her flush of temper receded. "I think you underestimate me, sir. The method of travel is the least of my concerns. Setting aside the issue of extra time, a route up the Cavalla in itself is neither prudent nor safe."

"I don't understand."

As usual, her hands accompanied her explanation. "First, some of the Cavalla River territory was the scene of major uprisings against government taxations in recent years. A lot of the mission stations along your chosen route were deserted for safety's sake. I cannot guarantee that some of the people we encounter won't still harbor hostility."

"All right, so we go armed and carefully through those areas."

Her brows knit together. "More importantly, Nana Mala recently made a bid to become a Paramount Chief, one who rules over several villages near him besides his own."

He stood unmoved, not understanding. "So?"

Her hands' abrupt rhythm signaled her frustration. "His bid failed, placing a great strain on relationships with the villages directly to the east of Pahn territory, where your route takes us."

"Does that make those villages more hostile to us?"

She shook her head and more mahogany tendrils escaped the bun at the back of her head and waved in the wind. He stopped from reaching to push them out of her way. "Probably not…"

"Then I fail to see the issue."

"Nana Mala is the issue. He will wonder if we are plotting with those villages."

"Surely you can reason with the man and explain when you vouch for me."

Her laugh held no trace of humor. "Reason with a man who goes to war with little provocation? He almost killed the last missionaries who graced his compound. He will listen to me, but the danger to you is increased from your travel plans alone."

She dropped her eyes, and the tight band around his heart eased until she spoke. "Mr. Hastings, you made an arrangement with Bishop Michaels for my guidance. You must take my advice and disembark at Garraway."

"I appreciate your counsel, but there are many things about my position that you don't understand. As to Nana Mala, if he can't be managed through your influence… well, isn't that the point of your employ? No, what I *must* do is disembark farther down the coast at Harper. Too much is riding on my timely completion for me to do this any other way."

The muscles in her jawline tightened. "From my understanding, all that's riding on your timely completion is more money. Are you so filled with…with…greed you'd traipse me all through the countryside at your leisure, taking advantage of my financial need and not considering that I might have other needs, as well? Not to mention you're ignoring sound advice. Is money so important you must obtain it despite the potential cost for both of us?"

She might feel inconvenienced, but he had a job to do, a plan to meet his deadline and a vow to keep to his mother. Too much at stake to pull his punches now. "My greed, as you put it, is also out of desperation. Desperation to establish myself with my own employer and to earn the money to save my sick mother from an early death. For her, I'll do whatever it takes, even if it means inconveniencing you."

Her eyes widened. He tried to soften the revelation and pleaded for her acceptance. "Miss Baldwin, we must move past this misunderstanding of the terms of your employment. Your bishop received funds from me in good faith. You yourself pointedly convinced me I had no alternative for a guide."

Her eyes lost some of their intensity. He continued, "You were happy enough with me in the beginning when you found my funds useful, so I'll ignore the judgment on my character for now. You wouldn't be the first Christian woman to prove herself quick to break her commitment to me when things didn't go the way she wanted."

She opened her mouth to speak, but he held up his hand again, silencing her. "The way I see it, we have two choices. The first is for you to fulfill your obligation to me as promised in the manner I specify so that my needs, the needs of the man paying your salary, are met."

Worry etched her face. He felt somewhat the cad for having placed it there, but the stakes were too high. If she was going to balk at guiding him where he needed to go, he had to know now. She was already plan B. He had no plan C.

She broke the silence. "And the second choice?"

"Obviously I cannot force you to honor your commitment. But if you refuse to do so, then I must insist we cable your bishop to return my funds by wiring them to Harper so I can attempt to replace you." If he was a praying man, now would be the time. Failure stared at him through the troubled brown eyes of his only known hope. He held his breath and waited for her answer.

Chapter Three

Anna retreated to her cabin after begging time to think and pray about the decision in front of her. She opened the door to find Mrs. Dowdy up and dressed. The small trunk with her belongings sat partially packed on the floor. Maybe she hadn't been to breakfast yet and Anna would get a few moments alone. Fortunately no one else had been assigned to the third berth in the tiny space.

"Anna, there you are."

She forced a smile. "I was up on deck." She raised her Bible.

"Oh, your devotions. I was putting mine off until I got my trunk ready for the steward to move back to my cabin with Mr. Dowdy."

Anna took a slow breath. Mrs. Dowdy didn't leave the ship until it reached Harper. There would be no way to keep this turn of events private. "About that. I may be continuing on to Harper, as well."

Mrs. Dowdy paused midfold of the skirt in her hand. "Oh. Will you still need a chaperone? Or is Mr. Hastings leaving us at Garraway?"

Anna recounted her dilemma and braced herself for her chaperone's poor opinions of Stewart.

"You are in a difficult position indeed, Anna. And I find I may have misjudged Mr. Hastings. Any man who would go to such great lengths for his mother is more honorable than I had believed. I would hope to find such devotion in my own grown sons if I were in need." Mrs. Dowdy placed the skirt on top of her trunk and sat on her berth. "On the one hand, you might be walking away from the only chance to save your young convert and prolong your own time in the village. Ask yourself this. If you had understood the itinerary from the beginning, would you still have agreed?"

Anna sat on the opposite berth, ducking her head slightly because of the bunk above her. She was shocked to hear counsel instead of complaint. She thought hard. "I don't know. As the bishop pointed out, I had no other immediate provisions. He was convinced this was God's plan. Even had I known, I still would have faced the problem of returning to the village before the Poro school began."

Mrs. Dowdy leaned forward. "I've been in this country a lot longer than you, dear child. We still have at least four more weeks of rain. And at least a couple more after that before the rice is dry enough to harvest. I've traveled up the Cavalla several times with my husband to look at property when we first arrived in Liberia. Once we went as far as the rapids, and it took approximately ten days. Of course, we weren't loaded down with much in the way of supplies. Still, it seems to me if you manage your land travel, set a steady pace for yourself and your porters, you could both accomplish your goals."

Hope flickered inside her. "Perhaps so, as long as we didn't encounter any major setbacks. But Mr. Hastings has declared his need for time to prospect along the way once we get within the mining concession area. I considered explaining about Taba, but how can I burden Mr. Hastings with choosing between his own mother and a boy he's never met?"

"Exactly so. And it is unnecessary, my dear. Once you get within reasonable traveling distance of the village, you could journey ahead if needed. Leave him some competent help so he can follow later. That will even give you time before he arrives to talk to the chief about Mr. Hastings's business in his territory. In fact, it is what Mr. Dowdy likes to call 'a selling point' for your need to arrive ahead of Mr. Hastings. If Nana Mala remains hostile, then Mr. Hastings will not be in danger's reach. You can send word so he will remain safe."

Anna's heart flooded with relief. This wasn't the disaster she feared. Perhaps if she hadn't spent a lifetime being subject to the impulsive, poorly conceived plans of her father, she might have been able to see this for herself. "The other point to consider is that Mr. Hastings's concern for his mother will drive him to continue on without me. And it's clear how little he really understands of this country."

Mrs. Dowdy reached over and patted Anna's hand. "Exactly, my dear. Most men need a strong guiding hand. Why, I can't imagine how Mr. Dowdy would manage here without me. His dealings would be an epic failure without my input."

Anna resisted the impulse to laugh. Poor Mr. Dowdy might wear the literal trousers, but not in any way that mattered. Stewart did need her experience, but she couldn't picture him ever allowing a wife of his to dictate his life down to the smallest detail the way Mr. Dowdy permitted. It was as unthinkable as Anna imitating her mother's cowed obedience in all things. Were all marriages doomed to such an imbalance of power from one side or another? What would it be like to marry a man who honored and respected God as well as his wife?

Mrs. Dowdy stood and smoothed her skirts. "I can see you're thinking hard on this. I'm going to go to breakfast and give you time alone to pray and seek God's Will. All the good counsel in the world can't take the place of God's peace and direction. I'll have a plate fixed for you."

Anna gave her a grateful smile. When the cabin door closed, she slid off the bunk and knelt on the floor.

Lord, I need Your guidance. Your peace that this is the right decision. You've called me to Nana Mala's village. You opened the heart of Taba to your salvation. You alone hold Taba's life in your hands. I know You can provide for all our needs, so if this is the way, then I don't want to miss Your Will. Not for myself, or Taba, or this hurting man you've placed in my path. Please, show me what to do here. I choose to stand on Your will, not my reasoning or my fears.

A deep peace settled over her. She needed to fully embrace God's provision and trust Him. And surely by trusting God in His provision, He would give her the strength not to be drawn in by a few frivolous romantic feelings.

Now to convince Stewart to keep her on. He'd given her the choice, but clearly he wouldn't hesitate to dismiss her and ask for his money back. She prayed she still had a chance.

Stewart stood on deck after breakfast and listened with growing consternation as Wilson regaled him with the difficulties to expect in his travels.

Wilson said, "The translators, and mind you they

speak Liberian English or a pidgin, are usually already hired by the traders, such as myself. They've no desire to go on an interior expedition, and even if they did, most were raised in or near the coastal towns. They won't be experienced enough with interior tribes to be of much value."

"What do you suggest?"

"Depends. Where exactly are you headed?"

"Eventually I'll base near the Putu Mountain range."

Wilson took on the look of someone about to reason with an asylum patient. "Cannibal territory?"

"Yeah, everyone gets that same look once I tell them my destination."

Wilson slapped him on the back before he walked away. "Can't help you there. Farthest my men will venture is about a day or so out of Harper. Talk to some of the traders in Harper."

Stewart watched Wilson's retreat. Giving Anna an option to get out of the contract was a big mistake. And now that he'd changed their destination, he realized the barrier that language might become. In his haste, he hadn't thought this through.

He stared out at the distant yellow sands, focusing on the rhythm of the breakers hitting the shore as his mind worked on his latest problem.

Eventually the hint of civilization peeked out above the distant treetops. Garraway's tin roofs winked in the bright sun. The transfer of passengers and goods by surf boat would soon commence and cargo would be taken on all through the night. A maddeningly slow process and the sound of the winch would preclude sleep.

Once at Harper, what would he be able to accomplish on his own?

He faced the hard facts. This was a problem of his own making. He could have insisted and gotten around Mrs. Dowdy to have more time to talk to Anna, if he had felt confident about relying on Anna in the first place, or any other pretty face with so much at stake. Yet there seemed to be much more than beauty where Anna was concerned. So why, with one little missionary in hand, did he balk twice about relying on her in the bush? He lacked the most basic understanding of this country, no matter how many maps he'd studied.

Truth was he still had reservations about relying on her or any other woman after his experience with Julianne arranging his future and then wiping it all away in an instant. He recognized that allowing his actions to be influenced by his past was poor business, but yielding his trust again was no easy thing. He had to seek a compromise before Anna refused him outright and left the ship. Surely his mother's situation would soften her heart.

All around him, deckhands suddenly stood straighter. Stewart turned, expecting to see the captain.

No, not the captain. Anna appeared on deck. Her effect on men's postures was profound. He, however, honed in on the absence of the small japanned steel suitcase she'd held when boarding from Monrovia. Did this mean there was hope?

As she came nearer, he caught himself straightening, as well. Must be an automatic male reaction. Did she know her effect on men? Most beautiful women did and used it to get their way. In the war between the genders, women fought with an unfair advantage.

He pinpointed the moment she caught sight of him. She tensed, her smile seeming forced. His mind raced to find the right words to say to regain her help. How hard could it be to apologize to one little missionary woman?

Her head tilted upward as she came to a stop in front of him. He looked into her face. His chest tightened. This would be harder than he thought.

Before he got out the first word, she spoke. "Mr. Hastings. I've come to apologize after reacting so poorly to our misunderstanding."

In war, this same feeling followed the concussive shock of artillery fire. A complete disorientation that had the ground of expectations shaking under his feet. It was too easy. She must have reconsidered the loss of funding. So much in life came down to the money.

She continued, "I'm afraid I don't take well to surprises or having my plans dictated to me, a character failing I need to work on." Her cheeks pinked up as she spoke. "And to accuse you of greed…well, that was uncalled for on my part."

Didn't like her plans dictated? Maybe they had something in common, after all. "Nonsense, Miss Baldwin, I'm sure to someone like a missionary, I do appear to be a fortune hunter, but I take family responsibilities seriously. My delay in discussing the itinerary earlier is to blame."

"How generous of you to say so. That you risked your life to save me back in Monrovia should have informed me better of your character without having to be told about your mother."

Her manner and sincerity sliced away at his general distrust. "I did what was necessary at the time, like I'm trying to do now." His breath waited on her next words.

"I prayed about this and am willing to take the longer route. I would, for my own needs, prefer to chart the course to minimize delays, but I will honor my agreement with you."

Hope rang in his heart and he took in vital air. "I am quite relieved to hear so, but concerned that we still have a problem. Wilson bent my ear concerning the difficulties of our travel outside of Harper. The more I learn of this country, Miss Baldwin, the more I realize the bonus I was offered by my employer may have been given to encourage me to do the impossible."

She smiled and his pulse elevated. "If you give me more details, perhaps we can form a plan together to deal with the issues he raised. After all, you'll be traveling with a missionary. We perpetually believe our God is able to do the impossible."

"I'll put more trust in our planning, Miss Baldwin. In my experience, your God isn't always available when it comes down to practical matters. I doubt God will stoop into our affairs to give you the name of a willing translator in Harper for the different dialects we'll encounter. I fear we will be reduced to hand gestures for communication."

Her smile broadened; her eyes caught a glint from the sun. "You're concerned about obtaining a translator?" No sooner had the words left her mouth than she dissolved into laughter.

She'd gone from apologizing to him to mockery?

"Miss Baldwin!"

She clutched her side and took a couple of deep breaths. "I'm sorry. Back to your practical realities. When the bishop said we were a match made in Heaven, he was right, after all."

"I'm not making the connection. Exactly what is funny here?"

Anna reached up, her hand resting on his shoulder

while she tried to dampen her grin. She failed. "God already met your practical need."

"What do you mean?"

His serious tone appeared to sober her, and her hand slid back to her side. "Languages have always been my gift. Which is one reason I was assigned to a post with such an obscure dialect. Native translators want nothing to do with Nana Mala on a long-term basis. Without the ability to translate, my sermons would be quite short and poorly understood."

Incredible. "What about all the areas we'll pass through before we get there?"

"Mr. Hastings, at the risk of sounding like a braggart, or 'bluff boy' as the natives say, translation will not be a problem, even if we fail to find any pidgin speakers."

"How is this possible?"

She sounded embarrassed. "I speak a total of fourteen languages fluently, not counting a few more odd dialects."

An offensive blast grenade would have stunned him less. Every time it appeared he would fail, his luck turned. An impossible plan might be in reach, all thanks to this modest little missionary. He didn't stop to think as the sheer joy of the implications for his and his mother's future overwhelmed him. He picked up the tiny bundle in front of him and swung her around in celebration. As he put her down, he said, "I thought all my plans were doomed to failure. Miss Baldwin, if you weren't a missionary, I'd kiss you senseless."

She grabbed the rail, dizzy from the spin. When her head lifted, he recognized the mistake he'd made. Passengers and crew members stared, reinforcing the impropriety.

Her voice trembled. "While I appreciate your...enthusiasm, I'm afraid I must insist on a couple more things in our association."

"Anything."

Wide eyes held his gaze. "No spinning your missionary like a children's top. And definitely no kissing. Ever."

Anna longed for the comfortable deck chairs and the tea trays they'd left behind two days ago. After a full day, including six hours of rain, on the wide, muddy waters of the Cavalla River, her cramped legs begged to stretch themselves outside the tight confines of the eight-man canoe. She dreamed of the luxury of a covered, motorized boat to traverse the river.

But hadn't she given up a prison of luxury to come to Africa in the first place? The real sympathy belonged to the long-legged Stewart in the canoe trailing hers.

She'd nixed the idea of sharing a canoe upriver to avoid the close confines and to reinforce the necessary bounds of behavior between two unmarried individuals. Clearly he'd meant nothing improper by his actions on board the ship. He'd been like a child with an unexpected Christmas present when she'd revealed her ability with languages. She'd been caught off guard, that was all.

She'd worked hard since to banish the thought of how safe and secure being in those strong arms made her feel. God was her true source of strength, and with His help she'd conquer this sudden longing to feel secure in a man's arms. Another reason for separate canoes until she overcame her failing.

Fortunately, between Mrs. Dowdy's presence and the eventual sight of the red-tiled roofs of Harper, Stewart had stuck to the business at hand after that moment. Remarkable how fast things came together once they'd crossed the beach and reached the town. A virtual whirlwind ensued as she filled supply lists, gave him instructions for securing rowers when he'd insisted on taking care of the hiring himself and searched out lodging for Stewart separate from the quarters the mission university provided for her.

All that hurry and now nothing for entertainment beyond the occasional parrot in the endless landscape of piassava palms and mangrove trees along the river's banks. The cadence of her Kru rowers singing to keep the rhythm threatened to lull her to sleep.

Earlier they'd passed several villages and one occupied missionary post. But it had been too soon in the journey to do more than say hello, stretch their legs a bit and gather information. She hoped their last source was accurate. Judging by the low-hanging sun and the lifting rain, if they didn't come across another village soon, they'd be forced to make their own clearing and camp for the night.

Not a pleasant thought. She hadn't seen any crocodiles so far, but she worried that the nocturnal, river-loving pygmy hippos might not be obvious until they made camp.

Thoughts of wildlife vanished when Stewart's canoe pulled alongside hers. She addressed her concerns. "I'm not sure we should have pushed on from the last signs of a village, Mr. Hastings. We might be forced to camp by the riverbank. Not my favorite location."

"I hate to waste good daylight with early camps this soon in the journey. Especially since our rowers couldn't help slowing down in the hardest part of the rain. What about those drums I've been hearing? Don't they mean we are close to a village?"

"Possibly, but hard to say with any accuracy. Those

are talking drums. Their sounds travel hundreds of miles."

"Are you having fun at my expense?" His head canted.

"No, not at all. Drums telegraphed village messages long before Mr. Marconi ever thought of sending signals through the air."

"Amazing how people make progress in their own way."

"I think you'll find a lot of things here to surprise you, if you keep an open mind. You might spend time watching local blacksmiths. Most villages have one. They do a lot of work in iron."

Stewart raised his eyebrows. "Interesting. Ironwork speaks to not only inventive thinking, but also tells me they are familiar with the metals and minerals available."

"Yes, but they don't value some metals the way we would."

He smiled. "Better for my company if they don't."

Surprise threaded her voice before she thought to conceal it. "You would deliberately take advantage of their ignorance of the rest of the world?"

He shook his head. "Of course not, but it will allow us to negotiate affordable terms. Mining here will be an expensive proposition."

"I guess I'll hear your terms for myself if I'm the one doing the translating."

His eyes widened almost imperceptibly and then narrowed as he looked past her shoulder. One hand reached down and gripped the stock of his rifle. "In the area of translating, does your gift for languages extend to drum talk?"

"No." She laughed. "Drum is not a language I've mastered."

"Too bad." He nodded to a spot behind her. "If you

had, we might know if that rather formidable display of warriors holds spears of welcome or imminent death."

Stewart was relieved to see that welcome prevailed. But three hours into the evening's festivities, relief no longer sustained him. What he wanted was quiet and his bed. If Anna had not explained the courtesies and customs, he would have cut the evening short and lost the goodwill of his hosts.

The sheer skill of the drummers, their intricate beats accompanying displays of impressive athletic prowess, were all fascinating at first. He'd thought Monrovia exotic with its marketplaces full of colorfully dressed Kru men and the impressively tall Vai and their wives walking down the streets side by side with roaming cattle and pigs. But Monrovia hadn't prepared him in the least for the sight of those fierce-faced, spear-laden warriors. He felt as green as new recruits on the front lines when reality didn't meet the idealized expectations of war.

And watching the petite Anna confidently lift her unfashionably long, rain-sodden skirts and step out of the canoe to speak to them before he even got to the riverbank? It was enough to induce a stroke in any man. After tonight, he intended to talk with her about her own safety. Even though he was only one man with one gun, walking away from your only source of protection was unwise. She might know protocol, but he understood the logistics of safety.

Observing her then and now was quite the education, not only about the country, but to a new side of the woman he'd hired to guide him. What a revelation when she spoke to those men. He'd scrambled to her side and listened to the translated conversation, one which allayed any lingering fears that a five-foot-three-inch brunette from Connecticut really spoke the language well enough to communicate. Only a few words from her and warlike countenances dissolved into smiles, postures relaxed, and they were elevated to the status of honored guests.

According to Anna, a mission station had existed here years before, so their hosts were quite enthusiastic at their arrival. The chief insisted on presenting them with a ceremonial gift of white kola nuts, water and salt. Anna reciprocated with a tin of tobacco, a fathom's measure of cloth and a few fishing hooks from the items she'd had him purchase in Harper as an expected courtesy to their hosts, which she called a "dash."

Food appeared in front of him. His stomach rumbled in anticipation. He smiled at the young woman who served the meal and quickly averted his eyes to his food, so as not to stare. She was clad in only a few necklaces and a country-blue trader's cloth skirt tied at one hip. The wooden bowl held an abundance of rice with some colorful bits mixed in, local vegetables he supposed. The pieces of fish he recognized as such. But what was he supposed to do with the smaller bowl of fragrant oil?

Anna rescued him. "Follow my lead." She poured her oil over the rice mixture. With her fingers, she stirred and formed some of the rice into a small ball. She leaned closer and said, "This is a type of palm-oil chop with bits of fish added. Rice and palm oil are staples here, but this late in the rainy season, rice is usually scarce until October when the weather dries out. They have served precious reserves because we are guests. Try to eat at least a small portion to be polite."

"No worries. My appetite will do this meal every courtesy. I'm just glad my mother can't see me. Eating with my fingers would cause her to despair and believe all her efforts to instill manners were to no avail."

Anna choked on her food a bit while laughing. Before he could pound her back, she recovered and said, "No one's mother prepares you for what you'll encounter here. Polite and acceptable are always relevant to a particular culture. As to the food, do take it slowly, since it can be a little difficult on the inexperienced palate."

After watching her eat, he doubted it would be a problem. He imitated Anna: he formed an oil-soaked ball of rice and popped it into his mouth. He chewed and swallowed. His eyes stung and commenced watering. His tongue…the burn… Through blurry tears, he saw Anna cover her mouth. A poor attempt to hide her laughter. He reached for the cup placed in front of him to put out the fire, and Anna's eyes opened wide. She shook her head, but all he cared about was dousing the flame in his mouth and belly.

She laughed till she cried when he clapped both hands over his mouth to keep the drink from erupting. He swallowed as the fire in his mouth traveled down his throat and enflamed his stomach.

He reached for his canteen. When he regained his ability to speak, he asked, "What was that?"

She wiped away big tears of laughter rolling down her cheeks and gasped for breath. "Fine Liberian cooking, Mr. Hastings. There's a reason the Portuguese called this the Pepper Coast."

The drums ceased and he realized that some of the fire in his throat was from trying to talk over them. He lowered his voice. "But I saw you eating and assumed it was fine."

"I've been in the bush long enough that food without it tastes bland. And I tried to warn you, but you were too quick. Most rice dishes will be this spicy. They call it 'sheeting' the rice with peppers. Discourages the vermin."

"And the drink? I notice yours remains untouched."

"The beverage is palm wine, a staple in the bush, or anywhere in Liberia, for that matter. It can be quite intoxicating."

"Ah. I thought my swallow had a kick. They won't mind if I stick to the water in my canteen, will they?"

Her head tilted and questioning eyes met his. "You're a temperate man, Mr. Hastings?"

"Are you surprised, Miss Baldwin?"

"I'm more curious than anything."

"For me the choice of drinking or not was easy. Years of living with a drunkard left me no taste for spirits and their destructive powers."

She nodded approval. "A decision like you made takes a lot of strength. Most would have found drink the easier path. You said on board ship you weren't a churchgoing man, but there must have been a strong moral example in your life."

Whether it was the flickering firelight dancing across her face or the intensity of her gaze probing his very soul, he found himself answering, telling her what he'd never spoken of to another. "My mother was a pillar. She instilled a strong sense of right and wrong, drove me to get an education, but also protected me from my father's abuse until I was finally old enough to protect her. All the while, she insisted life could be different. When I was twelve, I learned how different hers had been until she'd married beneath her and her family disowned her. She'd been the daughter of a merchant. Not rich, but a good life. She knew there was more to life than drinking every paycheck." He paused, remembering.

A gentle touch on his forearm brought him back to the moment. “She sounds like an extraordinary woman, your mother. To retain hope in the midst of such misery.”

“When I was nine, she defied my father and started attending church with me in tow every Sunday she didn’t have to work. Like you, religion means a lot to her.”

“So you did attend church, despite what you told Mrs. Dowdy.”

Yes, but he’d rather face a shelling from the Germans than discuss his reasons for walking away from religion. “Only as a child. But enough on me. You asked a simple question and I practically gave you my life story.” How did she manage to extract such confessions from him? He turned back to his bowl and rolled more rice into a ball. Eating it was a high price to pay for changing the subject. Still, if the dainty little woman beside him could eat this stuff…

Anna stopped his hand with one of her own before it left the bowl. “I kept a few tins—peaches and smoked-salmon filets—out of our supplies. I can slip them to you in your hut.”

Before she could say anything else, the same maiden who brought his meal presented herself and held out a hand to him. He looked to Anna. “What does she want?”

Anna addressed the young woman, who promptly dropped her hand and moved away. “She finds you quite fascinating. She was encouraging you to join the other men in dance when it starts again.”

“Oh, no. Not me. I have two good feet, but they are both oriented to the left when it comes to dancing.”

“I doubt the young woman will care. You’ve caught her fancy and now she’s looking for any excuse to interact with you.”

“Ah, I see. So perhaps this would be a good time

for me to find my bed and call it a night. Then my lack of interest won't hurt her feelings or bring any trouble. Which way through that maze of huts to my lodgings?"

Anna stood and brushed off her skirts. "I think that would be for the best. I appreciate your sensitivity to the matter. Come. I'll take you there myself and get you those tins I promised."

He stood. "No food. Just rest. Frankly, I don't know how you are still on your feet. You must need sleep even more than I do."

She smiled and shook her head. "My evening's not over. I don't want to miss the opportunity to share the Gospel with these people. I'm used to the late hours."

He followed her through the narrow paths until she stopped in front of a hut that looked suspiciously like all the others. "This one is yours. You should find your personal gear inside." She pointed to a hut two down on the opposite side. "I'll be right over there later should you have any trouble at all."

"I promise you, Miss Baldwin, the only chance for trouble will be found solely in the land of my dreams."

Barely two hours passed till Anna headed back to her own sleeping quarters. Time well spent. She rejoiced that her preaching had born fruit. The chief and two elders made decisions for Christ and invited her to stay on as their missionary. She regretted her answer, but too much yet remained for her to accomplish at her own mission post. She'd send a relayed word to Bishop Michaels. She prayed someone would heed the call and fill the need.

Ah, Bishop Michaels was right about a Divine hand in this arrangement. These results alone were proof. Who knew, maybe even Stewart would come to know God before the trip ended. She hoped so for his sake. From their conversations, it was clear his lighthearted exterior covered a painful past. No small feat. She knew all about painful pasts and keeping them hidden.

When he'd mentioned his father's drunkenness, it was with a calm detachment. But once Stewart spoke about his mother's encouragement in the face of such difficulty, his eyes had projected both his admiration for her and the hurt he carried inside. Part of Anna wanted to do more than reach over and touch his arm, to find some way to comfort him and relieve his pain. But she knew better than to build on the vulnerability of the moment, lest her empathy go so far as to create an emotional connection where none should exist. And from the way his memories touched a chord in her, that would be a dangerous path to travel.

In time, she could easily find herself suffering a romantic attachment of true depth for this honorable and troubled man. Serving God in such an untamed land was difficult enough without entangling herself in a relationship with a disparity of faith between them. No wonder God's Word issued warnings on the subject, seeing as how easy it would be to open the door to those feelings.

But how different Stewart was from her expectations. Not just the temperance and sense of humor, but his quick understanding and response to the problem with the young woman. He might not believe in God, but Stewart's behavior was beyond reproach. She'd worried about his deportment without cause.

She crossed the compound near the waning central campfire. Revelers had long since sought their own beds. Embers glowed but cast little light. She passed several huts, light snores from some, the sounds of restless children from others. Ahead, Stewart's hut came into view.

She hoped he'd been able to sleep. She'd forgotten to warn him about the Liberian version of a bed.

Oh, no, he was still awake? Movement at his doorway. A twinge of guilt assailed her conscience. She should have had the porters unpack the camp beds he'd bought for the trail. No. Wait. The height was all wrong. More movement and the moonlight outlined a small, lithe figure in country-blue trader's cloth skirt leaving Stewart's hut.

Anna clutched her chest. Pain stabbed her and took her breath. The pain of betrayal. How could he? After making her believe he was an honorable man?

Easy. He was like every other man in her life before the mission field. His painful past, one with elements so close to her own, had blinded her to the truth. She'd cast him in a good and virtuous mold where none existed outside of God.

She used all her self-control to force her feet past his hut once the girl was gone. Anna couldn't confront him tonight.

Not quietly.

She reached the confines of her hut and sank onto the sleeping platform. Despair cloaked her earlier joy. Taba's life would be preserved by continuing on with Stewart and completing the job, but would Stewart's behavior undermine her work? If this was how he acted after only one night in this village, what would it be like in the weeks he'd spend with the Pahn? Everything she'd preached and taught would be nullified through their association.

No, there was no choice here at all. God would have to provide another way to meet her and Taba's needs. In the morning, she'd send Stewart down the Cavalla for a fast trip home on the prevailing current. She'd pray for his mother's needs, but she'd ensure that Stewart Hastings never set foot in Nana Mala's village.

Chapter Four

Stewart bent to exit the low doorway of his hut. His head no longer ached, but everything else did after sleeping on a pallet made for a much shorter man. And the wooden neck block for a pillow? Living in the trenches had changed how he viewed comfort, but if this experience typified the sleeping arrangements in the villages, next stop he was breaking out the camp beds the trader in Harper suggested he purchase.

Anna considered them an unnecessary extravagance. Last night convinced him the beds were money well spent. Besides, she was the one that insisted on loading them down with kerosene, adding to the expense and weight of their supplies. How many lanterns did she need to light?

A dozen or so tendrils of smoke rose above the myriad thatched roofs. Breakfast fires? After last night, his ability to taste anything was questionable. If they spiced their breakfast the same way, the tinned foods purchased in Harper might not last long.

He walked toward the hut Anna occupied. Was she still abed? Who could sleep after the roosters announced dawn a good hour earlier than the sun?

Silence met his call at her doorway. He tried again. He ducked his head through the opening. Unoccupied. Could she be off preaching this morning?

Maybe she left to ready the rowers for an early departure. He'd start looking at the river and hope to find her before he got too lost in the village. They might as well get as far as possible before the rains slowed them down. All he needed was breakfast and to grab his pack.

As he neared the bank, he heard indistinguishable chatter and one distinct feminine voice. He parted the ferns and drank in the sight of Anna with her back to him, slanted sunlight shining off her hair. He missed the long curls he'd glimpsed the night he'd saved her, when her hair was in such disarray. Now they hid in a prim bun.

From her tone, she was giving directions to the head rower. The man shook his head, folded his arms across his chest. Her hands went to her hips. Before the clash of wills went further, the recalcitrant rower noticed Stewart and pointed.

Anna turned, her classically beautiful face holding a storm of emotions. None of them happy. Preaching must not have gone well last night. She advanced on him like one of his old drill sergeants. What was wrong?

"Good morning, Miss Baldwin. Problem with the rowers?"

"Only partially. Our headman requires a confirmation of my orders from you."

So serious. "Certainly. What is it I'm confirming?"

"That you'll be returning to Harper. I'm dividing out our belongings. I'll travel overland without you from here."

A cold wave washed through him. "Miss Baldwin, why would I want to return to Harper?"

"I have no intentions of continuing on with you, sir."

Was this some kind of waking nightmare? "For what reason? We parted on fine terms last night, so why…?" He stopped cold. Only one thing could have upset the normally even-tempered Anna. She'd seen the young woman leaving his hut last night.

"I can tell by your face, sir, you've deduced exactly why. I can no longer in good conscience vouch for you with Nana Mala."

Icy shards claimed his gut. "Are you going to even ask me my side of this story?"

Her eyes narrowed. "Are you saying there is some defense for your actions? Because a lie will not save you or your business venture."

Stewart struggled to keep his composure. "There is nothing to lie about, no action to defend. The young woman in question was promptly rebuffed."

"Mr. Hastings, the last man that lied to me found that truth will often make itself known. His deception ended our engagement. In a matter as serious as this, I cannot be expected to just take your word."

He took a deep breath before answering. Antagonizing her wouldn't help. "You speak the language. Go question her yourself."

"Fair enough, but I guarantee it will not occur to her to tell anything less than the truth in this matter." She turned on her low-heeled boots and stalked back toward the village.

Stewart glanced at the grinning rowers gathered on the bank. They were entertained, even without a translation. Women troubles must be universal. And always more amusing if you weren't the object of them.

He went to his hut to retrieve his pack, wondering which direction he'd be traveling this morning. If the young woman didn't exonerate him, all his plans ended here. Getting around that little bundle of righteous indignation named Anna Baldwin if she blackballed him with the chief would be impossible.

If the young woman was honest, and if calm reason prevailed, he might have a chance. Right now *calm* didn't describe Anna at all. So different from the fragile woman he'd placed on Momma Elliott's davenport. A depth of serenity had looked back at him from those brown orbs. Nothing like the flashing anger he'd just witnessed. It had to be due to the fiancé's lies she'd mentioned. Was he being judged by another man's actions?

He groaned at the thought. Hadn't he done the same when it came to comparing her to Julianne? The irony of losing all he'd worked for to a woman who used the same inaccurate yardstick of comparison he himself wielded... No. He'd done no wrong. He'd have to make Anna see. He took off down the same path she'd traveled.

His frantic wanderings led him to an open area with a large cook fire. Behind an enormous iron kettle, an older woman modestly covered in a bright red cloth stood stirring. He'd gotten turned around. Where was Anna?

The red-dress woman pointed and directed him to a path on his right. His confusion had needed no translation. He found Anna and the young woman from last night. They both cut their gazes in his direction. Serious looks he couldn't read. Might as well resolve this now. He moved forward to meet his fate.

Anna's mortification increased. No sooner had the amused girl finished telling her tale of surprise at her ouster from Stewart's hut, but there was the man himself. No time to pick and choose her words of apology. His stride hitched when their eyes met. Little wonder after her display at the riverbank. The poor man.

In either bush world, he struck a fine figure. More than one young maiden had approached Anna last night asking about his blond hair. She hadn't translated so he wouldn't know the extent of the interest his presence created and fall prey to temptation. Instead he appeared immune to temptation and in need of inoculation against her hasty judgment.

Lord, give me the words to make this right.

Now giggling, the smitten girl leaned closer and asked a question.

Stewart's head tilted as if better hearing were his barrier to understanding. "What is she saying? I can't defend myself if I can't understand her accusations."

Anna dismissed the girl, who left reluctantly. Anna called on every bit of inner strength she had to meet his eyes. "She confirmed your story."

"I see." Stewart stood quietly and stared, the relief on his face telltale of the turmoil he'd experienced at her hand.

She swallowed hard. "I'm sorry, Mr. Hastings. I failed to get all the facts before drawing a conclusion. I was wrong and I pray you can find it in your heart to forgive me."

His continued stare gathered up time and held it still. What more could she say?

"Mr. Hastings?"

He blinked, as if coming out of a stupor. "Of course, Miss Baldwin. Now perhaps we can put this aside and return to the business at hand. I'm anxious to get farther up the river today."

"Um…certainly. I'll inform the rowers of our intentions immediately."

He still looked at her as if she were a rare and unexpected specimen of Liberian wildlife he hadn't presumed to see. "Good. I'll grab my gear."

Anna turned to go.

"Miss Baldwin?"

"Yes?"

"I've never heard those words from a woman before today." The edges of his lips quirked a bit to one side. "My experience with most women has been that they would sew their own lips shut before admitting something wasn't the man's fault."

Even though he spoke with no rancor, the thought brought her up short. "But it clearly was my fault. I was even the one telling you on board ship that there is always more to a story than first meets the eye. Proverbs tells us that, but in the heat of the moment, I forgot myself and all that God's Word counsels."

He stepped forward, shortening the distance between them. His voice lowered and held gentle understanding. "From what you said before, I think that some of that anger was not intended for me. Perhaps one day when you meet the man you'll marry, you'll realize that all men are not liars like your former fiancé. I'm sorry that he hurt you." He turned and left, calling over his shoulder, "I'll be at the river."

She formed a denial that died a quick death before leaving her lips. Was he right? His hasty retreat brooked no further discussion. He must have taken her silence for agreement. Deep in her heart a small voice of truth clamored to be heard.

Without knowing anything of her life before she'd come to Liberia, Stewart Hastings defined a clear fault within her, even if he misjudged the only reason as a broken engagement. How could he possibly have understood her when she had been so blind to the obvious?

Her erstwhile fiancé's plans and promises about their marriage had been a lie, all designed to get her to the altar. Her own father had fed Reginald the words to woo her, telling him how important her faith was and how she valued the freedom to minister to others.

Reginald had had no intention of letting her do anything after marriage that didn't fit his own needs, and his profession of faith was a sham. The only thing he'd valued was her outward appearance and how he would look with her by his side. The curse of a beautiful face.

Even worse were her father's machinations to gain social connections and financial opportunities by marrying his only child into even older money. Both men had lied, thinking only of their own needs, but her father's betrayal had brought the most pain. Surprising how she could still be hurt by him, considering all the lies he'd told throughout her life.

And clearly she now had even more reason to beware of getting too close to Stewart Hastings. The lure of such a perceptive man, one who so easily forgave the injustice of her accusation and who took the time to try to understand her, was far more dangerous to her heart than the innocent flirting she'd steeled herself to resist. If she wasn't careful, she'd find herself dangling from an emotional hook that would compromise her faith far more than anything she'd considered possible.

Dear Lord, give me strength to stand strong lest my own emotional needs get in the way of my witness for You.

For now she'd be more careful, not only about jumping to conclusions without hearing the whole story, but also about guarding her heart against unexpected tugs of attraction that could distract her from her true mission, spreading the Gospel message of forgiveness and God's love. She refused to allow any other love to have a part in that mission at all.

Stewart would never understand women, religious or not. Something had changed in Anna and he feared the worst. When they spoke, he felt a barrier between them, one she'd erected after their misunderstanding over the village girl. Her apology rang sincere, and he'd expected the easy camaraderie between them to resume. In some ways it had, but he had this nagging feeling that she was no longer comfortable with talking about anything remotely personal. She steered all attempts to get to know her better back to the mundane or trip-related talk.

It wasn't quite the moodiness he'd sometimes experienced with Julianne, but it was enough to make him renew the comparison he'd dismissed as unfair. Anna had the same unpredictability of womanhood stamped all over her.

A shame really. After watching her shrewd bargaining in Harper and her expert handling of every situation they'd encountered so far, he found himself chagrined over ever not wanting her as a guide. Could he possibly have found anyone more capable? The bishop might have credited God, but Stewart knew God wouldn't bother interfering in mankind's affairs.

Anna would surely disagree. Or she would if she'd resumed their normal banter long enough to hear his opinion. Would she loosen up any on the jungle portion of this journey?

It was a question he couldn't answer, despite the time to contemplate. Perhaps she was just tired. She preached tirelessly. At times Stewart couldn't help but wonder if the jungle provided a refuge for her. Was she running from a broken heart? Maybe she'd cared more for her former fiancé than she'd realized.

One of the rowers in the front canoe called back, and Stewart's own bark moved toward shore. They'd reached their last stop before the falls, and well before the afternoon rains. From here they'd travel by foot. A gaggle of children stood on the bank to greet them.

He'd given out small gifts at each stop, one or two for the children to share. Had the drums passed the word? This was quite the turnout.

Anna alighted and was surrounded by a bevy of small nut-brown bodies, some completely unclad. The mothers, wearing more than their offspring and adorned with jewelry of bones and iron, watched, smiling. Anna handled the children's excitement and greeted each adult present. Perfectly at ease.

Just not with him.

He stood to join her just as his canoe bumped the bank. Trying to correct his balance rocked the bark vessel. Arms spinning, he went backward into the water.

Cold enveloped him. His pith helmet swam away on its own. In two strokes, he grabbed it and returned to the far side of the canoe edge, seeking purchase on the river bottom. Too deep. To the amusement of the gathered crowd, he worked his way around to the bank, where two strong rowers hefted him onto dry land.

He sluiced his face and ran fingers through his hair. If he changed before they left, at least he'd be dry for the first part of their march. Fortunately his 88 Winchester lay safely in the canoe bottom instead of joining him in the river.

Miss Baldwin, on the other hand, looked resplendently dry. Her eyes crinkled in amusement at his predicament. The first sign of unrestrained emotion he'd seen since the misunderstanding.

She asked, "Are you all right?"

"A bit waterlogged, but that's nothing new."

She turned to answer a shouted question from behind her and then told him, "They quite enjoyed the show."

"This is the rainy season, so I know they have seen a wet man before." He ran his fingers through his locks once more. "Has my cowlick taken a turn for the worse?"

She laughed. He'd forgotten how captivating that sound was. "No, it's the color again."

"I guess I do stand out."

"A wet giant with hair like the sun? Yes, you do."

"Always happy to make someone laugh. If mining doesn't work out, I might have to consider a career in vaudeville."

Her face sobered. "Another reason you stand out, Mr. Hastings. Most men would be too concerned with their own sense of dignity to make a joke and be comfortable with others laughing at them."

Her unexpected praise warmed him, but not enough to shake off the Cavalla chill. "Since the show is over now, can I find a place to change into dry clothes before setting out?"

Her head tilted. "Of course, but we won't leave until tomorrow morning at the earliest. Negotiations could take hours."

"What is there to negotiate besides where to secure the canoes?"

Her eyebrows almost crossed each other in the center. What wasn't clear? Sitting in a village for half a day would waste valuable time. Was she hoping to preach again? She was a paragon for preaching at every stop.

"A certain protocol must be followed to get the help

we need, Mr. Hastings. But why ever would we need to secure the canoes?"

"Our men can't be expected to transport all these canoes and our supplies. The logistics of that are inconceivable. Unless you know something I don't?"

Her face took on the look of someone working an impossible equation. Tentatively she said, "Nothing that will have us traveling before morning or require securing the canoes."

"Then what shall we do with them if we are not leaving them here? Won't our rowers need them when they return from Nana Mala's village?"

Her eyes widened. Finally she understood.

"Whatever made you think the rowers would take us overland?"

His stomach took on a waterlogged feel to match his exterior. "I promised them a handsome salary."

All traces of amusement fled from her face. "Oh, dear, Mr. Hastings. Just how much did you promise them?"

She blanched when he quoted the figure. "No wonder we've had so few complaints along the way. It's a veritable fortune in their world."

"Exactly. Enough to carry us to our destination."

Her head shook. "No, it's not. A Kru rower is a man of the waterways, the ocean even, but overland into the interior? Only for short distances. If you want a coastal Kru man to travel distance, it had better be on a boat."

He'd failed to ask the *right* questions of men like Wilson, and he'd insisted on doing his own hiring in Harper while he'd sent Anna for supplies. All in the name of efficiency. And being in charge…

He'd prefer to fall back in the river again than play the fool in business dealings. He hadn't felt this embarrassed since he'd dined at the country club with his potential in-laws for the first time. He'd proved himself as out of his element in a fine dining room as he was in the jungle. He swallowed the huge lump that was his pride and asked, "How will we proceed?"

"I'll know after I negotiate with the chief and elders to obtain carriers."

"If they say no?"

"Highly unlikely, Mr. Hastings. Please don't worry. Providing carriers for travelers such as us is a common form of hospitality. Add in the help of some of your trade goods, and we'll do fine. 'No' is not an answer I expect to hear."

"No" was exactly what she heard. As a woman, Anna sat outside the official male-only palaver area on the low stool provided her. Her meal of cassava and fruit settled into a lead ball. Three village elders sat next to the chief, all festooned with their necklaces of animal teeth and the small horns strung and used as a fetish. Each man's hand involuntarily moved to touch the horn around his neck for protection when she'd asked for carriers westward.

Stewart seemed unaware of her dilemma and was still picking his way through the cassava dish he'd been given. After his earlier distress, she hated to tell him about this new issue. If she could resolve things first…

Stewart chose that moment to look up from his food. "Is there a problem?"

He was too perceptive by far. And not just about her. "Nothing I can't overcome."

"You do realize how awkward it is to sit here like a decorative appendage on this stool and not understand a word anyone is saying."

"I'm sorry. I'm afraid I've spent so much time in the

interior by myself I don't think about someone else's limitations."

Stewart's lips quirked in his trademark half smile, revealing the hidden dimple. "If I gather that by 'limitations' you mean my inability to speak fourteen languages..."

Realizing how her words sounded, Anna said, "I didn't mean to imply—"

He flicked his hand. "Of course not. Indulging in a bit of teasing when everyone's so serious is habitual with me. I know you weren't maligning my intelligence. Please, just translate."

So much for solving the problem first. "Of course. Right now the chief and his council are worried about rumors of a secret society active in the jungle. The devilman, the stern-looking fellow in the elaborate headdress, insists their people would be in danger even though the supposed problem is closer to our destination."

"A secret society? In the jungle? Are we expected to believe this bit of fiction?"

"Actually, yes. The interior is rife with stories of secret societies, all based on animal totems. Early explorers documented many encounters with them. The one they are concerned with is the Leopard Society. You have to understand, these rumors gain attention every time someone is found after an attack by an actual leopard. While the real Leopard Society has a long history here, the government cracked down on them several years back. Reprisals are fierce if one is even suspected to be a Leopard Man."

Stewart asked, "So why would anyone become one?"

"Age-old purposes found in every culture. Belonging, feeling superior or special and, of course, power. In all these societies, power comes from fear and superstition."

"What is their particular fear?"

"Death, mainly. No death is ever simple here in the interior. However, most deaths are blamed on witchcraft, not secret societies."

Stewart shook his head. "Sounds like a great tale to raise the price of our transaction."

"Villages rarely try to extort travelers. An ingrained code of hospitality leaves them feeling obligated to help. Their willingness to ignore the custom tells me they believe these rumors, even if they are unfounded."

Stewart interrupted, "So what do we do?"

"Leave the negotiations to me. I'll get something worked out here. I'm sure God didn't bring us this far to have us turn back. I need to maneuver around the devilman. His talk is fueling their concerns."

Stewart's lips thinned. "Given my prime example of negotiating skill, I'm more than happy to leave the process in your hands. My only advice is to not make this into some kind of religious battle between you and the devilman. Try economics and see if you can negotiate something that gets us on the trail and doesn't bankrupt me."

"Shh! Let me listen." The increasing volume of the devilman's comments caught her attention. She listened and then turned to Stewart. "In this case, money is going to be exactly the currency Heaven uses to get us on our way."

"Why, what did he say?"

"This devilman is a sly one. He proposed creating specific charms of protection for both us and the carriers. For a fee, of course."

"Aha! So it was all about money."

"I hate to fuel your cynicism, but in this case, apparently it is. Plus, the devilman elevates his own status when his people believe they need his special charms to protect them. However, as a believer, for me to wear his fetish charm is out of the question."

Stewart shook his head. "I am not going to let the superstitions that either of you believe in compromise this journey...."

She put her bowl down. "You agreed not to compromise the Gospel in the villages we pass through. Wearing a fetish charm as a form of protection sends a message that our God is powerless to protect us. We simply can't do it."

All his fears of leaving his fate in this woman's hands reasserted themselves. This wasn't happening; not again. He launched his appeal. "Miss Baldwin, what other options are available? I can't afford to use precious days backtracking for a different route at this point." How could she smile when his world was falling apart?

"Relax, Mr. Hastings. You won't have to, not once I offer an extra bit of dash, or gifts for their trouble."

He sat. "But you just said—"

She interrupted. "I said wearing a charm was out of the question. Making a payment and calling it part of the dash is not. The chief can buy protection charms with the money if he wishes. This is a wonderful opportunity to show them that wearing a fetish object is not the true source of power. If neither of us wear one and yet remain unharmed, it sends a strong message."

The tension fled his body. "Miss Baldwin, you are a genius. You'll manage our needs, their fears and spread your Gospel all in one fell swoop."

She stood. "You know what they say about counting chickens. Let's be sure the chief agrees before we celebrate."

Stewart stood with her. After a few moments of speaking, Anna told him, "The chief is happy with the terms." She raised her eyebrows and canted her head slightly. "Apparently so is the devilman. He claims he can have enough charms ready for us to leave in the morning."

"Convenient."

"I'm about to tell him not to make any for us. He's not going to like my refusal, but he told the chief he'd make enough by morning, so he won't be able to back down."

His admiration for the uncompromising little negotiator grew. He was the only one who'd almost ruined things with his mishandled travel arrangements. She'd bailed him out at every turn. Even now she appeared to be holding her own against an unhappy devilman. "Anna, what is he saying?"

"The devilman is trying to regain the upper hand by reminding his people how he alone protects them and how foolish we are not to rely on his magic."

The devilman gestured, touching both of his hands. Anna translated his words. "He's emphasizing the terror of the Leopard Men. They have iron claws in place of hands. They rip their victims to shreds. No one is left alive to tell tales."

Stewart asked, "Unless they wear his charms, I suppose?"

Anna ignored him and kept translating. "The Leopard Men are powerful. Careful. They watch and wait till someone is alone."

"Assure them we will post armed sentries. I have extra Winchesters with me. Are they familiar with their use?"

Anna nodded. As the devilman continued, she stood intent on his every word.

"Anna, what is it?"

She ignored him until the devilman finished speaking and stood arms crossed, chin up. Clearly the man thought the advantage had gone to him.

Anna turned to Stewart. "According to the devilman, the Leopard Society is steeped in cannibalism."

Stewart asked, "How is that any different than the Pahn?"

"Nana Mala may eat his enemies to gain their strength, but in most cases it is an honor to a defeated warrior. From what the devilman says, Leopard Men look for innocent sacrifices."

The devilman spoke up again. The chief and elders nodded as his tirade continued.

Anna waited patiently and then spoke words to the chief. He gave a rather lengthy answer punctuated by the entire council rising and leaving.

Stewart looked at Anna. "So I gather we've been dismissed. Where do we stand?"

"We leave at first light."

He whooped for joy. "That's wonderful news!" He reached out to pat her on the back.

Anna took a wary step backward. "This isn't where you attempt to spin me like a top again, is it?"

He stilled himself, arms at his sides. "No, Miss Baldwin, this is where I thank you and acknowledge how my own ignorance almost derailed this undertaking. I may have led men in the Great War, but you've shown me your knowledge, your experience and your ability to deal with these people are all more than adequate."

Either it was a trick of the sun glinting, or Anna Baldwin just teared up.

A rapid blink removed the evidence, but emotion thickened her voice. "Your compliment means a lot to me, Mr. Hastings."

"Only what you're due. By the way, what was the last bit about? The chief's speech there at the end."

Anna hesitated. "The chief related his own story of the Leopard Men. As a young child, he stumbled upon an attack in progress and hid before the pack saw him. He described their leopard-skin headdress, their yellowed skin and how they used those iron claws attached to their hands. I'll spare you the details. Suffice it to say he believes these rumors to be true."

"Do you believe him?"

"Yes, his recounting of the memory was strong. But he told me that with us traveling with his men, he would rest easier for their safety where the Leopard Men are concerned."

"Does he think your God more powerful than the devilman's charms? Are we some form of superstitious protection now?"

Anna cleared her throat. "No, they still believe we might encounter the Leopard Men as they look for sacrifices of blood to help increase the leopard god's power."

Stewart's suspicions grew. "How does any of this make him rest easier?"

Anna answered, "The chief said we would be their main targets and not even his devilman's charms could protect us. He believes if the Leopard Men learn we are here, they will leave his people alone and deliberately seek us out for what they believe to be the uniqueness of our blood. He fully expects we will be the ones sacrificed to the leopard god."

Chapter Five

After two weeks and three different villages, Leopard Men no longer worried Anna. The hours of unrelenting daily rains, the chill that followed them into the evening and the treacherous wet trails they brought were the real problem. As soon as she could finish assigning loads to their new porters, they would make as much progress as the morning allowed.

All around her, the village children watched every move, mostly hoping for a glimpse of some new wonder to be found in her packs. Despite taking the time to answer questions from less shy members of her audience, the process went quickly. Some packs needed no adjustments, still falling under the forty-pound mark that each man would carry. Others needed consolidation since they'd been lightened through personal use and trade. And each one needed checking lest the oiled baize cloth not be wrapped and secured properly and the contents fell victim to the rains. The last one in front of her held the items she'd promised for the porters' services.

As she dug through the pack until she found the fathoms of suitable cloth she sought, the children's chatter ceased. She glanced up and saw Stewart headed her way.

The attention of a dozen pairs of button-brown eyes left her and looked toward Stewart expectantly. He reached into his pack and brought out a small, round wooden object that he fumbled with and then cast from his hand. Only then did she see the string. Both she and the children watched in amazement as the disc climbed back up the string and returned to his hand time and again.

The children broke their reverent silence and clamored to try the disc. Anna set the cloth down and moved closer to watch. Stewart raised one hand and waited until he had silence, then proceeded to launch the disc again. With each up-and-down motion, the children's animation grew. Anna pulled her attention away from the display long enough to catch the look on Stewart's face. He bestowed his broad grin easily on the little ones. His ease with the children, his willingness to entertain them, amazed her more than the novelty of the disc.

A man who bothered to play with children. Before she'd gotten to know him better, she would have thought he saved his charms for flirting with pretty young women, as on board the ship. Seeing a grown man playing children's games wasn't in the realm of her experience.

Packs forgotten, Anna stared harder at the man engaged in play, children giggling all around him. Her own father was too concerned about appearances to be so… so…undignified. Stewart Hastings acted downright silly with the little ones.

No hasty or mistaken judgments about him in this. He would truly make a good father. She pictured him with a large brood of his own, listening to them, playing with them. She envied the woman who would stand by his side. Except for his unbelief, Stewart behaved toward children exactly like the kind of man she would want to marry.

As soon as the thought laid siege to her brain, she threw up her defenses. What did it matter to her, his potential as a father, his potential as a husband? Allowing any creep of romantic feelings toward this man was a serious mistake.

True, he'd saved her life. He complimented her for her abilities and not her appearance, something no man had ever done…and he took time with children, treating them as precious and important, not something to be cultivated and displayed. Or worse, ignored.

But his unbelief was a true stumbling block.

Stewart handed the disc to one of the older boys and walked toward her. Her thoughts scattered, a disturbing sign that time spent in his company was affecting her more than she realized. Was she so needy from the lack of attention in her childhood that she'd allow the simple sight of a man lavishing attention on the young to capture her thoughts so?

He set his pack down near the stacked goods and brandished that smile like a weapon against her heart. "Can I lend a hand?"

The simple question stymied her. She was glad he couldn't know how much he'd begun to intrude on her thoughts.

At her hesitation his gaze took on an investigative slant. "Miss Baldwin, are you all right?"

She scrambled for an answer to put him off the scent and found an easy truth. "Yes, but as mesmerized as the little ones with your disc on a string."

His eyebrows went up. "My bandalore?"

"Is that what it's called?"

"You've never seen a bandalore? They were prized in

the neighborhood where I grew up. I thought they were a common toy."

Oh, dear. Such a simple thing and her ignorance revealed so much based on the look on his face. "Not in my household, apparently. I've not even heard the name before now."

"Maybe you heard it called a quiz? A Phillippine kid in my neighborhood once called it a yo-yo, but I doubt that name has spread." At her continued head shakes, he asked, "Were you raised in isolation? Bandalores have been around since the Greeks. What kind of toys did you and your friends play with, Miss Baldwin?"

She tried for nonchalance. "Not bandalores, as you can tell. Although I did have an extensive doll collection." Never mind that they were considered too precious to serve as actual playthings. Best to take the spotlight off herself. "But tell me, how is it that you carry toys with your supplies? Doesn't sound very businesslike to me."

His color heightened. "If you must know, there is a practical aspect to the toys. They generate goodwill for my employer."

None of his behavior with the children looked like a ploy. Maybe his argument would be more convincing if he'd maneuvered his encounters to take place in front of the parents. "I've observed you in several villages so far. Most men wouldn't spend the time with little ones that you do. Admit it, sir. You have a genuine fondness for children. If I were a wagering woman, I'd bet you have plans for your own large brood."

A deep and sudden sadness crossed his features. Had she said something wrong?

"You caught me, Miss Baldwin. I confess that I've always had a soft spot for the little ones. As to a brood of my own, I can hardly speculate or plan without a wife involved."

"I'm sure that will be no problem for a charming and handsome man as yourself."

He nodded toward her sorting of the trade goods. She followed his gaze and noticed the cloth she'd laid out had been opened and examined by several of the men serving as porters.

Stewart said, "They seem to like the cloth. Have we settled the issue of their services yet?"

Now who was changing the subject? She recognized the tactic easily as her own. She set aside her curiosity and turned back to the matter at hand. "Yes, but I had to give a little more than before. This group is even more agitated about the Leopard Society rumors."

He removed his hat and ran his fingers through his hair. "Seems the farther in we go, the more we hear these tales. And yet, no Leopard Men have attacked us." He replaced his pith helmet.

Anna gathered up the length of cloth and tried to return it to its former neat fold while she talked. "Two actual deaths in this area credit their fears with worth. You and I know that the blame most likely lies with a young male leopard establishing himself. We must finally have reached his range of territory. We should continue to post armed sentries. A young male leopard will aggressively defend his new claim."

Before she could protest, Stewart grabbed one end of the cloth she struggled to fold and stepped back, tightening the cloth's slack between them. "I agree, Miss Baldwin. Even if we never cross this animal's path, I'm glad you stay so prepared. You're a capable woman. I am still amazed at how you turned disaster into a workable plan back in the riverside village."

His continued compliments left her off balance, not unlike when he'd spun her around on board the ship. "Thank you. And you don't have to help with this cloth. I can manage."

"Nonsense. I learned from helping my mother that large items fold easier with two at the task." He followed her lead as she joined the length of the cloth edge to edge and then held the new sides taut. He moved toward her with his end and they met in the middle to fold it in two. Their hands grazed as he took her end from her. *Just fold the cloth,* she admonished herself, even as she breathed in the familiar faint hint of bay rum. She grabbed the new edge at the bottom and stepped back to pull it tight. He advanced to meet her end for a second fold and she made a desperate bid to seem nonchalant about the whole process. She could never reveal how empty she felt after his hands pulled away.

Stewart knew he'd flustered her when their hands met at the fold. It wasn't his intention to make her uncomfortable, only to help. He enjoyed being in her company more than he could admit. Right now he'd give anything to have more cloth to fold.

His mind wandered further, wondering what it would be like to casually fold laundry, spend time at mundane tasks with a woman he loved.

What was she saying?

"You are right about them liking the cloth. Here men do the weaving, and this piece is wider than they are able to achieve. They have to sew strips together to achieve this dimension because of the way their weaving apparatus is constructed."

She took the now manageable bundle from him. He pulled a blanket out of the open packet and added it to the small pile. "And here I thought you were going to compliment my folding skills and how well we worked together."

She ignored his comment and secured the lightened pack for travel. "You say you helped your mother? How is it you lent a hand doing what most men would consider women's work and beneath them?"

He laughed. "Disobedience had its consequences in my household. If I didn't want a switch to my backside, I did as I was told. But one look at how tired she was after a long day of scrubbing and cleaning other people's messes, and I never considered refusing to help her with anything needed in our own household. Some of those skills later helped me supplement my scholarship by working for rich fraternity boys. I knew how to manage everything from making a bed to laundry."

"Where did you go to school?

"Harvard."

"I'm impressed."

"Don't be. My scholarship didn't help me read the maps of this country or understand that our rowers wouldn't double as porters."

"But you did manage to choose very viable trading items for someone so new to the country. I only shopped from the list you gave me." She finished tying off the pack and straightened. "Besides, anyone new here might have thought they could rely on those maps. I made my own share of mistakes when I first arrived. Fortunately, I had the Mayweathers to help guide me away from the more serious ones."

His voice thickened before he gained control. "As I have had you."

For a too-short moment their gazes met and his lungs refused to fill with air as they had that night they first met. Anna broke off first, taking a sudden interest in her feet, allowing him to breathe deeply once again.

He ended the silence by clearing his throat. "And fortunately the contact I met in the tavern before I crossed paths with your attackers was a good source of practical information."

"A tavern? But you're temperate."

"Don't look shocked. I may not drink, but I met a potential guide there for an interview. The timing of that meeting may have saved your life."

She motioned for one of the remaining porters to take the last pack. "I'm grateful. Such a shock to be a victim of a random attack in a place where I expected to be safe. I take comfort in how God managed things for both our benefits."

Stewart disagreed. "I hate to say so, but on reflection, I don't believe that attack was random at all. Those two likely targeted you specifically."

A sudden chill swept through her. For what reason? No one would go to such lengths. "No, what happened had to be no more than a chance occurrence."

"Two Liberian natives with chloroform? How would they have such a drug? Then they happen to find a lone American woman walking home? There was no *chance* about it."

She tried to hide her fear, but her rising pitch was such a tattletale. "Who would want a bush missionary for a captive?"

He must have seen through her defenses. His eyes held a barely banked humor when he smiled. "Another possibility exists. I've seen your temper firsthand. You wield a serious umbrella when the situation demands. Is there anyone back home or in Liberia you've angered?"

She shook her head. "I can't think of a soul."

"I was only kidding, but it looks like your thoughts have taken a serious turn."

She nodded. "I suppose the idea, while absurd, gives me a chill. At home, I have no one but my parents and the maid who raised me. Neither is likely to have orchestrated such an act."

"Does this maid harbor a grudge against you?"

Anna laughed. "Marie? Not possible. She raised me from a young child, put me to bed, sang me lullabies. She introduced me to Christ, and her church raised my support to come here."

Stewart's head canted. "Your parents didn't take you to church?"

How did she explain parents like hers?

"Only on special occasions such as Christmas and Easter. They were unhappy with my decision to come here."

"So unhappy they may want to kidnap you or harm you in some way?"

"No, of course not." Despite her father's drastic steps to keep her from her calling, his telegram while she traversed the Atlantic made it clear he'd washed his hands of her. "My parents are far too worried about trying to make a mark in society or finding the money to continue their social climb, especially since I left."

He stepped closer. "What do you mean, especially since you left?"

Anna hesitated. "I'm not used to telling my private business to people, Mr. Hastings."

The zeal to know drained from his eyes. "I apologize. I've overstepped."

Would he understand? "My parents don't serve God.

Their religion is wealth and status. My leaving prevented them from using me to acquire more of both."

"But if someone knew you previously had a maid, a lot of people would assume you were wealthy. Could your parents be known as people who had enough money to pay a ransom?"

"If they were kidnappers, they were destined for great disappointment. Knowing my father, even if he could get the funds, he'd only pay to have me back if I agreed to his disastrous marriage plans. Which I wouldn't."

Stewart's brows knit together. "The fiancé you alluded to before?"

Anna forged ahead. "Yes, a wealthy man. Old money. My parents hoped for an elevation in social status and their finances by arranging a marriage between us."

"Usually money flows to the husband, not the other way."

"Not in this case. Reginald promised to pay handsomely to assure I graced his arm. Ours was an ill-fated match in many ways, even before I felt the call to missions."

"Ill-fated how?"

"My fiancé deceived me into thinking he was a believer so I would agree to marry him. Despite his insistence once I uncovered the truth, I would never marry an unbeliever."

Stewart's eyes narrowed. "Not to be indelicate, Miss Baldwin, but with a face like yours, other marriage-minded men who shared your faith, wealthy or not, couldn't have been in short supply. You mentioned my potential as a family man, but what about you? Don't you want a family, too?"

Did he think her so unfeeling? Anna blinked back the moisture gathering beneath her eyelids. She directed her attention to the children's antics with the bandalore while she gathered her emotions into control. "I would love to have children, but sacrificing my calling or settling for a man who didn't actually share my beliefs is out of the question."

Consternation spread across his features. "Has no man who shares your faith asked for your hand? I find it hard to believe you wouldn't have had a suitable proposal by now."

She brushed off her skirts. "Many proposals, but none suitable. Ardent young men have made offers, some even impulsively after our first meeting. Once they realized I possessed strong ambitions as well as a porcelain complexion, their ardor quickly cooled."

He shook his head. "Hard to believe, Miss Baldwin."

"Tell me, Mr. Hastings, how many men do you know who would desire to share their wife with the work of a remote jungle mission?"

"Other missionaries? I bet some would jump the Cavalla rapids for the chance."

"Poetic, but no. For now, my students are enough for me. If God wants otherwise, I trust he'll send the right man into my life, one who will see my heart."

Stewart's voice took on an unexpected fervor. "Perhaps he did. Maybe your standards are the problem. Are you sure you'd recognize him even if he stood in front of you?"

Anna took a hard look at the man in front of her. She'd warned him about flirting with her on the ship, but this was a more serious tone. Had his flirting concealed something deeper? Maybe she'd cultivated this in him, failing to conceal her growing interest in him as well as she'd thought. Or maybe she was misconstruing his intent. Best to get it out into the open now and put the issue to rest. She just had to keep her tone as light as possible in case she was mistaken. "Mr. Hastings, are you suggesting you're the man God has sent for me to marry?"

She'd stolen a page out of his big book of teasing scenarios, the one he used to keep things light and casual and unsuspecting women at bay. As if a woman like Anna would have anything to do with someone like him except as a joke. Even laying aside the faith issue, it would be like one of Grimm's tales: the one about the beautiful young maiden and the hideous beast. Difference was, Stewart's ugliness lay concealed beneath his shirt. And the son of a dockworker was no prince in disguise.

He'd developed some tenderness toward her that hopefully she would never realize. But love or anything like it had no place between two such disparate people. He could never be happy with a religious woman. He answered, lighthearted tone in kind, one hand across his heart, "No. I promise I have absolutely no interest in even applying for the position."

Her expression turned to relief. "Good, I'd hate to think I'd sent out the wrong impression."

Not all teasing, then, but some real worry, too. He should put that completely to rest. Maybe that was why she'd been so distant.

"No, Miss Baldwin, neither myself nor any other man like me who spent time in your company would feel driven to propose. Your calling is clear. You are safe from any impulsive proposals from this quarter. I…"

He watched in horror as her face flamed in embarrassment to match his own. Unless he was mistaken, the words he'd intended as reassurance actually implied that no man would be interested in her after getting to know her. "I mean… I…"

She fanned her face and looked everywhere but directly at him. "No, Mr. Hastings. Don't apologize. I'm not very good at the lighthearted side of things and I made a hash of it by trying to joke around about a serious subject. Of course you have no interest in someone like me. And truly, most men wouldn't."

"But I didn't mean…"

She held up a hand. "Not another word. Your true meaning was clear. Now, if we are to make progress today, we should set out as soon as we present our dash to the chief."

Stewart did what any sane man would in the situation. He shut his mouth and followed her lead while he tried to figure out how to walk with one foot still firmly planted in his mouth.

Stewart hacked at the vegetation in front of him. He was used to hard work, but nothing like wielding a machete through the never-ending maze of jungle growth in this heat. The muscles in his arm clamored for a rest as much as he itched to unbutton his high-collared shirt and cool off, even for a moment. Unfortunately, exposing the ugliness beneath the cotton was not an option.

He stopped to catch his breath and reached for his canteen. Heat or not, the machete work would be worse once the rains cascaded down. He took a swig of water and diverted his thoughts to his surroundings. They'd started on a worn, single-file pathway near the village and then moved to climbing over massive tree roots skimming the ground. His geologically trained mind knew the granite lying shallow beneath the loam wouldn't let roots burrow to any significant depth, but his bruised body suspected the soaring cotton trees possessed murderous intent, deliberately tripping unschooled feet.

The dense vegetation was worse. The undergrowth yielded only by inches and with much reluctance to the blade in his hand. He consoled himself with how exhaustion might bring sleep, and keep him from replaying an endless review of his last conversation with Anna.

Little moments from their talk plagued him, popping up as he lay in his camp bed like three-dimensional images on a stereoscope. The small quiver of her lips when she'd said her students were enough told him about the tenderness of her emotions. Anna Baldwin wanted a family. He knew the pain of that want. Only, unlike his own, her dream was achievable.

Next was the fear that had crossed her face when discussing the possibility of her attackers having targeted her. A fierce protectiveness rose up within him. Someone might try again and he wouldn't be there to protect her. And he was drawn to protect this woman even more fiercely than he had been his mother.

But when he got to the last stereoscope slide, the picture of Anna, Bible in hand, preaching her beliefs every chance afforded to her, he could never picture himself at her side. There was no place for someone who couldn't share her faith. And he never would.

He renewed his attack on the vegetation. He sorely missed canoe travel. He understood Anna's concerns about his routing now. The jungle made him earn his deadline bonus every day. He was foolish to have insisted on this route over Anna's objections. They were only now entering the boundaries of the proposed mining concession. He'd have to manage his time carefully to deal with the mountains near the Pahn.

He looked back. Anna remained out of sight. The

single-file trail snaked backward for some distance. When he remembered his question to the bishop about proprieties, he could only laugh. Anna was accompanied almost everywhere she stepped. Porters made endless requests to hear her "stories" after dinner and later vied for the honor of sleeping in front of her tent to serve as a guard.

This group was so protective they'd been upset when she'd refused to ride in the hammock chair left over from a long-ago exploration expedition. She insisted she would not be carried—no special treatment for her. Even when she spoke until all hours, she always had a kind word for anyone who wanted her time. Mammy Anna, as she was called, set an exhausting pace for herself. The circles under her eyes were growing.

Ahead of him, shouts of triumph. He pressed forward and found the men happily divesting themselves of their packs in a small clearing with a wider path leading forward. Till now, the trail had made their usual noon break impossible. He eyed the forming clouds. The daily downpour was coming soon. Best to eat while they could enjoy the experience.

He sheathed his machete and reached for his canteen. Almost empty. The last swig went down as Anna came into sight, a flock of porters on her heels.

She held out her canteen. "Here. Don't let the heat disable you before we reach an adequate stop for the night. Drink more and slow down a little."

"I'll not take water away from you. Just because you weren't swinging a machete doesn't mean you aren't in need, as well. Walking is difficult, too."

She lifted her pith helmet and brushed damp tendrils of hair off her forehead. "Don't be foolish. Our men say we'll cross a major stream very soon. I'll purify more."

He weighed her nearly full canteen in his hand and then drank deeply before returning the remainder. "Thank you."

She reseated her hat. "You're welcome. We'll make better time now that the machetes can be sheathed."

He couldn't help but laugh. "Until the rain slows us down. I finally understand why they measure distance here in days of travel instead of miles."

A porter appeared at their side, handing out bananas, mangos and plums. They sat and ate while they could do so and remain dry.

When they'd finished, Stewart said, "You, Miss Baldwin, are a woman of remarkable restraint."

Her head canted to one side. "Restraint? In what way?"

"You've had any number of occasions to point out the folly of my travel plans. Soon we'll need even earlier camps so I can have the daylight to adequately prospect."

"In the rain? And you know how fast night falls with the trees blocking out so much of the sun." Her eyes took on an uncharacteristic twinkle. "I guess I won't complain about that, either, since Proverbs tells me 'It is better to dwell on the corner of a rooftop than with a contentious woman.'"

Brave to make a stab at teasing him after his last disastrous response to her attempt. Maybe his sense of humor was rubbing off on her, even if it ran to the biblical. Or, ever gracious, she was giving him the opening that eluded him, allowing him to move past the awkwardness he'd created at the start of this leg of their journey. He chose his words carefully.

"For once I defer to the wisdom of the Bible."

Her face lit up. "You might be surprised at how practical God's Word is for our lives."

He hadn't meant to encourage Bible talk. "And that, my dear Miss Baldwin, is my cue to call for our march to continue."

Anna called out the signal to move on. Stewart picked up his pack and turned to go. Her soft voice, no trace of joking, stopped him.

"Mr. Hastings?"

He turned and stepped aside while porters sluggishly moved past.

With a beatific smile to soften the blow, she said, "You can march away as far as you want, as long as you want, but God will always be there waiting."

A strong pressure formed in his chest, constricting his breath. She couldn't know she'd echoed his ever-hopeful mother's parting words. "You've got it all wrong, Miss Baldwin. In my experience, men will always be waiting on God. And He will never show up."

Anna climbed up and over yet another massive downed tree blocking the path. She considered Stewart's words and the barefaced pain that delivered each syllable. What had happened to bring him such sorrow and unbelief?

He'd shared about his father's drinking, but he kept the rest of his past as tightly buttoned up as his shirts. No buttons undone, ever. She must have touched a real sore spot for him to have voiced those feelings. Ahead, she lost sight of that familiar white Arrow shirt as he disappeared around a bend in the path. Carriers following him winked away, as each one rounded the same dense corner of vegetation. The loud commotion that followed set her to a run.

She reached the site to see men backing toward her in haste.

"Drivers," Suah, the headman they'd hired at the last village, said.

A common-enough sight, the black ribbon stretched across the path, its regimented motion unmistakable. She gave orders and Suah sent men to follow out the line to either end.

Stewart said, "Ants? Can't we just walk over them?"

"Only if we have to and then very carefully. These are driver ants. Common in the jungle. Don't get too close, Mr. Hastings. They'll leave us alone unless we provoke their attention."

He moved for a closer look. Just like a man. Tell him to stay away from danger and the little boy deep inside moves in for a better look. Next, he'd start poking them with a stick.

His voice filled with wonder. "Fascinating. They move like an army maneuver. The bigger ones flank the smaller ones and make one long marching column of soldiers."

He stood a little too close for her comfort. "Soldiers with a vicious bite who won't let go easily. Traveler's lore says some tribes use them like sutures to close a wound. Others use them as a form of punishment for wrongdoers. Most just stay out of their way."

He straightened and stepped back to her side. "What happens if you disturb them?"

"They'll fan out several feet on both sides, looking to attack. You don't want them turning in your direction. They eat anything in their path and their bite is quite painful."

He stared at the undulating trail with a grim fascination. "Not a fate to be envied. Do we wait or go around?"

"Depends. Drivers sometimes run for miles in one solid, unbroken train."

He gave a low whistle. She pointed to the returning scout reporting to Suah. The head porter came over. "Not good, Mammy Anna. Drivers long."

Stewart asked, "We can't wait for them to pass?"

"We have no way of knowing when the line will stop. We'll cross."

"Then let me carry you over the line. I don't want you hurt."

She looked at him quizzically. "I appreciate the thought, but I've done this a lot. It would be safer for both of us if you just followed my lead." She picked up her pack and secured it.

Suah gave orders to his men. They all walked up to the continuous sea of scurrying ants. To Stewart, Anna said, "We take wide steps and start stomping where our feet land." She lifted her skirt above her boots. "Follow me, and whatever you do, don't stop pounding your feet until we are well clear. If some of them get on you, the force shakes them off."

He stooped to tuck his pant legs into his boots. "I think I'll minimize their chances."

"Smart man. Now follow my lead." She took a broad step, moving rapidly while stomping once she crossed. She examined her boots before dropping her skirt.

Stewart joined her. "Not so bad."

Their porters walked on past them.

"This time. Most columns are small. Occasionally a whole colony picks up and moves en masse, creating a serious problem for anyone and anything in their way."

Once the last man cleared the ant line, Anna followed them down the trail, Stewart at her side.

Stewart mused, "At least we can see them before we have a problem."

"Not always. One missionary I know ended up spending the night on the top of his kitchen table holding his hysterical wife when their home was overrun. Drivers ate everything, but he didn't see a bug, rat or any vermin for some time after that night."

"What prevented the ants from climbing the table legs?"

"Remember the kerosene I bought? Most is for lighting, but if you pour some in tins and set the legs of your furniture in it, the ants won't bother you. They'll cross narrow water, but not kerosene or fire."

"Miss Baldwin, I take back all my thoughts of how much money I thought wasted on those containers."

The trail narrowed. A few minutes later the clouds opened and let loose the first of the downpour. Anna removed the slicker from her pack against the worst of the rains. Stewart did likewise and took the lead. For hours, the caravan became one long straggling line, Stewart behind Suah, who led the way. Both were barely visible through the deluge. Three porters slowed and stayed with her.

Next time she looked, Stewart and Suah were out of sight in the diminished visibility. She rounded a bend and found the carriers huddled under the tree line surrounding a clearing. Immediately ahead was the steep downward bank of a river. A V-shaped bridge of vines swayed over the snaking waterway, as Stewart tugged and tested the security of the structure.

She called out, "Those will need more than a good jerk or two to bring them down."

He returned to her side. "There must be another way instead of using such a flimsy structure."

Anna slid her pack to the ground. "Flimsy? Those vines are several inches in diameter. As long as they are maintained, they are safe."

"I hope so, otherwise we swim once we hit the water."

"Either we cross on the bridge or climb down to the banks, build a makeshift raft and lose a substantial amount of time. Don't worry. They're trickier in the rain, but the sides help you balance on the narrow bundled bottom vines. Follow my lead and all will be fine."

Stewart rubbed the stubble on his chin, dislodging the clinging drips of rainwater. "I don't need my hand held here, Miss Baldwin. I'm cautious, not fearful. Permit me a bit of checking before I entrust your safety to a bridge whose structure is somewhat suspect. The fall would be a significant risk."

Her safety? First he wanted to carry her over the ants and now this bridge business. He took a few tentative steps onto the bridge and returned. She cleared her throat to cover the amusement threatening to bubble out once she noticed his serious expression. He was really concerned. A warmth she couldn't identify started in her chest and spread. She couldn't remember a time anyone wanted to protect her before this. Well, except for the attack, but that was an extreme situation. Despite the fact that she'd been in the jungle longer and knew more about the dangers than he could imagine, to have someone worry and try to take care of her was touching.

She pulled her mind back to the moment at hand, lest the feeling overwhelm her. "Mr. Hastings, we'll have to make camp in another hour or so. A couple of the men want time to hunt monkey for dinner. We need to go forward if you're satisfied so they have time."

He walked over to reclaim his pack, unaware of how his simple concern had affected her. They stood together until the porters passed over the bridge. "Anna, have I eaten monkey before? I've tried not to ask the contents of some of those dishes."

"For the record, you've eaten some fine goat and chicken, but no monkey meat so far. It's tasty, but I struggle with their cute little faces when I eat it."

He laughed. "Here I thought you were a practical woman. Surely you wouldn't want one of those as a pet. Such noisy, smelly things always screeching at us and chattering in the canopy when we come across them. I prefer the beauty and sound of the parrots."

"As do I, but I have seen smaller species on the shoulders of some natives. But I wouldn't know what to do with a pet anyway. I understand they require a lot of care."

"Have you ever had a pet? A dog?"

She denied sadness an outlet. "Not really. My father didn't want the bother."

"So no pets, no bandalores. What did you do for fun?"

"Needlepoint, piano and all the arts for a young lady to be considered successful and catch a good society husband. To this day I have an aversion to sewing and only do so out of necessity."

Stewart gave a low whistle. "So, your parents planned to push themselves into high society through you from an early age. After watching you in the jungle, with the local peoples, I can't even imagine you sitting still with needlework in your lap." He shook his head. "Strange, I always envied people with more money than we had. Envied them almost as much as I disliked the very rich." One side of his lips curled when he spoke of the rich. "From what I can tell, despite the fact that your family had decent enough means to keep the one maid, there was more fun to be had in my slums."

He didn't realize how wealthy her family actually was. She searched back in their conversations and realized the assumptions they'd both made. His own mother came from the merchant class originally. He'd probably assumed Anna the same. He thought she had only one maid? More like one maid for her and one maid for everything else. They weren't Rockefeller rich, but quite wealthy, even if her father always lived above his means and wanted more.

Would Stewart be so protective if he knew she was one of the class of people he so despised? He'd talked about his mother cleaning up their messes.... This was another complication she hadn't anticipated, one she'd deal with only if necessary. That hadn't been her life since the day she'd left home.

She hefted her pack onto her shoulder. "It's never something like money that makes the real difference in life. People are the same, Mr. Hastings, whether they are in the Liberian jungle or locked behind rose gardens and stately homes."

The last of the porters headed across the bridge, their packs balanced on their heads and one holding the vine on that side. Before she followed, she said, "I know you wish for wealth from this trip and what it can provide, but money is only a tool. Having more doesn't bring happiness or change a person's true nature. Don't forget that, if you manage to achieve your goal. Money, or the desire for more, can drive men to things they wouldn't normally be capable of otherwise."

She pulled her hand from the scar on her cheek where it had instinctively crept as she spoke. It was better that she didn't call attention to the visible proof of that statement and end up revealing more of her background. Their relationship had finally found an equitable balance. Considering Stewart's barely concealed anger over his mother's treatment by wealthy employers, would he even want to keep working with Anna if he knew the extent of her family's wealth?

She sighed. In this case relationships and rope bridges had a lot in common—one misstep on either could prove fatal.

Chapter Six

Stewart noted how nimbly Anna crossed the rain-slicked bridge, just as he'd noticed the unconscious hand to her cheek. He recognized the motion as one he often made when talking about the war. His went to his chest or just below his collar.

When he'd first noticed her small scar, it had been a welcome relief from her perfection. Now its presence angered him. Who'd hurt her? And what did it have to do with the wealthy? Her fiancé again?

Every time he thought he understood her, she presented another dimension. She was a jigsaw puzzle with the pieces being doled out to him sparingly. The emerging puzzle didn't resemble the picture on the box he'd first drawn in his mind. But he'd have to ponder the mystery of Anna later. For now he had to cross this bridge without embarrassing himself.

He held the vine rails and put one foot in front of the other. The wobble disconcerted him, but if that little bit of a thing crossed in a skirt, he'd manage. Only question was how foolish he'd look as he traversed the span. This could be like his dunking in the Cavalla River all over again.

"Raise your head for better balance, Mr. Hastings. Watch me and not your feet."

So much for hiding his ineptitude. She'd crossed as if it were nothing more than a Sunday sidewalk stroll, so he followed her advice. Especially the part about keeping his eyes on her.

The wobble diminished, and she continued to coach him. "Walk faster and the crossing will be smoother."

He picked up his pace. Right again. When his feet touched solid ground, he tried to keep the relief from showing.

Anna walked up and patted him on the back. "You managed. Not bad for the first time crossing a vine bridge."

She'd seen right through his nonchalance. Might as well be a good sport. "Your advice was exactly what I needed, Miss Baldwin. Bring on the rope bridges—I'm ready for another." He lowered his tone to the more serious side. "But I'm still checking them all before use."

She rewarded him with laughter. "This territory is new to me, and all crossings are not made alike. Checking is a good idea."

Despite the cloud-obscured sun, her smile lit the jungle. Even those little wisps of curls that first popped out in the humidity managed to look appealing dampened by the downpour and plastered to her cheek. Movement out of the corner of his eye diverted his attention and saved him from being caught in a scrutiny he couldn't explain.

"Then we'll expect the unexpected. Like right now..." He pointed over her shoulder. "Our porters are leaving us behind. We usually have to inspire them onward. Quite a new spring in their step since we crossed the river."

She turned. "They're hoping the rain is about to let

up, and I think they're eager to make camp. Suah said they have a spot in mind."

The rains stopped as if on command. He'd never get used to the suddenness of their coming and going. It was like turning on the spigot back home. The open area by the water's banks allowed them to walk side by side, a rarity. There was no polite way to mention how he'd noticed the touching of her scar. Maybe he shouldn't. He never discussed his. Of course, he also hid them from sight. He wrestled his curiosity and concern until they gave up and allowed Anna her privacy. For now, at least.

Suah rejoined them. "Mammy Anna, camp late for best place?"

Anna asked Stewart, "What do you think?"

He considered the lay of the land. "Sure. By my calculations, we've barely crossed into the territory that the mining concession covers. Nothing to prospect yet, so let's move forward."

Suah trotted off and sent two men to hunt.

A couple more hours of hiking brought them to a large clearing. "This crew is industrious, Miss Baldwin. The cook pot is in place around the stones, and a fire underneath. I do believe your tent is already up."

She smiled. "My pace allowed them a good head start, but don't let your stomach get too excited. Meat and rice won't make the plate for a while yet."

"What, no cassava?"

She yawned. "You will get a lot more variety in the Pahn village. Now, I know the sun is still up, but I'm going to rest a bit in my tent on that camp bed you bought for me. I can't thank you enough. I appreciate the comfort and privacy both items afford me on the trail."

"You already thanked me before we left Harper.

You're more than welcome. Only a cad would buy one for himself and leave a lady to the hard jungle floor."

"I'm used to sleeping on the ground. I had to watch my budget when I got here. I decided to do without the luxury."

He couldn't resist the opening to tease her. "I guess that's one advantage I have by not working for God. My employer is more generous with the earthly rewards." He glanced around. "Speaking of which, I wonder where mine are."

Anna pointed beyond the stacked bundles on the other side of camp. "If I'm not mistaken, behind the pile of packs."

He looked askance. "And to think, on board ship, you said being male was an advantage here. I've yet to see how. Every crew has doted on you. My needs are met, but you are some kind of royalty."

Anna looked up, down and anywhere but at him, obviously trying not to laugh.

"Why is that funny?"

She shook her head in mock seriousness. "I guess that even with a heavily funded employer, you can't have everything. However, I could tell you how to get the same level of treatment. You need do only one thing."

Okay, he'd bite. "What might that be?"

"Quit your mining job and become a missionary."

Anna eyed the wide, flowing water in front of them. She dearly wished for another rope bridge, but the terrain near the river was broad and flat. From the distant hilltop that morning, the water had appeared as a narrow blue ribbon among the lush green. At the banks, the ribbon turned into a wide band. In the dry season, a crossing might prove easy. But rains had swollen the waters and the current hinted at a viciousness underneath.

Suah stood beside her. Anna asked, "Can we wade across? Hold a rope for safety?"

Suah shook his head. "We build raft. Too deep. Much fast for mammies or even the giant man."

She approved and Suah left to organize the process. She hid her amusement at his description of Stewart. Suah's people were a handsome race, much like the nearby Pahn, but unlike some of their Vai cousins, his people barely topped the Kru in height.

Stewart joined her. She asked, "How are your raft-building skills?"

"Fair. I'm no Huckleberry Finn, but that's not the Mississippi, either."

"For our purposes, it might as well be. I'll keep one man to help and I'll cook extra for our supper to save time in case we cross late. You can join Suah and construct our conveyance."

He nodded. "I'll need you to translate my overall plan to avoid any misunderstandings with Suah's pidgin."

How to tell him gracefully? "I only asked about your skill to see if you wanted to help. These men are accomplished raft builders."

He grinned. "Guess I have a habit of taking charge, even when others know better how things work. Made the same mistake with you."

"Well, I was trying not to be too direct, but since you mention it…"

"Point taken. Don't worry, I'll leave it to Suah and add my labor to the mix." Stewart followed Suah.

Anna directed her own helper to cast his net by the riverbank. Fresh fish hadn't been in their diet since the Cavalla.

By the time the pot boiled and the rice softened, six fine specimens of African catfish found their place in the mix and Stewart and the other men had dragged the last of the newly hewn young trees to the bank.

The few porters who owned Western shirts stripped them off. Stewart only rolled up his sleeves, baring muscular forearms to the elbow. There was a distinct tan line at the point where he'd rolled them. How odd he never unbuttoned even the top of his shirt. Perhaps he was being overly modest for her sake. Unnecessary and even dangerous in this heat. He'd been so concerned for her safety, maybe he was equally worried about what a missionary might consider proper. She'd have to put his mind at ease for his comfort and health's sake.

Anna called for lunch. Grateful men made their way to the cook pot.

Stewart grabbed his mess-kit utensils. "Fish? I guess this delay brings some positive points. I'm ravenous."

She placed a generous portion on his plate. "There's a log over there out of the sun where you can eat. You should take more care not to become overheated. Becoming acclimated to the temperatures enough to do heavy labor safely takes many months."

He'd already forked a mouthful of the dish and had to finish chewing to answer. "May I point out I managed the machete on the trail without succumbing to heatstroke? Or should I just say 'Yes, Mother'? Next you'll be counting out the grains of quinine for my daily dose."

She threatened him with her serving spoon, which only made him laugh at her. "No, I'm serious. At least consider removing your shirt when you work so hard. Please don't let my presence stop you. I assure you, I will not take offense at the sight of a man in his undershirt, especially not when it's prudent for your health."

His smile vanished and the gleam in his eyes flattened. "Thank you, but I'm okay as I am, Miss Baldwin."

He walked off. Suah offered her his bowl to fill and she mechanically dished up another portion.

What happened? One minute they were joking and the next he'd turned cold. Over propriety? She ate her lunch alone and cleaned up while the raft came together, torn between waiting for the opportunity to apologize and hoping he'd realize he may have overreacted and apologize himself.

After the multiple trips across were finished and the men hauled the conveyance out of the water, Stewart still kept his distance. She shouldn't let a simple mistake fester and there were still logistics to discuss.

He crossed his arms and waited at her approach. She stopped a couple steps from him to discuss the business at hand. "We might as well make camp near the banks. We won't have to haul water so far. Makes it easier to purify a good quantity before we travel onward tomorrow."

Discussing the practicalities thawed his countenance. "You'll have plenty of time for that. Look how sharply the river bends." He pointed. "And farther up, there are signs the river once ran more to this side of its banks. If there are any alluvial deposits in this immediate area, these would be places most likely to hold evidence. I can take advantage of what light is left to me today and get set up. I'll need more than one afternoon."

"All right. But why does the sharp bend hold such promise, and what are alluvial deposits? I thought you were looking for gold."

"Alluvial deposits are areas where the smaller, lighter sediment once carried by active waterways finally comes to rest. Over time the course of a river can be diverted by many things, or it can dry up completely. The old river paths have a characteristic look to the trained eye and they can signal the presence of gold in the ground. But not always. A sharp bend like that one allows for more erosion and is more likely to expose a gold-bearing gravel layer."

"And here I thought it was more in shallow creeks or mined from mountain caves."

"It can be there, too. What I'm going to do here is called placer mining, looking for gold that over the ages has been carried from its source by water. Gold is also found in veins in connection with quartz and in rock beds."

"Well, I'm not sure how much help I can be, but I don't mind learning something new." Especially if it would help him get past his offense at her earlier suggestion.

"Good. Tomorrow I'll dig trenches and set up a sluice box to run the dirt for any gold present. Maybe do some spot panning like I've done several evenings before. You can help with that part if you like. There's an art to panning, but it's easy once you catch on."

Did she have time to learn that art? She eyed the skies reflexively. The daily deluges that marked the rainy season were still with them, but their duration had begun to shorten. Most of the time, dramatic thunderstorms the natives called tornadoes signaled the end was near. But the rains could also end with little warning. Up until now she'd been confident of arriving back at her post before the rice harvest. This sounded like a longer enterprise than she'd expected. "How long of a delay are we talking about, Mr. Hastings?"

"A minimum of two or three days. Longer if my efforts show any significant color."

"Color?"

"Color is gold. Once you wash out the lighter-weight materials from your pan or sluice box, the gold contrasts against the iron-laden black sand left behind and stands out. Hence the term 'color.'"

"I see. So, longer than two to three days if you find evidence of…color?"

"Yes, but I can't say how much longer until I see what, if anything, is here. I'll need the pack labeled Mining No. 2 so I can run a few core samples first and focus my search. Could you have Suah bring that one when you locate it?"

"Of course."

"Thank you." He walked off toward the bend.

The possibility of a longer delay was worrisome, but she'd wait until he'd had a chance to prospect and knew more. She called to Suah, who ran right over.

"We'll camp by the bend for the next two nights, maybe longer. But definitely no travel tomorrow or the next day. Before we pitch tents, I need you to help me find a pack that contains tools Nana Stewart needs."

Suah vigorously shook his head. "No, Mammy Anna." Then he lapsed out of pidgin into his own dialect, his agitation growing with every word.

Stewart noticed and came back to her side. "Something wrong?"

She said, "Yes, Suah is refusing to camp here. But I don't understand what has upset him so."

Suah spoke again, more insistently.

Stewart interrupted. "Not this again. I've heard the word for *leopard* so many times that even I can translate that one. Not once have we had any hint of trouble."

"I know, but he's determined not to stay here at night."

"This is ridiculous. A total nuisance. Can't you insist?"

Suah interrupted, still in his own dialect. Anna translated. "No, I don't think so. Suah states the Leopard Men prefer to attack their victims near bodies of water. If we insist on staying here, the men will desert, leaving us and all our equipment."

Stewart walked the ten minutes from camp, carrying a bucket and a folded canvas stool. Behind him several men carried shovels, the components of the sluice box he would build and the other tools he hadn't wanted to leave unattended at the river last night. He set the men to work, some digging near the bend and others digging deep into the area where the river had once run its course. He decided to pan some of the pay dirt from yesterday's shallow digs before he built the sluice box for a larger operation. No point in taking the trouble if the site had nothing to yield. Although he could finally see the Putu Mountains in the distance, there was no way to tell if this river originated there or had ever carried gold from anywhere.

He unfolded his stool, filled a bucket with water and squatted beside the piles of sediment trenched from various spots he'd designated the previous afternoon. He filled a fourteen-inch round miner's pan with the dirt and added water. He used one hand to swirl the pan, while his other rubbed the errant remains of sleep from his tired eyes.

Behind him, an unstiffled yawn announced the arrival of Anna. They had both paid the price of those Leopard Men legends, having to take shifts through the night alongside their normal sentries. Even with compromising the location of the camp, they'd found it necessary to personally patrol, not to prevent an imagined threat from a secret society, but to forestall desertions of fearful men during the night. He would have traveled on after first light, rather than spend another wakeful night if this site didn't practically boast of hidden gold.

His decision plagued him with guilt at the sight of an exhausted Anna covering her mouth a second time. His protests over her insistence on taking her own shift had been met with stubborn refusal. He accepted the sheer logic that he could not patrol all night and work all day. But after only one night of this, the circles under her eyes were darker than the rain-laden clouds that laced the skies.

He set his pan down and stood to greet her. "Might I persuade you to try your hand at panning? The site looks promising. I'm still hoping for some plunkers." If she agreed, he'd seat her in the shade with a bucket and pan. He could keep an eye on her and make sure she didn't overexert herself. Chances were they had another long night ahead of them.

Anna perked up at the suggestion and rolled up her sleeves. "Put me to work." Her head tilted in a becoming manner. "But what are 'plunkers' and how will I know one when I see it?"

"Plunkers are a prospector's term for small nuggets. They are large enough to make a plunking sound when dropped in the pan, unlike the paper-thin flakes I found yesterday. Sit on my stool and I'll show you how this works."

She sat and gave him an eager grin. "I have another question."

"Ask me anything."

"Do I get to keep the gold I find, or does this all go to your employer in the end?"

"Looking to find the same riches you warned me about, Miss Baldwin?" He handed her a large round tin pan filled with their diggings.

She grasped it and shrugged her shoulders. "The Lord's work costs money. If He wants to provide out of this river, who am I to argue?"

"Be careful. A little success here and you might contract gold fever like folks during the Dahlonega gold rush or the '49ers later in California. And yes, you may keep some of your find. As far as I know, individuals may still prospect at will unless someone claims ownership of the area."

He squatted across from her and showed her how to dip a tilted pan into the water, swirling until she had an emulsified mix. "Once the water mixes well, dip again—" he demonstrated "—tipping your pan enough to let the top layer, which we call the overburden, wash out. Then repeat until you get down to the black sand. If you watch closely, most of the action is in the wrist."

"Won't the gold flow right out into the water?"

He continued his motion, washing away each subsequent layer. "No. Gold is the heaviest substance. The weight drops it to the bottom of your pan. As long as you get a good, watery mixture going and tip at the angle I'm using, you won't lose any gold." He stood and held out his finished pan so she could see the small amount of dark black sediment and a few flakes of gold intermixed.

"Oh, my. You found some. Is that real? Such tiny little flecks. Where are the plunkers?"

"It's real, all right, and if I knew where the plunkers were, my job would be easy. These flakes have smooth edges. That tells me it's likely they've washed downstream quite a ways from their source. We may or may not find bigger nuggets." He pulled a small glass vial from his pocket, removed the lid, touched his finger to the flakes and placed them inside. He held up the vial for her to see the small accumulation. "When we have enough, we'll dry these out and meld them into one lump by baking our find inside one of those sweet potatoes we'd planned to eat. Easier to manage and weigh. It can be tested for purity later."

Her face took on a focused determination. "That I have to see, but after I conquer this pan." Water splashed onto her skirt. "I'm not very good at this."

"Takes practice. You'll get the motion down before long. Let me help." He moved behind the stool and held her arms at the elbows so he wasn't indecently close to her. "Relax and let me lead." He reached around and adjusted the angle of her wrists, guiding her motions until she was able to do it on her own, all the while breathing in the clean scent of the soap she'd used that morning.

He stepped back and picked up his own pan again, and his arms felt empty. For a moment he allowed himself the daydream of what they might be to each other in a world without his scars, and minus her missionary zeal. Just two people who could be in love, talking for hours together in front of the campfire, getting to know one another instead of always being so conscious of propriety's needs and adjourning to their tents at opposite ends of the camp.

He'd come into this jungle with a predetermined view of Anna Baldwin, missionary woman, but moments like these, her excitement at seeing gold in the pan for the first time, or when she'd spoken so casually to men with spears, reminded him she wasn't just a pretty face attached to a Bible. She was so much more than the stereotype he'd held. When he'd agreed to have her as his guide, he'd feared trusting his future to someone like her because of his past. He didn't worry about enjoying her company too much or the problems of wishing for an impossible future. He realized his concerns had been misplaced. Losing his heart to her was the real danger.

Nearby whispers reminded him that he'd forgotten his audience. When he looked, some of the men stood leaning on their shovels, grinning. He had probably looked like a besotted calf staring the way he had at Anna. At least she hadn't seen him.

She looked up as the whispers grew, and he nodded in the men's direction. "We have an interested audience, Miss Baldwin."

She went right back to the swirling sands in her pan. "Probably because their 'Mammy Anna' is finally behaving more like they expect a woman to behave."

"What do you mean?"

"A lot of the manual village work is done by women. Planting, carrying water and many other things. Even though I sometimes share the cooking as expected, they find my role as a leader in this journey confusing. Now you've put me to work with the pan, which is closer to what they would expect."

"So the women are relegated to most of the daily work?"

Anna swirled her pan more naturally. "Like I said on board ship, the roles of men and women are very specific. Women rarely, if ever, lead, and outside of an expedition like this, the men who brought water this morning would never stoop to doing something they believe is a woman's job. But you sound surprised, Mr. Hastings. Do you find customs so different in our world?"

He didn't need to think to answer. "No, I guess not. My mother spends most of her life in long hours of servitude to one of the big houses, scrubbing and cleaning for a pittance and no appreciation. Then she returns to take care of her own home. When my father was alive, he put in a full day at the docks, but never helped at home, not even if sober. Part of my determination to provide for my mother came long before she was sick. As I saw it, women like my mother held two jobs and worked far harder than the men in their lives."

"Exactly. I noticed the same thing when I was about ten and finally realized how hard the servants in our house worked, a fact I might have missed had I not spent so much time in their care while my parents ran off to someone else's country house that summer. The ones who didn't live-in were like your mother, responsible for two households. I was constantly amazed at their ability to carry such a heavy burden. I find the women here have that same strength."

The realization of what she'd said struck him dumb. Servants, plural. Country houses. Anna Baldwin came from wealth. Had she deliberately hidden her background from him or had he made assumptions? Real or imagined, he couldn't shake a feeling of disappointment.

He looked down to see her pan tipped and dirt spilled in her lap. The widening of her eyes said she realized what she'd revealed. He'd made little secret about his own background or his contempt for those from hers.

The realization of who Anna really was did more to dispel his inappropriate daydreams than her fervent faith. No wonder he'd compared her to Julianne. They were more alike than he'd realized. He tried to temper it, but an air of accusation hung on his words. "You're from money. Real money. You lived in luxury, while people like my mother spent their days scrubbing your floors, unnoticed and overworked. Why didn't you tell me?"

She gripped the edges of her pan as if it were gold itself. "Mr. Hastings, I never deliberately hid my background from you, but it was hardly a factor in my employability. And after some of the things you said about your mother and all…well, I didn't realize until recently you had mistaken my comments about my parents' finances. I didn't choose to be born wealthy any more than you chose to be born poor. In a way, we both looked for a way out of the lives we'd been born into." Her words carried a plea for understanding.

"Working your way out of poverty is hardly the same as walking away from luxury." He'd deluded himself to think they could have anything in common. "But it does make for a strong irony, doesn't it?"

"What do you mean?"

He refilled the sediment and tilted his pan into the bucket to mix in water, the better to put some distance between them. "That someone from privilege like you is now employed by the son of a lowly household servant."

"But I'm grateful God used you in my moment of need. Society may sometimes make class distinctions, but God doesn't and I certainly don't."

Society always made distinctions. She was kidding herself if she thought she didn't, too. He tilted his pan and sluiced again. "Now I understand why you ended up out of contact with your parents and no funding. I bet missionary service wasn't quite the standard tour of the Continent your parents had in mind for their socialite daughter."

Her hands stopped. The swirling water kept moving and once again wet the fabric of her skirt. Her voice quieted. "No, it wasn't."

Why would anyone walk away from a life of ease? He pushed for another piece of the puzzle. What more was she hiding? "What I don't understand is why someone like you, coming from a life of privilege, would walk away from everything that entails."

Anna stayed still, watching him intently.

He added more water to his pan and continued, "I know what I'm doing here in the middle of the jungle, but you traded having anything you could have wanted in life to be here. Why would anyone in their right mind do such a thing? You're lucky your father didn't lock you up until you came to your senses."

The look on her face brought him up short. He'd allowed himself to speak too freely. They were both suffering from a lack of sleep and here he was picking at her like a dog trying to uncover a buried bone. He needed to drop the subject and take time to sort out his own feelings, talk again when they were both rested.

Her pan and all its contents slid from her fingers to the ground. Twin spots of red stained her cheeks. "You and my father would get along famously, Mr. Hastings. Insane and needing to be brought to my senses was the conclusion he came to, as well."

She stood and he rose from his squat. She looked as directly into his eyes as their eleven-inch disparity in height would allow. The intensity of her gaze and the import of the words that followed made her the taller person. "The fact that I survived such an attitude to get to the jungle and minister is a testament to God's grace. Otherwise I might not have survived being imprisoned in my family's attic, enduring my father's persistent attempts to beat his particular brand of sense into me."

Chapter Seven

Anna grasped her hands to stop the shaking. She'd never spoken of those times to anyone and shouldn't have now. Why had she felt such a need to defend herself? This was a wound her unforgiveness had only allowed to scab over, not heal. And now she'd spewed the vile contents of that sore out at the smallest provocation. It was a wonder God's grace had ever prevailed in her life to place her here as a missionary, considering what an example of godliness she was turning out to represent. Her failure to guard her lips against this breach made her far more angry than anything Stewart had said.

Anna mustered her tattered dignity and continued to meet Stewart's gaze even though she'd rather do anything else. The distress she saw in his eyes threatened to overwhelm her.

"Miss Baldwin, I..."

She couldn't talk about this now. She needed time to collect herself. "If you'll excuse me for the moment, Mr. Hastings, I could use the privacy my tent affords for a few moments. We are obviously both too tired to have this conversation on a subject so personal." Anna turned her back and started to walk away.

"No..." He reached for her arm and maneuvered himself in front of her. "First, allow me to apologize."

She searched his face. Contrition filled in the etching. He couldn't have known what he was saying, not really. She took a deep breath. "No, this is my own fault. Instead of taking offense, I should have heard your pain, the hurt you feel over your mother and her difficult life. I had no business thinking of myself when I should have been helping you see how God cares about your situation and wants to be there to help and heal those emotions. Please put my dramatic statement out of your mind and let us talk later about these things that burden you." She tugged and he released her arm from his grasp.

"I can hardly place such a statement out of my mind. Surely you must know that."

Anna glanced toward the porters. "We still have an audience. I don't want them to think we are in dissension when they are already fearful about staying."

His reluctance filled the air. "Then let's talk later, if you will permit. I want to understand."

She started to shake her head, but he pulled out a trump card. "Please don't dismiss my request. If for no other reason, I need to know at least enough to consider if what happened in Monrovia might be related. Maybe you were targeted as I suggested before. Not by a mysterious enemy, but by your own family."

"I don't believe my family difficulties have any bearing on that attack."

"You cannot know that for sure. What if there had been a second attempt at Harper and we weren't prepared? Not only could you have been harmed, but this expedition, as well. Keeping information from me puts me in a position where I can't keep you safe."

The determination in his voice convinced her that he believed in the possibility.

"No one, not even my father, is desperate enough to follow us into the jungle to lay hands on me. I will consider talking further. But for now, I need some time alone."

He nodded and she walked away, her thoughts bobbing in all directions over the concerns he raised. Once at the camp, she found a warm cook pot of rice and an absent Suah. He'd likely be gone some time on a hunt for fresh game. She sought the shelter of her tent, the comfort of her bed and the guidance of prayer.

Long after, she heard noise in the camp and left her tent to investigate. Perhaps Suah had had an early success. She peered out the tent flap and saw Stewart at the cook pot, his back to her.

She stopped and smoothed her shirt, uselessly pressing at the wrinkles that formed when she'd fallen asleep praying. She fortified herself with another quick prayer as she exited. "Early lunch, Mr. Hastings? Let me do that." She dished up the rice with an apology. "The meal is pretty plain. Hopefully, Suah will return with something to add later."

Stewart took the food she offered and sat on the fallen log the men had moved into camp for convenience. She joined him, but her stomach rebelled as soon as she lifted her fork. They sat in silence, an awkwardness between them she couldn't figure out how to breach.

"Not hungry, Miss Baldwin?"

She set her bowl down and glanced toward his. "You appear to have found the appetite I lost."

"I believe my taste buds finally adjusted to the level of spice in the food."

Ah, the safety of small talk. Anna smiled. "With a little help. I had cook tone down the peppers so the adjustment was more gradual."

"Ouch! I wrongly believed myself a bit superior for adapting so quickly. Instead—" he stuck out his tongue and pretended to try to eye it "—you, my manly taste buds, need to build more endurance."

His clowning broke the dark mantle of memories. She laughed. "You are quite the entertainer, Mr. Hastings. Do you always resort to humor in every uncomfortable situation? Or only with crazy missionary women?"

"I see I've infected you with the habit. I do find humor works well in most situations." He put his bowl beside him on the log and continued, "And it looks as if I'm right. You're able to make a joke and laugh again, aren't you?"

"Yes, I am."

He took her hand, swallowing it up in his two larger ones. "I didn't intend to suggest a woman deserved to be locked up or harmed for choosing to follow her convictions. I hope you will accept my sincerest apology."

"I do."

Sincerity had been his goal, she was sure. Not creating this connection, not jolting her into more of an awareness of him and the tenderness he hid behind his lighthearted exterior. She slid her hand out of his before asking, "What is it you want to know, Mr. Hastings?"

He stood, pacing to maintaining a suitable distance between them. He knew a father's fists, but how did he ask her of her experience? "Your father…did he…? I mean…" His nerve faltered. "Is he the reason you never married?"

"You are worried that my father's violence is why I

haven't married?" She slowly shook her head. "Certainly not what I thought you were about to ask."

"I'm still trying to understand the puzzle that is Anna Baldwin."

"You are not the first. Even in the Pahn village, my single status is questioned. Most men, no matter the culture, believe a woman's only place is to stand at her husband's side, to bear children, to create a harmonious household."

He prompted her to keep talking. "But you want something more."

"Yes, I do. God called me to evangelize. I don't seek a husband, only God's Will in my life."

"You can't have both?"

A small smile this time, but not reaching her eyes. "Many missionaries marry. But from what I've seen, marriage is not always a position to be envied or even desired. Certainly not with the man my parents demanded I marry."

"Did your parents really lock you up? They hurt you over your beliefs?"

Anna's hand lifted to her marred cheek and rubbed. "Yes, Father initially believed his disapproval enough to bend me to his will. Once he saw the steamer ticket and the packed trunk, he resorted to more drastic measures."

"Then the small scar on your cheek didn't come through some accident."

She dropped her hand. "A father's anger can be a terrible thing. He usually confined his blows to where they wouldn't be seen. He was horrified when he lost control and his ring drew blood on my cheek. He left the room and locked the door. With help, I escaped that night and boarded the steamer. Father cut me off without a cent, telling me in a telegram delivered to the ship."

The picture of what that night must have been like for her…and without anyone to protect her…flashed through his mind.

"You mentioned irony earlier, that a daughter of privilege was now employed by the son of a maid. The real irony was that privilege brought me only heartache and it took the actions of my brave maid for me to escape. Without her aid, I wouldn't be here in the first place." She smiled to try to put him back at ease. "So having a maid's son, and not wealthy parents, help me stay here is quite fitting. Don't you agree?" She didn't wait for his reply. "I believe it is substantial proof that God has a well-developed sense of irony. And He used you to prove it."

If irony were a fisted hand, Stewart felt sure he would be down for the count. The woman whose religious zeal he'd disdained along with her wealthy background had been through the trenches of her own war, just as much as he had in his own home and later in France. All because of her belief. Long-ago lessons from church gave him enough understanding to wonder, truly wonder for the first time since the war, if God was there and was working some kind of plan in his life. Had he been maneuvered into seeing another side of the religious equation, not by a woman, but by the God she served?

Admitting the possibility brought up a slew of problems, including his determination to believe that same God didn't exist. The belief in a God who was no more than a fairy tale carried less pain in its pages than a God who didn't show up when needed. Stewart had prayed for deliverance when he'd first realized the gas had gotten him. Prayer proved no barrier to the blistering burns. Where was God then? "Easier not to believe in Him at all."

Anna touched his arm, lifting him from the haze of memory. "Why is it easier, Mr. Hastings?"

"What?" he groaned. He'd spoken aloud.

"You said…"

"Never mind what I said. For a moment I forgot myself."

He met her gaze. *Look strong; brush her concern off as nothing.* The orders carried no weight against the compassion flooding those soft brown eyes. The hardened crust of his heart cracked.

Humor chose that moment to desert his front line of defense. Desperate, he grasped for another way out. Denial.

"Belief in God is useful if it comforts you. In a difficult time, I turned to it myself."

When she spoke, gentleness pillowed the words. "On the trail you said men will always be waiting on a God who doesn't show up. Is that what you refer to? You called out to God and He let you down in some way?"

Hope dangled itself just out of reach, but he was wise to its faithlessness and refused to reach for it. "Yes, Miss Baldwin, He did. When I served in France, the Germans launched a deadly, destructive offensive against the trenches, one of many such volleys. For a brief moment, I dared hope He was real. The hope died as men around me died a horrible death, or wished they would." He had wished for death so desperately that night and in the days that followed.

"How horrible."

Her gentleness cracked his heart further. He shored up his defenses as best he could. "What, no Bible verse to explain the horror? I heard a lot of those stateside." In a hospital ward. In the burn unit. "Useless words. Look at you, after all. God didn't deliver you from that beating."

She never flinched. "No, but He was my comfort and hope throughout. God doesn't promise to deliver us from pain or even death, Mr. Hastings."

"Then what good is He? Before I was big enough to stand up to my father, my mother suffered for years. Her belief never stopped his fists."

"In God, we receive the strength to walk through life's trials, whether we are delivered from them or not. Sometimes we find the way of escape, as in my case."

This conversation touched places he cared not to examine. He stood. "I appreciate the candor, even if I can't embrace your beliefs, Miss Baldwin. Unless you have something else to tell me about that affects this trip, I think we've cleared the air between us for now. With the rain holding off today, I need to return to prospecting. My morning panning showed promise."

A look of panic filled Anna's eyes as she scanned the empty skies. "No clouds, no rain yet today. I'm afraid this is the beginning. We may have crossed over into the dry season."

"You look upset. Isn't the change in weather a good thing?"

Her hands fidgeted with the folds of her skirt. "You asked if there was anything else that would have an effect on the trip." Her eyes failed to hold a steady gaze. "With the change in weather and your need to stay here longer, I'm afraid I must take two or three men and go on without you. I can leave Suah with you because he speaks pidgin."

"Absolutely not. Your impatience to return will only put you in danger. What's to prevent them from deserting you over this Leopard Society business, leaving you stranded and alone somewhere in the jungle? I don't understand what the weather has to do with anything, but I do know there is no argument you can muster to change my mind where your safety is concerned."

"But you must change your mind, Mr. Hastings. If I don't get to the village and intervene before the rice harvest ends, a young boy will die."

She'd have to go whether Stewart liked it or not. Would he consider it as breaking their arrangement? Or would Mrs. Dowdy's counsel hold true? She silently prayed. *Dear Lord, please help me explain and him to understand. I'd hate to come this far to lose Stewart's goodwill now.*

Stewart sat back down on the log. He removed his pith helmet, dangling it in front of him.

Anna allowed God's peace to wrap around her until the flare of panic smothered. Stewart's gaze never left her while she told him her tale.

"Like you, I have a critical deadline on this trip."

He dipped his chin, dismay evident. "You're just now telling me?"

"I expected to travel directly back to my mission post. When you changed the itinerary, I worried, but after calculating the expected additional time, I assumed we would arrive before the dry season began. While I feared for Taba's safety, I knew he would be unharmed until then and saw no reason to burden you with another person's well-being, not when your own mother was at the forefront of your thoughts."

One corner of his lips quirked as he silently considered her words. Finally he broke his silence. "Taba being the boy, I presume?"

"Yes, he is a twelve-year-old in my school who became a Christian and managed to convert his whole family. The devilmen have sought ways to make an example of him ever since."

"You've been gone a couple of months, Miss Baldwin. What makes you think Taba yet lives if these devilmen intend him harm?"

"They won't hurt him outright, but if the weather has truly shifted, he won't be safe much longer."

"How does the change of season affect the child?"

She took a deep breath. So far she was just confusing Stewart. Small wonder; he didn't understand the customs. "Shortly after the rains cease, the rice harvest begins, a process lasting about three weeks. Once the majority of the rice is brought in from the fields, children of Taba's age are enrolled in the bush school—the Poro for the boys, the Sande for the girls."

At his look of continued confusion, she continued, "The Poro is run by the devilman and his apprentices. Children live in a sequestered area outside the village while they learn about life, religion, relationships, everything."

"Seems to me like a good plan for a child's future."

"For most, but if you are a new Christian like Taba, the school becomes a death sentence because of this particular devilman. He opposed Dr. Mary before me, provoking the chief to lure her to her death."

"Obviously he didn't succeed."

"No, what the devilman had planned for evil, God turned into good with the chief asking for his village to have its own missionary. The devilman spoke publicly against the chief's decision to allow me to live among the Pahn, and the devilman was livid when Taba became my first convert." Despite her effort to stay calm, emotion cracked her voice. "And if the devilman gets Taba into the Poro school, Taba will never make it out of the sequestered area alive. His parents will be presented with his effects, told of some accident, when in reality Taba will have been sacrificed. It's a common enough practice."

Concern etched Stewart's face. "Tell me, Miss Baldwin, how do you plan to thwart this devilman?"

"The only solution I've found is to use a large portion of the funds you've paid me to put Taba into a mission boarding school at Newaka near Garraway."

"What of his parents?"

"They aren't entirely sold on the idea of sending him away. Their fear of the devilman's fetishes runs deep. They lack the power to openly defy him. Taba attending school away from home solves the problem, if they agree to the plan." She pushed back tendrils of hair, dampened from the humidity.

Stewart stood. "Wasn't the point of you guiding me here so you could stay on the mission field?"

"I will be able to remain for yet a while. My needs are limited. The supplies you bought in Harper for myself and the school will help. The village gives me the hospitality of a dwelling. My other needs are modest. Nothing compares to the importance of Taba's safety. I want to see him alive, educated and able to return to his people, not an unnecessary martyr to faith."

He replaced his helmet. "What happens when your funds run out?"

"If God does not provide, I trust He will have other plans for my life. Even if I have to return to my parents and throw myself on their mercy until another door opens for me."

"After having escaped your father's beating? I can see how serious you are about helping this child. What I don't understand is what causes you to believe I would be unwilling to inconvenience myself to save a child's life?"

Shame burned through her. "Nothing, Mr. Hastings. I only thought it unfair to ask you to choose between a boy you'd never met and your own mother's needs."

"What if we'd encountered major delays on the trail or the seasons changed before you expected? Had you been forthright from the beginning… Well, making significant adjustments now is no longer possible."

Having her own fears voiced aloud gave her a pang. Had she waited too long? She needed to forge ahead to the village. Would he continue to refuse now that he understood?

He stood and replaced his pith helmet. "It's too late to do anything else, so…"

No! He couldn't expect her to just give up.

"…to use our time efficiently, I'll need you and every man available to work this site for as long as daylight allows. Then tell the men to prepare. We will all be leaving at first light. Nothing is more important than a child's life."

Stewart followed as Anna, in her long brown skirt, white shirt and bobbing pith helmet, wove her way around every obstacle the trail threw at her. The bearers hustled to keep up with her. She'd marched a punishing pace since they'd left camp seven days ago.

He'd never question her strength or ability again, only his own self-control. He warred between wanting to shake her silly for not telling him about the dire plight of the child, and wishing to hold and comfort her and tell her everything would be all right.

Neither choice would be welcome.

Anna's willingness to do whatever it took to save Taba

inspired him to be a better man, and yet set an impossibly high standard for any other woman in his future. Surely other suitable women existed, good women out there with the strength of an Anna Baldwin. Maybe one of them would be able to look past his scars. He tried to focus on that hope, but when he closed his eyes, he couldn't envision anyone else. Only a fiery little missionary who would never return his love.

Love? Was this need to protect her, the admiration he felt, trying to grow into something else? Something impossible?

Anna called for a rest, and fruit was passed around.

He sat and peeled a mango, taking that first juicy bite just as the object of his thoughts dropped her pack at his feet, sat and struck up a conversation. "The heat is taking a toll on everyone, but we're almost there. We'll plan for a longer rest around lunch or once we find a large enough clearing on the trail. I'd feel better if we were all refreshed before dealing with Nana Mala."

Stewart handed her the canteen off the side of her pack. "I assumed you would check on Taba first."

She drank and reattached the canteen. "Protocol must be observed despite my worry. I wouldn't want anything to go wrong with the chief accepting you into the village."

"Are you still concerned about our reception?"

"Yes. Nana Mala was unhappy with everyone after his failed attempt to become Paramount Chief—even me. I suspect he believed his reputation would be enhanced with the prestige of having a village missionary and that somehow my presence would guarantee his bid. He failed, and now, after several talks with Suah, I think the rumors of the Leopard Society may have originated in Nana Mala's territory. That only makes things worse."

"How?"

"From everything I've pieced together, this Society is comprised of older men with a drive for power. Leopard Men create terror to support their own political plans. They might oppose Nana Mala's bid to expand his rule." She chewed one corner of her bottom lip.

"Is there no end to the problems these Leopard Men tales have brought? I think the stability a mining enterprise will bring might be the best thing for this region. If Nana Mala works with us, the economics might do more for his reputation than anything. So when do you think we'll arrive?"

"Certainly before dark. I'm not sure since I've never come from this direction."

"I'm eager to get to those mountains. The river area held some promise, but we'll have to see how the samples I took test out. I hold the most hope for the area around and in the mountains."

"You had so little time there, I worried my problems were undermining your job."

"My plan was never going to work the way I thought it would. Now that I'm actually here, I understand so much more. A lifetime of work is needed to adequately explore this jungle, but one good gold or gem find is all my company needs. They can send whole teams to scout once they have something to justify developing an operation here."

"But you've found gold. I've seen it in your pan and in those small vials you've been filling."

"Sure, but only enough of a yield to justify prospecting for an individual miner in any one area. So far, nothing I've found is significant enough for a large operation."

"Well, perhaps those mountains will yield results

more to your liking." She stood and called for an end to the rest.

The trail narrowed. "After you, Miss Baldwin. Looks like we're back to single file."

He walked behind her for a couple of miles. The porters, even Suah, exchanged glances and sparsely furtive speech. He marched on, keeping himself alert in case of trouble.

Finally, another clearing. Anna signaled and grateful men collapsed in the dirt, leaning against their cargo. And not a one of them ceased to watch the trail.

Stewart approached Anna, who had commandeered a small, hollowed log to sit on. Not squeamish about the bugs, that one. "Are we breaking to eat, as well?"

She shook her head. "No, according to Suah, we're less than an hour out. We'll partake of a meal in the village after we arrive."

He pointed his thumb back to the porters. "They seem a little jumpy."

Anna scanned the resting men. "Desertions are to be expected at this point, out of fear of Nana Mala. I'm surprised some didn't drop their packs already and slip off into the jungle out of fear. It's not uncommon for one tribe to take members of another hostage until a ransom is paid by their village, which is why they rarely venture past the territory of the nearest village."

Suah approached. "Mammy Anna..." His eyes rounded as he stared past Stewart's shoulder.

Anna spoke softly. "Stewart, slow moves and keep your hands where they can be seen. We have company and they're armed for war."

Chapter Eight

Anna counted fifteen armed warriors. She spoke calmly in Pahn, calling to several by name. "I am happy to greet you. I have returned as promised, bringing friends."

Gardiah, Nana Mala's son, stepped out from behind the wall of foot soldiers, and the strings of tension in Anna let loose.

Gardiah said, "I am happy to greet you, Mammy Anna. The children will be glad of your return. Who is this you bring? Have you taken a husband?"

Anna laughed. "No, Gardiah, I am still unmarried." She motioned for Stewart to step up and spoke to him in English. "This is Gardiah, Nana Mala's son. He speaks a little English, but for now, I'll do all the talking."

Turning back to Gardiah, she returned to Pahn. "This is my friend Stewart Hastings. He wishes to explore."

The young warrior broke into a wary smile. "If his stories from the book are as good as yours, he is welcome at the fire. Tell me, why do you travel from a new direction? We expected to hear drums from Nynabo of your arrival."

Anna weighed her words. "My plans changed because

of Mr. Hastings, but he is not a missionary. He brings no stories from the book."

Gardiah looked at Stewart with a questioning face. Anna asked, "Why are we greeted with so many warriors?"

"Much happened, Mammy Anna. We patrol to keep Leopard Men away, but also the district commissioner. Neither shall enter our territory."

She translated for Stewart, who said, "Not surprising on the Leopards, but I thought the district commissioner or his soldiers never came here."

"Nana Mala would make them pay dearly if they tried. Maybe there is a new push from the government to enforce the Hut Tax." She turned back to Gardiah and asked in Pahn, "What is happening with the government men?"

He answered, "The drums tell of villages many days away where tax men come. We will not pay or allow them to take our people as slaves."

Anna replied, "I see your concern."

Gardiah grinned. "Today, no government men. Here we find happiness on our trails in our friend Mammy Anna. We will escort you back to the village."

"Thank you. But tell me, how goes the harvest?" She hoped the keen ears of Gardiah didn't hear her heart stutter to a stop waiting for his answer.

"The fields are ready soon. Does Mammy Anna wish to gather rice with the other women?"

A weight lifted. They'd arrived with time to spare before the bush school started. *Thank you, Heavenly Father.* "No. Mammy Anna wishes to teach as soon as my friend is settled."

Practically giddy, Anna turned to Stewart. "Gardiah says the harvest hasn't started yet." She squeezed his arm in glee. "We're in time."

Stewart patted her hand. "I'm glad for your and Taba's sakes."

"I can't wait to see him for myself." Her gaze wandered to where a few abandoned packs lay on the ground. Most of the men remained, shifting from foot to foot beside their loads, exchanging silent glances. "First, I'd better take care of our men."

Anna asked, "Gardiah, our men wish to leave. Can we get others to carry our belongings?"

He nodded. "We will leave a guard and send back for what cannot be carried now."

Grateful bearers backed away, disappearing into the heavy overgrowth. With guard duties assigned, thirteen of the fifteen warriors took packs.

Gardiah asked, "We are ready, yes?"

Anna agreed and walked beside Gardiah. Stewart remained a steady few paces behind.

Gardiah looked back at Stewart. "Mammy Anna, why does this man walk behind? Do men in the white bush serve the women?"

Anna snorted and motioned for Stewart to flank her other side. "No, they do not. Mr. Hastings was a soldier in the white bush's Great War. He probably believes it is better to guard us from that position, since most of your men walk ahead."

Gardiah assessed Stewart with new respect. "He must think you valuable to take this position. Perhaps he wishes to be your husband."

Gardiah was worse than Dr. Mary. "No, I'm sure he does not."

Gardiah shook his head, disbelieving. "Men of the white bush cannot be so blind."

Anna turned the subject. "Mr. Hastings comes to do

business. To explore. He looks for iron, gold and things that are valuable in the white bush."

The planes of Gardiah's face sharpened. "Mammy Anna, I fear my father will not approve." He swept an arm in a wide arc. "This is Pahn land. Everything here belongs to the people."

"Of course, and the people will benefit if they do business with him." Anna hesitated. The government licensing of this area had to come out at some time. "The people he works for have been given permission to seek these things."

Gardiah stiffened and his eyes narrowed. "This permission means nothing to us."

"Yes, I know, but the government is desperate for the money this would bring. They might send soldiers if you oppose them. But Mr. Hastings is not a government man. He means no harm. If he finds minerals here, the village gains prosperity. Think of how the money would pay taxes. Then the government wouldn't have an excuse to take men away to work."

"The Pahn have never had men stolen by the government for slaves to pay taxes. My father thinks not of wealth. His mind is on that which is denied him, a position as a Paramount Chief. You will find his mood little improved since you left."

"I am sorry to hear so."

"You should also know he is angry because your missionary god didn't raise his status with the other villages." He gave her a pointed look. "And you know how he has treated outsiders in the past."

"Yes, I do."

They walked on in silence. The scrub thinned out and the path widened. Anna sought the words to convince Gardiah to help gain his father's trust. The smell of village cook fires grew stronger. "Gardiah, I need your help with this."

Gardiah halted and smiled at Anna. "I must bow to the wisdom of my father and the elders, but I may know how to help them decide if your friend can stay."

"I see your smile. You are ever the thinker and planner."

Gardiah smiled more broadly. "Your father is far from here, Mammy Anna, and my father still embraces you as a daughter. If your Hastings asked to marry you and paid my father a bride price, then Hastings might be allowed to live."

Stewart walked beside Anna while she bantered with the chief's son. He was a strapping young fellow, a little taller than his men, but far shorter than Stewart. Gardiah appeared to be no more than twenty, and all warrior. His head was shaved, one short oval tuft remaining at the top. Nothing for an enemy to grab in combat. He wore a woven loincloth, tied at the sides. A necklace of animal teeth surrounding a small fetish pouch at its center partially obscured a strangely surgical-looking scar slashed across the right side of his chest. The mark crossed other more intentional scars. A patterned design started midchest and ran down his torso. When he smiled, teeth filed to sharp points issued a stark reminder of the Pahn's true nature.

Despite his outward appearance, Gardiah seemed friendly enough. Stewart couldn't understand a word, but the conversation frequently involved smiles and laughter. Then they both grew serious, Anna stiffened and glanced at Stewart.

"What's wrong, Anna?"

She averted her eyes. "Nothing."

"Miss Baldwin, let us not start to keep things from one another."

"Gardiah proposed a solution for you to stay if his father does not first approve your visit."

"What kind of solution?"

"Not a workable one, a measure of last resort."

"What exactly does a cannibal consider a last resort?"

She shook her head. "I'm not sure you want to know."

"I prefer to know exactly what I'm walking into, Miss Baldwin. I'd not like to end up in this fellow's cook pot."

She lifted her skirt hem and accepted his arm as she maneuvered over a downed limb. "Gardiah tells me their patrols are actively watching for government agents. They wish to prevent any attempts to collect the Hut Tax."

"Why should they pay taxes? If enforcing a tax on these people is an attempt to solve the government's financial crisis, then the capital is in more trouble than I realized. Selling mining concessions is one thing, but taxing people without providing benefits in return?"

Anna responded, "I know, but it's the law. The government boasts many members who are descendants of repatriated slaves, brought here by a group called the Maryland Society. Few of those immigrants ever had any ties to Liberia. The new colonists modeled their government after what they came from, not what they came to. Now it's as if there are two separate societies in one and neither understands the other."

"No wonder the Pahn fight to keep the government men out."

"Politics to the side, what you need to understand is that more incursions by the government make Nana Mala more skittish about outsiders right now."

"And Gardiah's solution?" Stewart waited. Was a blush creeping across Anna's cheeks?

She softly cleared her throat. "Since Nana Mala holds me in high regard, Gardiah suggests your marriage to me would offer protection from any drastic repercussions the chief might otherwise impose."

Stewart choked.

Anna handed him a canteen. "Here, drink."

The tepid water relieved the condition. He kept swallowing small sips while he collected his thoughts.

Gardiah looked amused.

Stewart tried for a mild tone. "I may not be religious, Miss Baldwin, but I consider marriage to be a serious undertaking."

Anna nodded. "You know my thoughts on marriage, Mr. Hastings, but Gardiah worries over my unmarried state. He probably thinks this an ideal solution to finally securing me a husband and to save your job, possibly even your life in the process."

A fist seized Stewart's stomach. Marriage or death? What was he willing to do to secure the funds for his mother's care? Or his life? If not for Anna's beliefs, marriage to such a smart, beautiful, principled woman would be ideal. Knowing her, she would do whatever was required to save him, but what man wanted a wife to marry him out of sacrifice?

On the other hand, what man wanted to become a literal sacrifice? He'd conveniently put aside her admonition back in Monrovia about how this plan could turn deadly.

Anna interrupted his thoughts. "Not to worry, Mr. Hastings. An unmarried woman of my age goes against the customs of Gardiah's world. He is constantly trying to rectify what he believes is a problem."

Stewart's face must have given away his feelings.

Anna laughed. "Oh, my. You look like a prisoner given a commuted sentence."

Stewart found a chuckle. "Exactly how it feels." As soon as the words left his lips, he realized how his words sounded. "I didn't mean to imply marriage to you was a fate worse than death, Miss Baldwin."

Anna smiled. "I took no offense, Mr. Hastings. We can remain on friendly terms and still agree that any union between the two of us would be disastrous."

Disastrous? He struggled with a heart that grew more tender toward her every day. Clearly she didn't have the same problem with him.

They walked on in silence until terrain fell away to a valley fronting the mountains. The palisade walls of the village came into sight. From the hilltop, he gained a clear overview. Off to one side, ripening rice fields. The village was large, with tall, heavy walls constructed with timber, not the flimsy barriers he'd seen elsewhere. Conical thatched huts were tightly packed around an open square, and more bled out from there. At the rear, there was a second gate, and inside to the right, a separate area walled four huts inside. "That's some fortification."

Anna nodded. "Matches their warlike reputation. The walls are a strong deterrent to their enemies, but past history alone keeps most at bay."

Stewart whistled low as they moved closer. "Considering their wall decorations, I understand. Are those skulls?"

"They certainly put a hitch in my step when I arrived. Dr. Mary and her husband, William Mayweather, came close to becoming martyrs here."

"What exactly happened to them?"

"Nana Mala tricked them into believing a baby Dr.

Mary delivered was sick to get them to come to the village."

So the chief was the devious type. "Why?"

"Egged on by the devilman, Nana Mala wanted to acquire what he believed was Dr. Mary's magic. The possibility of acquiring the power he believed to exist in her medicine caused him to lure them here to get it any way he could, even through cannibalism."

Stewart said, "Cannibalism is something I can't fathom. But, in some ways, the Liberian people seem no different from people elsewhere. Everyone wants power or prestige."

Anna said, "Human hearts are the same. Only the culture and customs change."

Stewart considered the implications. "Good."

Anna blinked. "Good? How is this good?"

Stewart answered, "Human motives being what they are, my plan to woo the chief with trade goods and future prosperity should work. With your help, of course."

Anna countered, "Human *nature* aside, Mr. Hastings, you cannot count on your plan working. Nana Mala is not so predictable. If he decides you're a threat..."

Stewart went straight for the humor that had served him so well in the past. "Then, my dear Miss Baldwin, you might have to resort to extraordinary measures to earn the other half of your fee. Should we negotiate a bonus now in case we're forced to marry?"

Anna entered through the familiar gates of the Pahn compound and blinked back sudden tears. Several of her students, including Taba, had come out to greet her. She embraced each in turn, trying not to single Taba out from the others, and promised them all answers about the tall white man once school started.

Gardiah walked ahead and spoke to a warrior who'd come forward to greet him. She'd thought this place lost to her, and yet she was here, able to stay because of Stewart. He'd half joked about a bonus for marriage to keep him alive. For an instant she wondered exactly what she would do to keep Stewart from true jeopardy.

She'd refused a marriage to one man to serve her calling. Would she now be forced into a marriage to save a man's life? The results for her mission work would be the same either way.

Stewart brought her back to the moment. Nodding toward the children scurrying off, he asked, "Your students seem quite happy you've returned. Which one was Taba?"

"See the tall, thin boy in the beaten bark cloth to the right of the others? That's him. I'll introduce you and show you my school later."

"Will we be allowed to rest or do we go straight to the chief?"

Anna removed her pith helmet and smoothed her hair. "I'll get you settled and then present myself to Nana Mala. I'd prefer to approach him alone at first."

Gardiah returned, gripping his spear as if about to go into battle. What was bothering him? His face stoic, he spoke. Anna translated, trying to keep her features even and her silent prayers rapid. "Gardiah says we are both to go immediately to meet his father and the elders."

Anna caught the slight narrowing of Stewart's eyes as he said, "I'm guessing this isn't another kola-nut and salt ceremony, from the look on Gardiah's face."

She motioned for Stewart to follow beside her as Gardiah led the way. "Mr. Hastings, let me speak to the chief first. You smile and follow my lead."

"Don't worry. Our trek together has taught me the

folly of taking things into my own hands. This is your show."

Anna prayed as they were escorted to stand just outside the sheltered palaver area. Fond of her or not, the chief would never allow a woman to breech the males-only space.

Nana Mala and the tribal elders stepped outside the space. The devilman exited last. The chief barked orders and Anna's nervousness turned to horror. Warriors surrounded them; the ones in front directed their spear tips toward Stewart. Anna launched herself in front of him, a futile barrier to iron, and prayed she'd been wrong—not prophetic—when she'd told Stewart that the bishop's plan might get him killed.

Stewart fought the cold sweat of fear and grabbed Anna's arms from behind. He lifted her rigid body despite her resistance and shunted her behind him. "It's my job to protect you, Miss Baldwin. At the very least, stand behind me for safety."

She issued a terse whisper. "Do you have a death wish? Stop talking and leave this to me. If there is any part of you that does believe in God, I'd strongly suggest you pray."

The temptation to fall back on making pleas to God was there. But prayer failed against the mustard gas. Iron was far more substantial. Right now the only thing he could focus on was the stubborn little missionary trying to place herself as a shield in front of him, as if the weapon tips wouldn't pierce her just as easily.

Low murmurs carried through the crowd when she managed to succeed. He moved her again. As their silent tug-of-war continued, unexpected snickers came from the crowd. Spears pointed upward and a couple of the younger warriors grinned. "Miss Baldwin, I do believe we've gone from target to a source of amusement."

She looked around. Apparently satisfied with what she saw, she moved to his side. She smoothed her shirtwaist, a wasted attempt to regain dignity in the face of the crowd's amusement. "We're not out of danger yet, Mr. Hastings."

The warriors facing them parted, revealing a man who could only be the much-vaunted Nana Mala. Even without knowing the man's reputation, Stewart recognized the danger standing in front of him. Nana Mala, his face an angry mask, was shorter than Stewart expected. This was a man who'd go to fat soon, but for now the coming corpulence was only a hint layered over a muscled, squat physique. His oiled braids gleamed and were devoid of the top hats, bowlers and other Western wear chiefs in other villages prized.

Up close, Stewart counted every pore, noted each tattoo marking. Century-long seconds ticked by until the chief grunted and turned to Anna. He spoke in harsh, guttural tones. Stewart wanted to tell her to translate, but contained himself in mute frustration at the rapid concert of tones played back and forth. The chief's staccato rang out and was answered by Anna's even melody. After a battering of guttural tones, her melody shifted to carry a hint of desperate insistence. Enough. If his fate was being decided, he deserved to know. "Anna, what is he saying?"

Both parties and the surrounding crowd quieted and stared at him as if he'd declared God dead in a room full of preachers. Nana Mala crossed his arms across his bare, muscled chest and said something to Anna.

Anna paled, her eyes flared rounder, and she shook her head at the chief.

"Anna, translate."

"He is angry you have come. . . ." She spoke as if the words stuck sideways in her throat. "He says the government has no right to give you permission to the land of his ancestors." She swallowed and dropped to almost a whisper. "He wants to kill you as an example to others who would try to come in the future."

The last time such lead had filled his veins was when the mustard gas had hit his trench. He kept his tone even. "Is there any hope of negotiating further? The trade goods, a promise of riches to come?"

Looking again at the tattooed face, Stewart stopped. This was not the face of a man to be won over with novelties or promises. Stewart had miscalculated. Badly.

The chief leered and issued a guttural command. Warriors pushed Anna aside and placed his arms in grips like iron manacles. A sudden jerk backward threw off his balance. Dimly he saw the drag marks his boots were leaving. He struggled to regain his footing. Anna pleaded with the chief. Nana Mala ignored her, looking over her head and watching as Stewart was pulled away. Stewart's last sight of the chief was of his satisfied smile and the two rows of gleaming pointed teeth he bared.

Chapter Nine

Anna was led back to her hut under escort. Her fruitless attempts to reason with Nana Mala left her with a bone-deep exhaustion and no reprieve. Her biggest worry had been arriving before the harvest's end for Taba's sake, not how to save *two* lives. The thought of the funny, kind man she'd grown fond of being executed in front of her left her with a cold emptiness. How could she even manage to remain here preaching God's love and forgiveness if Nana Mala executed Stewart?

Up until today, she'd thought herself equal to any task involving bringing the Gospel to an unreached people.

How mistaken she'd been.

She'd lost her composure when Stewart was taken off to be imprisoned. The change in Nana Mala since she'd left for Monrovia was drastic, or was this the unmasked face of the true man he'd hidden from her?

At the next crossing in the paths, Gardiah appeared. With the exception of Taba and Jayplo, a secondary wife of Nana Mala, Gardiah had been the most receptive to listening to the Gospel, but he resisted making any commitment. He dismissed her escort. "I am sorry, Mammy Anna."

"What of your earlier plan? Can I marry Stewart and stop this madness your father intends?"

Gardiah's pity was apparent. "No, then you would be a widow. My father's anger has found the target he lacked."

"Killing Stewart will bring your father's fears to pass. The government will be angry. They need the money Mr. Hastings's company will give them."

Gardiah said nothing. She knew him well enough to know he would think on her words.

"Gardiah, unlike the government who takes from you, the company will pay the village. You can palaver until you reach an agreement that is best for everyone."

Bolder now, she pressed on. "The village will not have this chance if Mr. Hastings is killed. The government will use his death as an excuse to send their soldiers."

Gardiah stopped and stared, a feral gleam in his eyes. "Let their troops come. The Pahn will not allow them to enslave our men or hang our chief as they have done to many of the Kru." He looked every inch a taller version of his father at that moment.

She'd gone too far. He heard a challenge, not a warning. He had no idea the weapons available to the Liberian Frontier Force soldiers.

Heavenly Father, I need Your wisdom and help. I cannot do this on my own. Your Word says you move kings' hearts. Please move Nana Mala's heart and save Stewart.

Gardiah crossed his arms over his chest. "Because he is important to you, Mammy Anna, I will speak to my father. He might banish your friend when I explain how the other, weaker villages might be destroyed and blame him if the soldiers come. My father still hopes to become a Paramount Chief. A war with the government would hurt his chances."

The roaring desperation in her head subsided. “Thank you, Gardiah. Anything that saves Mr. Hastings’s life.” She thought about Gardiah’s reasons. “How is it your father thinks he can try again to be Paramount Chief after his first bid failed?”

His eyes slid away for a fraction of a moment. “Those villages to the east have given us grave insult by refusing my father as their Paramount Chief.”

Revenge? No, that wouldn’t get him elected. “Isn’t that their right?”

“They may choose, but he vows to succeed.”

Not unless something changed the minds of those who opposed him. She’d save her questions for another day. “I wish to see my friend.”

“The day is gone, Mammy Anna. You should return to your hut for the night.”

“I will not be able to rest unless I see him unharmed.”

He spoke with reluctance. “For a moment only.”

“Thank you, Gardiah. I am grateful for your kindness.”

Gardiah shrugged. “You missionaries have been kind to my people.” He traced the diagonal scar on his chest. “Even to the saving of my life by your doctor. I have not forgotten.”

“As I will not forget what you are trying to do for me now.”

He grinned. “Your words on the trail said you did not bring a husband, but now I think you wish him to be. Do you love this man, Mammy Anna?”

“No! But he is a friend. I would not see him harmed.”

“As you say.”

Meaning he didn’t believe her. She didn’t love Stewart. She couldn’t. Anna hurried behind the warrior’s long strides, anxious for proof Stewart was indeed unharmed.

* * *

Stewart sat on the dirt floor of the hut, nursing a set of sore ribs. The two armed guards at his doorway had made their wishes clear. He tried to quell his fears for Anna's safety.

While light remained, he studied the hut's construction for eventual escape. The walls were a hardened mud mixture and lacked any window, the thatch roof a noisy possibility. No easy out here. The guards' vigilance doomed any attempt for now. Later, he'd take the wooden sleeping platform apart and fashion a crude weapon. Turning the other cheek when a fellow tried to kill you might be a missionary strategy, but he'd go down fighting, not like a lamb to the slaughter.

Minutes ticked by. The unmistakable rustle of a Western woman's skirts interrupted his mental planning. Was Anna being imprisoned, too?

She entered. He'd never seen a more beautiful sight after having tortured himself with what danger he might have brought upon her. Never mind that her clothes were travel-stained and her hair had escaped its bonds during their tussle.

He rose to meet her and reached out, intending to clasp her hands in his. The first touch of her overwhelmed him and he crushed her to him, the relief at her safety overwhelming every bit of propriety. She stiffened and then relaxed. He held her until she gently pulled back.

He whispered, "I feared he had harmed you."

Her voice betrayed the strain she was under. "I am fine, Mr. Hastings. Nana Mala is unhappy with me, but not murderously so."

Any news she had must truly be bad if she wasn't indignant in response to his embrace. He made a weak attempt to fall back on humor. “Does this mean we’re engaged?”

She dropped her gaze. “Marriage and these circumstances are no joking matter. I did ask. I would have agreed to go through any ceremony they required, despite the fact there could never be a real union between us. Gardiah said his father was too angry to be amenable to the plan. The execution proceeds with or without our marriage.”

This couldn’t be the end. He had to find a way out. “I appreciate your effort.”

“Of course. To save your life, I would do whatever it took.”

If hers was one of the last faces he would see, he’d prefer a memory of her smile over this grief he saw written there. “From your look, I gather marriage to me would be only one fateful step below the death promised me.”

A tiny smile. “Of course not. No marriage here would be valid. But at least you would live.”

What had he expected? He’d escape and they’d live happily-ever-after?

Twin trails ran down Anna’s cheeks. “Mr. Hastings, if Nana Mala cannot be dissuaded, you will be executed in two days.”

A gaping hole, apparent only to him, opened in his chest. He resisted the urge to pull her close again, clasping her hands in his. “Is there no hope, then?”

“Hope still exists. Gardiah agreed to try to get his father to give you a reprieve of sorts.” No point in telling him yet that banishment was the other option. One worry at a time.

“Miss Baldwin, you do understand I won’t sit and wait for an execution. We need a plan of escape. I do not trust what might happen to you if I go missing.”

She shook her head. "Getting beyond the walls is difficult, but possible. The problem is the warriors would have the advantage in the jungle and we have no weapons. The closest place is Nynabo, but we'd be bringing trouble to the mission station. We'd have to travel much farther before we'd be safe." She gave his hands a reassuring squeeze and let go. "But you might have a chance on your own. My pace would slow you down, and I cannot leave Taba. You could hide and retrace our route till you were beyond his reaches."

"I can't leave you here with a threat hanging over your head."

A small smile, devoid of joy, appeared. "Mr. Hastings, every missionary that sets foot in this land does so knowing death might await us. Because of the malaria here, almost half of us never make it past our first year. As much as I've appreciated your efforts to keep me safe, some things are in God's hands alone."

An attitude like that would ensure her fate. "Are you so ready to throw away your life, so eager to die in God's name?"

Pain played across her face. "I have no wish to embrace death early, but I trust God. If it is His plan for me to die here, then I will."

Silence reigned for several moments.

"I'm sorry, Anna."

She looked puzzled. "Why? I am the one who failed you."

"I was a blind fool not to heed your early warnings. To think I knew more about how this world works than a woman who had experience to back her."

"If you were blind, it was desperation's fault. You were lured by the hope of great gain at a time when you needed it the most. No man is a fool who would risk what you have risked to save his mother."

"Kind of you to say so, but a dead son profits my mother nothing. You work on the chief and I'll work on an escape plan."

Gardiah cleared his throat and stepped in the doorway. "Mammy Anna, I must return you to your hut now."

She spoke in English after the Pahn, translating for Stewart's benefit. "Just another moment, please. We wish to pray together."

Pray? One look at her face, and Stewart knew better than to challenge her. He did the only thing any sensible man would do when faced with a determined woman on a mission.

He bowed his head and let her pray.

Long after the breakfast cook pots had been scoured, Gardiah entered Anna's hut, every muscle in his face taut. "I spoke long hours with my father. He agreed for your Mr. Hastings to leave unharmed. Warriors will escort him to the edge of our lands in the morning. From there he is on his own."

Anna's legs felt like the calf's-foot jelly the cook used to serve at Easter dinner. He wouldn't die, not by Nana Mala's hands, but alone in the jungle, no guide and no language skills when he encountered other tribes. "He does not know the jungle ways or speak your tongues. Surely you can send someone with him to Nynabo. They will help him get home safely."

"For you, I will try." With those words, he was gone before she thought to ask about seeing Stewart again. She'd have to talk her way past his guards. She hurried out the door, adjusting her hairpins along the way.

She refused to think about how she'd grown accustomed to his company and their banter. For now, she had to focus on how to ensure his safety for the duration of his travel. Should she leave with him to be sure he got to Nynabo if necessary? Not without Taba. The Poro school opened soon. There'd been no time to talk yet with his parents. Would they let her take him to Nynabo while escorting an enemy of the village?

Lord, what would You have me do? Choosing one over the other is impossible. Show me clearly how Your Will can be accomplished here.

Perhaps God was working all things to the good, as Dr. Mary had admonished her. Stewart leaving now might be beneficial to Anna. Gardiah was wrong about her loving Stewart. But when she examined herself closely, she found she had grown too attached to him. Unless she took more care, her feelings might become a snare and compromise her duty to the Lord.

She prayed again for peace and guidance as she neared Stewart's jail. A lone guard stood watch, the father of one of her younger students. He allowed her access without question.

She called at the doorway, "Mr. Hastings? May I come in?"

"Certainly, please."

She stepped in and gave her eyes a moment to adjust to the dim light. Stewart's face bore a haggard appearance, his beard, meticulously kept clean-shaved on the trail, shadowed his jaw. She wished she could get his kit so he could shave. Holding on to a touch of civilization kept one sane in the jungle. "Did you get any sleep?"

"Not a wink. I waited for a chance to escape. The guards never gave me one."

"I hope you will sleep better tonight. Nana Mala granted you a reprieve."

He studied her face. He took a step in her direction, but now that she was aware of her attraction, she took a step back.

A sheepish grin spread across his face. "Sorry. About last night, I hope you can forgive me for taking liberties."

"Emotions were high for both of us, Mr. Hastings. We believed you were about to die. Comforting one another in such an extreme circumstance is not unseemly."

"Well, when do I get out of here? I'm still on a deadline."

"Tomorrow. But the news isn't entirely good. The chief agreed not to kill you, but he's banishing you from his territory."

His face went still. He turned his back to her and paced. Should she say something? No, she'd give him a moment to collect himself.

When he stopped and faced her, a quiet strength was in place. "I am in your debt for saving my life."

"I wish things were different, Mr. Hastings. I'm sorry I can't do more."

"As do I, Miss Baldwin. Nothing here is your fault, but there is one small thing you can do for me to soften the blow."

"Anything. Whatever you need."

"Call me by my given name, please. I think Stewart is more appropriate than Mr. Hastings after all we've been through together."

For one day? What could it hurt to drop that barrier between them? "You're quite right, Stewart. I would be pleased if you called me Anna."

He rewarded her with a tired smile. "What happens next, Anna?"

"You'll be escorted to the edge of Pahn territory in the morning. I'm trying to get a guide to Nynabo, where you will be safe. Clara, who mans the station while the Mayweathers are gone, can make arrangements for further travel." She fought the catch in her throat. "I'm sorry this solution will not provide for your mother."

"You saved my life, Anna. My only regret is that after all you've done, I can't give you more time with your students."

"What do you mean?" Understanding pressed into her. "The money. Your company's payment?" She looked back up at him. "They won't..."

Her unfinished sentence hung in the air like a plea. The second half of the payment would have provided the rest of the funds to send Taba to school. Now Stewart was safe, but Taba was still in jeopardy.

He shook his head. "I'll try to convince them to give you something more in payment for getting me out safely. But the contract the bishop signed won't require them to do so. I can only hope they'll act in good faith when I report your efforts."

"I didn't think beyond the fear of your death. I've failed us all."

He reached a hand to her shoulder. "You are not responsible for Nana Mala's actions. Looks like we both lost our dreams today."

Iron shot through her spine. "There has to be a way. Only yesterday you were to die, and now you've been granted life." She reached out and grabbed both his hands in hers. Even in her own ears, her voice carried a new authority. "I cannot believe God will not honor a son's plan for his mother's care. Neither will I believe God requires Taba's life as a martyr. Prayer worked last night. We're just not done yet."

"Anna, we can hardly credit this to prayer. I went along with you last night..."

She insisted, "I believe enough for the both of us, Stewart. And you have nothing left to lose by joining me once again in prayer. What if you're wrong?"

He hesitated and she waited, pouring every bit of silent encouragement she had into him. Yesterday he was scheduled to die; today his life had been handed back to him. Could he not see that?

"Fine, I'll close my eyes while you pray, but that's all. And it's only out of gratitude for what you've done, not out of some sense of upcoming Divine intervention."

She decided not to push things any further and bowed her head, praying for Stewart's salvation and God's further intervention. Silently she also prayed for strength to conquer her straying thoughts and feelings for Stewart. Otherwise, how would she handle her growing attraction if her prayers were answered and Stewart was allowed to stay?

By the day's end, Stewart was ready to pull the hut walls down with his bare fingers. Pacing in tight circles only lent his mind the time to ponder his mother's needs and Anna's question. What if he was wrong? Twice now, his carefully constructed plans for his life had come to nothing. First when Julianne broke their engagement and now at the word of a cannibal chief. He'd agreed to pray once with Anna and his life was handed back to him. What if he was wrong about prayer? About God?

A day of enforced contemplation brought no answers. Passing voices in a language he couldn't understand and the rustling of insects in the ceiling were all that broke the silence. For distraction, he'd sunk to watching the occasional beetle scurry around after falling out of the thatch above, which was why he noticed when his many-legged companions went completely still, as if listening to something only bug ears could hear.

Their inaction ended without warning. The noise from the thatch increased. Insects from every corner made a unified mass exodus. Outside, people shouted, running past his doorway. His guard stuck his head into the hut and spoke urgent, unintelligible words.

What did he want? He spoke again, then shook his head and left.

Stewart stuck his head out the door. To his right, a group of women, babies on backs and toddlers in hand, crowded their way down the path, all moving in the same direction as the bugs. To his left more villagers came in a rush, chickens, children and small piglets squealing in their arms.

What were they fleeing and where was Anna?

He stepped out and went against the flow of bodies, determined to find her. Best he could tell earlier, this was the direction she'd taken when she'd left him. One older woman grabbed his sleeve and jabbered, clearly upset with him. She attempted to pull him in the opposite direction. He persisted and she gave up.

Were they at war? Being attacked? What kind of enemy scared off the insects?

He called Anna's name as he went. Whatever was happening, he had to know she was safe, even if he had to search the whole village.

He almost despaired before he found her. She ran toward him, skirt hem lifted in one hand, lantern swinging in the other. She yelled something. A few more steps and he heard her clearly.

Drivers? A line of ants caused this much panic?

She stumbled as she got to him and he righted her.

Breathlessly she said, “Drivers. We have to get out by the east gate and head for the water.”

He took the lantern so she could better manage her long skirts. “Why not stay out of their path like before?”

“Not a line, a mass attack. Possibly a whole colony. Our best hope is the nearby stream. It may be wide enough to stop them from bridging it. Pray they can’t reach us.”

Prayer? No, this was a time for action and he knew what kind. He grabbed her arm. “The kerosene.”

She shook her head. “Great for putting in cans with your bedposts or for routing a small line, but not a whole colony.”

“And if the stream isn’t wide enough? Do you want to take that chance with innocent lives at stake? What about fire?”

Her eyes sparked hope, but her voice held caution. “There might not be time to lay a line wide enough to route them.”

“Then let’s not waste time arguing. Where would the kerosene be stored?”

“The chief’s compound. He confiscated everything.”

“Show me. Then you get to safety in case this doesn’t work.”

“This way.”

They ran in silence until they got near the closed main gate. A few torches lit early against the approaching night guided them in the descending gloom. A clicking hum permeated the air.

Anna gasped, “They’re close to the walls.”

“Will it slow them down?”

“Barely. They’ll climb the walls and come down the other side.”

They passed the palaver hut where Stewart’s sentence

had been passed and arrived at the smaller walled compound he'd seen when they'd first approached from the trail. Inside the chief's deserted property, they scoured the area.

"There," Anna shouted.

Stewart recognized the packs, some plundered and scattered around. Silver cans with the word *kerosene* stenciled in red sat behind them. "Point me in the general direction of retreat in case this doesn't work."

Anna shook her head violently. "No. You can't stop them by yourself. The process will take the two of us pouring down a long, thick line of kerosene to route them. If the barrier isn't long enough, they'll just go around."

He weighed his options for a split second. "Grab some cans, then. But promise me, at the first sign we can't stop them, you run."

She nodded, grabbed two cans by their handles and fell in beside him. "Don't worry. I have no intention of dying today."

As they got near the gate, an animated black line danced at the top of the gleaming skulls and darkened the pitch points of the timbers. Were they already too late?

Chapter Ten

Anna gripped harder on the handles of the kerosene cans as the swarm of ants topped the skull-topped timbers. Stewart shouted and pointed to her right. He went left, pouring kerosene in a long line a few feet from the inner base of the stockade walls. She went the other way. *Please, Lord, let this work.*

The first can emptied too soon. She grabbed the other and kept pouring until she needed to return for more. No time. She looked to Stewart as the ants hit the ground. In the distance, he waved her away, a torch in his other hand. *Lord, let this work and keep us from burning down the village.*

She stepped back and he lit the kerosene.

A glorious flame crackled to life and ran down the line. She followed Stewart back to the kerosene supply and they loaded themselves down. Pungent smoke billowed off the line of flames, hampering their ability to see if they'd routed the ants. Anna surveyed the ground while she started a second row of kerosene.

Stewart motioned to her. "Leave your cans. I'll pour. You get the rest."

She ran as though the ants had chosen her as their next course.

She clutched two cans and headed back. Stewart took them from her and continued pouring. Legs burning, she returned for more.

Passing the palaver hut, she spied Gardiah in the distance, torch in hand.

"Mammy Anna!"

She didn't stop. The ants wouldn't wait. They met as she left his father's compound with her flammable burden.

He grabbed her arm, forcing her to clutch the cans even tighter. His words in Pahn flew at a furious pace. "Mammy Anna, what are you doing? All are at the water. I did not see you there but smelled smoke. You must come back with me."

He tried to pull her in the direction of safety and she resisted. "No, my friend is stopping the ants with this kerosene at the front gate." She thrust the cans at him. "Take these to Stewart."

He stopped pulling her. Her frantic certitude must have won him over. He placed his torch in a nearby holder, took the cans and ran. She went back for more.

When she caught up, Gardiah and Stewart were working in tandem. She fed them kerosene, and they poured. The roar of the flames drowned out any chance to hear if the ants still clicked. The men emptied the last cans, and Gardiah watched with grim satisfaction while Stewart lit the second, thicker line. Flames reached for the sky.

Both stepped back out of the billowing clouds, coughing. Water. Her throat ached with the need. She found a full jar in a nearby hut. She carried the container to the sooty men, who lifted it high and poured it directly into their mouths and over their heads.

Stewart held the jar for her and cool relief hit her burning throat. Water never tasted so good. She held out her hands for some to splash on her face. Too late she caught the spark of mischief in his eyes and realized his intent. He dumped the remainder right over her head and Gardiah howled in laughter, slapping Stewart on the back in male affirmation.

She sputtered and wiped the drips. "What was that for?"

"The heat. Your face resembled a well-roasted turkey ready for the dinner table. A dainty splash wouldn't accomplish much."

She turned to Gardiah, who still laughed. "And you? This is funny?"

A grin split his face from ear to ear. "It is funny, yes."

His grin infected her. She smiled and wrung the drips from her hair. "It was funny, wasn't it?"

Stewart set the empty jar on the ground and inspected the ground near the flames. She and Gardiah hurried to join him. "What's the verdict? Did we route them?"

"Can't tell for sure until the smoke dissipates more." He looked at her dripping self. "If we didn't route them, I'm guessing we'll have some very angry insects."

Gardiah walked the long line of fiery defense, his form soon swallowed by the haze of smoke. She stood beside Stewart and listened. The flames quieted. Was that clacking? *Please, no.*

Stewart stiffened and grabbed her arm. Ha! She wouldn't need any encouragement. If that insect hoard still advanced, she'd be the first in the creek joining the others.

She sucked in a deep breath when Stewart said, "The noise is retreating."

After another minute the *click-clack* was gone entirely.

Stewart let go of her arm and said, "Stay ready to run."

"I will, but I think we were successful."

The smoky haze thinned and Gardiah returned. "Mammy Anna, they are gone. I will send warriors to track their retreat."

Anna translated.

Stewart asked, "They might return?"

Gardiah nodded after Anna conveyed Stewart's question. "But not if we find their nest and burn them in it." Again, Gardiah clapped Stewart on the back. "I go now to tell my people the village is safe." He nodded toward Stewart. "Your friend is now our friend. My father can see it no other way. He brought luck to the village."

Anna cringed at the superstitious notion. Stewart's quick thinking saved the remaining livestock, a precious commodity to the people, and possibly prevented deaths if the angry horde of insects had bridged the stream. She told Stewart what Gardiah had said.

"So I'm a friend, their new good-luck charm. What does that mean exactly?"

"After what you did, the chief will most likely allow you to stay."

"He'll negotiate with me?"

"I don't see how he can't now."

"From the look on your face, I have to ask. What's the bad news?"

"Gardiah believes your presence is good luck. His father will believe so, too."

"So? What's the rub?"

"The rub, as you put it, is one of my worst fears about your presence here coming to pass."

Stewart slid his fingers through his hair, flinging wet droplets to the side. "Hey, you're alive, I'm alive, we managed not to burn the village down, and I may be able to stay. What is so bad?"

"From the beginning I feared for God's witness in this place being compromised. Your quick thinking physically saved this place, but the tribe judges your actions through their superstitions. After preaching for over a year, trying to enlighten them, I can only hope this hasn't set back my efforts beyond a point of recovery."

Stewart took in Anna's words and recognized the droop in her shoulders, the exhaustion in her eyes. She'd fought a hard battle. This was the emotional aftermath. "You're seeing things all wrong, Anna."

"I am?" Her eyes held a glassy sheen.

"You are. Reminds me of one of my soldiers. Your nerves were on high alert. Physically you fought a battle here today. This is the letdown that follows. Things will look better after some rest and a meal. Women weren't mean to fight battles like this. It's hard on the nerves."

She bristled. "Impugning my womanhood is a low blow."

Ah, success. "See, you're bouncing back already."

She heaved a deep breath, pursed her lips and rolled her eyes heavenward. "Point taken. But the problem is real."

He lifted one arm, theatrically referencing the charred battle lines and the walls behind them. "So was the solution. Anna, have you forgotten?"

Her brows knit. "Forgotten what?"

"The prayer. Did you not insist God would find a way for us both to stay? You're focusing on Gardiah's mention of luck. Perhaps it was not just quick thinking for me to remember the kerosene. As a missionary, shouldn't you be the one looking to credit Divine intervention here? Not that I believe it, but maybe you should see this as your answer to prayer."

Her eyes widened. "I stand corrected. God's hand is evident, and I allowed the exhaustion to blind me to His workings."

"That's my girl! I knew the missionary talk I've grown to tolerate would peek through that gloomy cloud."

She rolled her eyes. "Stewart, you are irrepressible, but I thank you for bringing me back to my senses. If the village sees you as lucky…I have an idea for getting Taba's parents' approval for my plan."

He bowed. "Glad to be of service."

"We should go talk to the chief while he is in a grateful mood."

"I agree, but we need only wait right here."

She turned in the direction he nodded. Gardiah walked beside his father, engrossed in an animated conversation. As they made their way to where he and Anna stood, the chief turned his attention from his son to Stewart. Grateful or not, the chief's gaze still sent a chill through Stewart's veins as if evil itself stared through him.

Behind Nana Mala, a corpulent woman trailed in her colorful swath of fabric and bangles. Further in the entourage was a beautiful younger woman with a small child in hand. She sported country-blue cloth draped modestly over her form and wore more adornment than most women he'd seen in a village. Warriors, some with torches, flanked the party.

Anna said, "The one right behind the chief is his first wife, Mammy Tarloh. She is Gardiah's mother. The younger woman is Jayplo, his second wife. The child is their daughter, Wonlay."

"How many wives does the chief have?"

Anna smiled at him. "Two. Unusual where a man may take as many as he can afford."

"Nothing I've seen about Nana Mala seems remotely usual, even compared to other villages. Before he gets to us, one quick reminder."

"What?"

"Translate as we go, please. No surprises at the end like last time."

She nodded. "Bargaining for your life left me with no time. And I couldn't take the chance you might unknowingly make things worse." She touched his arm. "Stewart, you need to trust me to do the right thing. I'll translate as I can, but patience isn't in his repertoire of virtues."

"He has virtues?"

She smiled. "Of course he does. That question is precisely why I can't always translate directly for you. Nana Mala is a harsh man. Keeping his people safe from their enemies has required things of him that we can't understand in our world. But in his own way, he is loyal and loving to his family, and since his experience with the Mayweathers, his attitude toward missionaries changed."

"Maybe it did, but now it seems more hostile."

"I wish I knew why. I suspect the political failure was too great a disappointment."

Stewart restricted his reply to a nod as Nana Mala and his entourage stopped in front of them. The chief spoke and Anna translated. "Nana Mala thanks you for the good luck you brought to his village. He knows how you stopped the ants and the chief says he wishes to extend the hospitality of the village to you."

Much preferable to being the evening's meal. "Please thank the chief for me and tell him…well, tell him whatever you think appropriate. I trust your ability to say the right thing or to negotiate anything I need."

Anna gave Stewart an approving look and proceeded to speak to the chief. How long did a thank-you take here? Nana Mala's eyebrows rose and he responded in a few short words to another long volley from Anna.

Finally the chief gave another short reply that he followed with a signal to his wives. They headed to his compound. Stewart waited until they were gone. "Well? What did he say?"

Anna grinned like a small child with a happy secret. "You were right about God answering prayer. I managed to get us what we both need."

His right eye ticked with suspicion. "You know I don't really believe in prayer, right? I just said that to help you. So, exactly what did you get *us?*"

"For now the chief is content to allow you to explore. If you find anything, negotiations will come later. He's allotted two men to help and an apprentice." Her grin widened.

"An apprentice? There isn't enough time for me to train a man. The language barrier alone is enough."

"For communication, Nana Mala agreed to send to the north for a man named Pennon, who translated for the Mayweathers. Pennon speaks a Liberian English, and your apprentice knows enough English for basic communication."

He hated to douse her lovely smile. "Anna, I'm no teacher. Can't you tell the chief thanks but no thanks on the trainee?"

She blanched. "No, I can't. It will ruin everything."

"All right. Don't worry, then. If the price of my prospecting is to train a man, so be it. Anything is better than the future Nana Mala originally had planned for me. But we'll have to be careful in other negotiations. The company may not like too many unexpected contingencies."

"Oh, this wasn't his idea. I asked permission."

"Why would you obligate me without asking? It doesn't seem like you."

She grinned. "Because the devilmen can't force Taba into their school if the chief has promised you the boy as an apprentice. This way he will be protected until you leave. When you travel home, he can go with you to Newaka and remain in the care of the school."

"Taba? So am I supposed to train a twelve-year-old boy or just keep him safely out of the way?"

She answered, "A bit of both. The Poro school starts soon and I'd prefer he weren't around for its start. This clinches his safety."

"What about his parents' say in all this?"

"Taba's parents will be greatly honored to have their son as an apprentice. It's the second part that's a little trickier."

"Now I'm almost afraid to ask."

Her gaze didn't quite meet his. "You're going to have to buy Taba from his parents."

Anna regretted not having time to explain beforehand. The horror on Stewart's face illustrated her blunder. He had no idea how missionaries wrangled the law and resorted to contracts and payment to save a child.

"This is your idea to protect him? Have him sold to me? Find another way, Anna. This smacks of promoting slavery. I will never own a slave in this land or any other."

She rushed to explain, "No, of course not. This is a

form of guardianship, a way to safely, legally remove him from the village so he can live to get a Christian education."

He shook his head. "I'm a single man, hardly in the position to parent a child. An apprentice is one thing, but there's no guarantee I'll remain in this country."

"No. Let me explain. Children from the bush are often sent to mission schools along the coast to 'receive book,' as they call getting an education. Sometimes there is a contract drawn up between the parties much like is done when a child is indentured to serve in a home in Monrovia. Those contracts call for the family indenturing the child to provide an education in addition to a small stipend. By giving a small consideration or payment to his parents, this binds them and keeps them from being pressured into changing their minds by the devilmen."

"And this is normal, that parents would indenture their children?"

"Yes, and they also pawn their wives. Wives to pay their debts, but children for the hope of an education. Of course, a lot of children have ended up in a home that promised them an education but simply used them as free labor. At least this way Taba will get his education, learn more about God and be allowed to choose his own future."

"So why not just have his parents make a contract with you?"

"In this case, you are better than a missionary. If Taba's parents give him to me to send to the mission boarding school, they risk the ire of the devilmen. This is why they hesitated before. But the chief believes you bring luck to the village, so a contract with you elevates their status, and the devilmen can't take revenge."

"So taking Taba on as my apprentice, in essence buying him, offers his family a form of protection?"

"Yes." She placed a hand on his arm in reassurance. "Stewart, Taba will want to do this."

"Hard to say no, even though, on the surface, you're asking me to go against a basic principle I hold. I'd feel better if I talked to the boy first. Twelve is still young to make such decisions. I also need to be sure we are all clear that I'm doing this to help save him from the devilmen, not to adopt him."

"I'll arrange for you to talk. You'll see that Taba understands these things."

Stewart stuck his hands into his pockets. "Fine. But if there is even one indication otherwise, the deal is off and we'll need to find another way to get him out of the village."

Anna surveyed the sixteen happy faces seated on the ground in front of her. Each one clutched a worn New England primer. The primers were ancient, but the fact Stewart had secretly obtained them for her children in Harper gave her as much joy as her students. Now that Stewart had acquiesced after meeting Taba and his parents, Taba would be safe and she could focus on teaching and preaching.

Eight-year-old Togar raised his hand. "Mammy Anna, teach words, please."

Anna instructed them in Pahn about the rules for the precious primers. Sixteen solemn faces nodded at her every word, but one page into the actual book and their attention wandered to a spot behind her.

Anna turned. Stewart stood with one booted foot propped on the low wall of the open-air school, his corresponding elbow resting on his knee and holding up his chin. Soft giggles came from behind her. She turned to keep both Stewart and her students in her field of vision. "Children, this is Mr. Hastings," she said in Pahn. "Let's thank him in English for our books."

"Thank you, Mr. Hastings."

Stewart stood straight. "You're welcome, children."

More giggles. Anna gave them a short assignment, walked over to Stewart and noticed the backpack at his feet. "Are you leaving now? Taba has talked of nothing else all day."

"We'll see how he feels after long days spent prospecting. Pennon arrived, so we leave shortly."

"How long will you be gone, Stewart?"

"Why? Are you going to miss me?"

Heat flowed up to her cheeks from under the neckline of her shirt. "It's… I…"

"I'm only teasing you. In fact, I can tell these children have enough of your attention to keep you from knowing I'm gone."

"I haven't meant to neglect you."

"Once you introduced me to the village blacksmith, I learned a lot from observing. Ingenious fellow with his functional furnace and bellows. Back to your original question, we're taking supplies for ten days or so. We'll survey the general area, get the lay of things and set up a base camp on the most promising site."

"Be careful. Post guards, especially at night. Keep your fires burning. You should…"

"Anna, if I didn't know any better, I'd believe you cared for me."

Of course she did, just not the way he implied. "I'd just hate to think after all God has done to get you here that a roaming leopard would be your final end."

"Since Gardiah and his men dug that pit and trapped

the leopard that's been terrorizing the area, I think you can put all those fears to rest, Leopard Men included. Only Pennon remains unconvinced. His insistence on a constant guard should keep anything else from taking us unawares."

Little hands tugged Anna's skirt. Six-year-old Donyen had something to say. Anna addressed the intrusion in both languages. "Donyen, it is important not to interrupt your elders."

Donyen dropped her head. Anna turned her attention back to Stewart after a raised-eyebrow glance toward her whispering pupils. "Pennon isn't the only one. Gardiah trapped the big cat, yet he still cautions me not to venture from the compound unaccompanied. He hints the threat of the Leopard Society is real but assures me the village is safe."

Stewart said, "Perhaps he is worried for your general safety and this is his way of protecting you."

"Gardiah is a bit overprotective. Reminds me of you."

Stewart raised one eyebrow.

Another small tug on her skirt. "Donyen, please go sit down." The tugging continued. "Excuse me, Stewart."

She knelt eye to eye with Donyen. "What is so important, Donyen? This is not like you."

Now that she had Anna's attention, the child breathed out one word. "Secret."

Stewart said, "Secret, right? What secret does this little one need to tell you?"

Anna answered, "Maybe your yellow hair has worked its spell with another young lady and she's too shy to say."

"Please, don't remind me. Just let her down gently."

Donyen leaned in and whispered in Anna's ear. Not

a childish crush. Anna reassured her and stood. Donyen skipped back to her place.

Stewart said, "She's happier now." He eyed Anna suspiciously. "What did you tell her?"

"She's content because she shared her secret."

"Why don't you look relieved?"

"She overheard our mention of the Leopard Men."

"We've scared her."

"Not exactly. Last evening she went later than usual to the stream where the women draw water." Anna took in a deep breath. "She ended up hiding in the brush."

A muscle in his cheek pulsed. "Why?"

"Because crouched by the stream, she saw three leopards."

"Gardiah trapped one. Leopards don't work in packs. Are you sure she isn't making this up?"

"No, Donyen is a sweet child, not given to guile. Her description is disturbing."

"How so?"

"Donyen's leopards stood on two legs, not four."

Six days tramping the mountains, four camped, and not a leopard of any number of legs in sight. Stewart stretched his aching back. After days of almost fruitless trenching, there was color found, mostly flakes, but some small nuggets. He looked downstream, where Taba worked intently on his new assignment. Thanks to him becoming fascinated by the different rocks in his pan and picking them out, Stewart now had excellent samples of the indicator minerals that signaled gold's presence: quartz, mica, beryl and garnet.

He wished Anna could have seen the look on Taba's face when Stewart had explained how those small reddish-brown rocks Taba found hid the deep red beauty of garnets.

Stewart wished for a way to polish them to demonstrate he was telling the truth. For now, the skeptical Taba was proud that he alone got to use the special sieving pan.

Stewart walked over to Pennon. "Finding anything?"

As Pennon gave the pan a shake, Stewart heard the small sound. "Sounds like you have a growler mixed in with those flakes."

Pennon asked, "What is a 'growler'?"

"A gold nugget not large enough to make a loud sound if shaken in your pan."

"Aw, yes, a growler. Is this good?"

"Yes, and I expect we'll find more as we work our way upstream."

"Yes, growlers. We can search for these on our next trip."

"Instead of making another trip, Pennon, why don't we send our men to the village to restock our supplies? I can send a list for Mammy Anna and she will know what to give them from my stores. Then we can continue working our way upstream."

Pennon shook his head. "Nana Stewart, I am coming to go just now."

Stewart puzzled on the contradiction of words. "Coming to go? I don't understand that expression."

Pennon explained. "It means I am leaving now or leaving soon. I will return when the moon is full."

The last full moon was two weeks back. Stewart couldn't afford more wasted days. "Pennon, I will pay more if you can stay for now."

"No, Nana Stewart. My bride's family waits."

"You're getting married?"

He nodded. "This work made it so. I have enough for bride price now."

Clearly a besotted bridegroom-to-be. Stewart knew

there was no more bargaining to be done. But he and Taba could still stay and send the men for supplies before he left. "Congratulations, Pennon. I wish you happiness. When you return, I will be upstream or in this area nearby. Could you instruct the men and send them for supplies so I can remain here?"

Pennon shook his head. "No, Nana Stewart. The men would not return if one of us does not go with them."

"Why not?"

"They will not want to leave the safety of the village unless we make them return. They fear the Leopard Men."

Stewart asked, "Leopard Men? The Pahn trapped a real leopard, not a man. I do not believe there is any cause for worry."

Pennon shrugged. "Leopard Men would like you to believe so. You must guard. Stay away from water after dark. Walk with friends, not alone."

Water. A familiar warning. A prevalent superstition.

Taba joined them. "A girl in our village saw five Leopard Men where we draw water."

The tale had grown from three to five, like all good rumors. "Taba, I heard her. She said three, and I do not believe they were Leopard Men."

Pennon asked, "Is this a spirit you talk to, Nana Stewart?"

"A spirit? No, a living girl."

Pennon spoke, his confusion evident. "This cannot be. No one survives them. Nana Stewart must be careful. Sometimes spirits take bodies and talk to us. The girl child may be a warning from your ancestors."

There was no point trying to dissuade Pennon from his superstitions. To Pennon and Taba he said, "Then I see no point in staying here any longer. Let's break camp and head back."

Pennon notified the porters, and they disappeared in the direction of camp. He and Pennon followed, Taba trailing behind. At the campsite, Stewart found the men working at top speed to leave. Maybe they were still afraid despite the leopard skin Gardiah was proudly displaying in the village.

Stewart gathered his own gear and took time to wrap his notes in oilskin despite the pointed looks and shifting feet of the porters beside their ready loads. A few extra minutes was a small price to pay to guarantee all his records and mapping weren't destroyed if he slipped in any of the creeks or swampy areas they'd tramp through. He still needed to secure his newest samples before he put them in his pack, but not while watching the men's dance of impatience. He couldn't take much more of this leopard nonsense. "Pennon, send the men on ahead. I can see they are ready to return to their home. We can follow behind."

Grateful men balanced their packs and set off. Stewart stowed the last of his samples. If they pushed, they'd make the village before nightfall.

When they reached a juncture of paths well over midway to the Pahn, Pennon signaled a stop. "This path leads to my own village. I will leave you now. The boy knows the way and there is enough daylight."

"Travel safely, Pennon."

Pennon nodded. "I will. Much safer in the direction I go home."

"Why?"

Pennon pointed to the east. "No Leopard Men sacrifices past Pahn village. My home is safe." Pennon vanished down the path and Stewart turned to Taba. "Down to just us, Taba."

Taba nodded and Stewart matched his pace to the shorter set of legs beside him. The silent walk turned his thoughts to Anna. Word of their return would pass quickly in the village. Hopefully, she'd come to greet him. Only because he'd still need her help to communicate beyond hand gestures with most of the residents. Or so Stewart told himself.

The busy search for gold helped during the day, but her face slipped into his dreams at night. American Mining's deadline wasn't his only reason to hurry. The sooner he left this territory, the sooner he could put his infatuation to rest.

If she knew, it would embarrass her and— The toe of his boot slid under a tree root. His momentum propelled him forward. He hit the ground, remembering at the last moment not to brace his arms for a bad break. His foot wrenched as his body hit the trail. A vicious root under his rib cage knocked the wind out of him.

"Nana Stewart hurt?" Taba stood over him, his small eyes rounded widely.

Stewart inhaled and a spasm stabbed through his ribs. He tried a more shallow breath before attempting to speak. "I will be fine, Taba."

Taba looked unconvinced.

Stewart dislodged his foot with a resounding hiss of pain. Taba's brow furrowed. Stewart pulled himself to his feet, brushed off the worst of the leaves and debris, and tested his ankle. Pain so sharp he saw spots stabbed through him. Hobbling wouldn't work. "Taba, I need a big stick to help me walk better." He mimed how he would use a makeshift crutch and Taba took off into the brush.

Stewart left his boot on. The tight leather would hold down the swelling.

Taba returned a few minutes later with a stout, Y-shaped branch. Extra-long but usable. "Thank you, Taba."

"This will help Nana Stewart walk?"

"Yes, you did well." The boy beamed at the praise.

Stewart cut the branch to length with his knife, took the blanket from his pack and cut a long strip off the bottom. He used the piece to pad the end he placed under his arm. He hobbled a few steps to test his creation. "We will have to go slowly. Lead the way."

Like any young boy with an important job, Taba stood a little straighter and his chest puffed out. Taba was a good help, but Stewart regretted sending the men ahead. The speed he could manage traversing on a makeshift crutch would put them back well after dark.

The slower he traveled, the faster precious sunlight dimmed. Time to break out the lantern before he took another fall.

Taba stopped stock-still on the trail. Stewart opened his mouth to ask why and then he heard the voices ahead. Someone had sent a search party.

"Taba, call out so they will know we are near."

Taba shook his head vigorously. "No, Nana Stewart. Enemies hear as well as friends."

Stewart only nodded. The child had more sense about the bush than Stewart.

The voices receded along with Stewart's hope of help.

They rounded a blind bend, bringing them to where they must cross the stream that trailed beside them down the mountain. Stewart dreaded navigating the slippery rocks. Taba took a step back, bumping into Stewart. Not normal for the trail-savvy young man.

Then Stewart saw why. The source of the voices stood in front of them.

Not their porters. "Taba, run, hide."

Three men with elaborate headdresses, spotted skins covering their yellowed bodies—no, make that four. From his right, an iron claw slashed out, driving deep into his unprotected side. Burning pain followed a burning realization.

The Leopard Men were real.

Chapter Eleven

Anna joined the search party forming at the gate. Gardiah spoke to the two porters who'd returned hours ago without Stewart and Taba. Despite their insistence that Stewart had told the men to go on ahead, she'd been too angry earlier to question them herself, afraid the un-Christian attitude roiling through her would find its aim in their direction.

Gardiah walked briskly toward her. Anna braced for the argument once he spotted her backpack.

"Mammy Anna, you must stay here."

"I'm going, Gardiah. If you leave me behind, I'll follow on my own."

He smiled. "The women of the white bush are undoubtedly fierce warriors, but the men of my bush are swifter without them, Mammy Anna."

Desperation to find Stewart and Taba warred with her common sense. Gardiah was right.

"Mammy Anna, I will find them. Offer prayers to your God while we search."

Anna nodded her agreement, not trusting her voice. Her prayers hadn't ceased since Jayplo, the chief's young second wife, brought her word about Stewart and Taba not returning. But still she had allowed her worry to wear her like a hair shirt. What kind of example was she setting for Gardiah about trusting God?

Relieved at her agreement, Gardiah issued orders, took an extra torch from one of his men and left with his party. She watched until the torch flames turned into tiny dots and finally disappeared into the forest. She stared into the dark for many moments longer and then returned to her hut.

When she got inside, she slid her pack to the floor and sat on the low stool to pray and wait.

Father, protect Stewart and Taba. Guide the men to where they may be found. Lord...

Her thoughts raced ahead of her prayers. Taba's salvation was sure, but not Stewart's. What if he died in the jungle? The porters should have known better than to leave.

Ah, unforgiveness, her most difficult foe. *Father, forgive me for harboring this bitterness and anger. I forgive them.*

Peace and the smell of spicy cassava wafted through her hut. Jayplo stood at the doorway, a large plate in her hand and her small daughter at her side. "Mammy Anna should eat."

"Thank you, Jayplo. Will you join me?"

Jayplo shook her head. "I have already had my meal."

"Then stay a moment and keep company with me." Anna patted her lap and Wonlay's chubby legs propelled her into the offered seat.

Jayplo reached for one of the pierced-edge plates hanging from Anna's wall while she laughed at her much-indulged daughter. "How will you handle food with such squirming in your lap, Mammy Anna?"

Anna enjoyed the distraction of the little one who'd

wiggled into just the right spot. "Wonlay is no bother. Besides, I have little appetite right now."

Jayplo placed the bowl in front of Anna. Anna's stomach growled and Jayplo smiled. "Mammy Anna's mouth says one thing, but her belly says another."

Anna poured the palm oil into the rice and mixed. Chubby little baby fingers inched toward the plate. Jayplo corrected Wonlay.

"Jayplo, let her have some. She and I will eat together and take my mind from worry."

"She is ever hungry, this one. She ate her belly full before we came. Sleep is not far from her eyes." Jayplo scooped the food, forming a small ball. Wonlay opened her mouth like a baby bird and happily popped it in. After the third time, Wonlay's head bobbed and Jayplo reached for the child. She snuggled her daughter into her arms, rocking to encourage sleep. "They will find Taba and your friend. Do not grieve. Eat for your strength."

Anna finished eating and said, "I guess I was hungrier than I thought."

Jayplo nodded. "Now we will wait together." She handed Anna the sleeping Wonlay and Anna let the comfort of holding the peaceful child seep into her bones while she continued to silently pray.

Jayplo cleaned the plate and slid it back over its wall peg. She checked the water jar and said, "I will refill this."

Anna considered her restless friend. "Jayplo, I have more than enough till morning. If I didn't know better, I would think you were the one with worry."

Jayplo's head dropped and she averted her eyes.

"Jayplo, I am sorry. I allowed my own thoughts to consume me and here you are with something on your mind." Anna gestured. "Sit and speak to me."

Jayplo complied. "I do not wish to burden, Mammy Anna."

Anna smiled at the self-effacing woman. "You are never a burden, only a blessing to me. Please, tell me what bothers you."

Jayplo hesitated. Anna waited till Jayplo was ready. In a sudden burst, Jayplo said, "Mammy Anna, I have become ugly in my husband's sight."

Anna was taken aback at the force of emotion that came pouring out. Jayplo with her high cheekbones, broad nose, expressive eyes and smooth nut-brown skin marred only by the customary tribal markings was far from ugly. As befit her station as a chief's wife, she wore the more modest dress that covered both halves of her body and many pieces of jewelry.

Perhaps in a land without mirrors, Jayplo didn't know her own beauty. Not something Anna's parents had ever allowed her to forget. "Jayplo, why do you say this? Do you not know how others see you?"

"I do not care for others, Mammy Anna. My husband is the only one who matters. Wonlay is long weaned, yet he pays no mind to me and spends his time elsewhere."

"Is he courting a new wife?"

Jayplo shook her head vehemently. "No, although Tarloh and I have urged this so we might have another to share the work. He must find me ugly for he chooses to be away from the village instead of with me. I think he goes secretly with his warriors patrolling the jungle trails." She stood and paced. "He is the chief. This is a job for others. He must find me so repulsive he would rather be elsewhere doing that which is beneath his station."

Before she could address Jayplo's concerns, Anna's

student Togar interrupted, breathlessly announcing himself at her doorway.

Anna tensed and gestured for him to enter. He shook his head. “Mammy Anna, please come. They have found them.”

Togar ran off before she could ask any questions. Anna handed the sleeping Wonlay to her mother and headed out the door, Jayplo fast on her heels.

By the time they got to the gate, torches bobbed down the hill in the distance. No one was close enough to make out any figures. She quashed the urge to run out and meet them, hanging on to the dignity her impatience demanded she shed. Stewart and Taba were found and the knowledge enabled her to wait.

When the line reached the gate, a serious-faced Taba trailed alongside two warriors supporting Stewart. Stewart’s shirt hung in ribbons on one side, caked in blood. Her heart seized. Dr. Mary had taught her only rudimentary medical skills for survival.

She directed the men to take Stewart to his hut. She grabbed Taba, turning him around for a quick survey. “Are you all right? What happened?”

His words raced. “Leopard Men, Mammy Anna. Nana Stewart protected me. He told me to run, but I stayed. His gun scared them away.”

“You were very brave, Taba. I’m sure Nana Stewart is as proud of you as I am.” Secretly, Anna was horrified. She looked at Jayplo. “Can you get Taba to his mother and then bring the basket of medical supplies from my hut? I need to go with Stewart.”

Jayplo nodded and ushered Taba away, distracting him from his distress with the antics of now-awakened Wonlay.

Anna hiked her skirts and ran till she caught up with

the men helping Stewart. His bloodless lips were tightly compressed. "Stewart, what happened?"

His speech came out in terse, tight bursts. "Attacked. Leopard Men. Not a rumor."

The men helping Stewart looked quizzically at her, not understanding the English. She ignored their curiosity, not wanting to spread panic. "Let's get you to your bed so I can look at those wounds. I've sent Jayplo for the medical supplies Dr. Mary gave me."

He protested, "No, Anna. I can't have you dealing with this."

Had she heard him right? "What do you mean, no? The risk of infection is too high in the jungle. You must let me treat you."

When he made it to the edge of his sleeping pallet, he waved off his helpers. Anna lit the lantern wick and waited, puzzled at his refusal of help.

Eyes downcast, Stewart said, "This is no job for you. Send your supplies with Taba. I'll do it myself."

He must be out of his head with fever. She lifted a hand to his forehead. He flinched at her touch. He looked up at her. "No, it's not a fever talking. Please, Anna, just get the supplies and let me handle this." He grimaced and squeezed his eyes shut. His hand reached for his injured side and stopped just short of grabbing it.

"Stewart, you're in no shape to handle anything."

He opened his eyes. She turned the lantern wick up to see his face more clearly. Exhaustion and pain battled there for supremacy. And something else that looked like shame, but that made no sense.

He managed another argument. "Weren't you the one who worried I'd compromise your witness in this village?"

"Yes, but..."

"No buts. This is the way it has to be to protect you. Your reputation."

"Fever or not, you must be out of your head with pain if you think propriety is important now. Besides, Jayplo can stay and assist me."

His head dropped in defeat, his chin practically to his chest. A desperate note echoed in his whisper. "Please, Anna. For my sake, just go."

Something was dreadfully wrong here, more than Leopard Men and propriety. Whatever the real reason he wanted her to leave, whatever he was holding back, his spirit was breaking under the weight of the effort. She prayed for guidance and grace. A gentle boldness came over her. She stepped directly in front of him, softly placed her hands on each side of his face and angled it gently upward till their eyes met. The sorrow and shame evident there broke her heart.

She spoke softly. "Stewart, tell me why you really don't want my help. You can tell me anything, and it will be all right."

He searched her face for a moment. "Telling you isn't the problem, Anna. It's when I show you that everything will be ruined. You've come to mean enough to me these past weeks that I can't stand that once you see, afterward you'll never look at me the same again."

Of all the things to occur, an injury that would expose his mustard burns to Anna's view was like a contrived scenario in a bad play, a tragedy where he knew the ending well before the last scene opened. Right now Anna's eyes held compassion. But if seasoned nurses lost their professional demeanor when they saw the damage, avoiding direct eye contact for the duration of his stay, how could a tenderhearted missionary manage once she saw what he'd kept buttoned away from view?

True, in a few more weeks he would be gone from here, but he'd harbored hope that American Mining might send him back to establish an operation if they bought the concession. He wasn't so deluded to think he and Anna could ever be anything more than they were right now, but to never be able to talk and tease or enjoy her company again grieved him more than he'd expected. Burns cost him a relationship with Julianne, and now the thought of Anna looking at him differently once she saw what he'd hidden left him with a gaping hole of despair.

He knew this was inevitable. He could never reach some of the places those iron claws had mauled. He had to live to do his job and take care of his mother. If he was to die, he should die for something worth more than just his pride and a relationship with no real future. He'd survived Julianne's rejection; he'd get through Anna's, as well.

He removed her hands from his face, clasping them in his own. "I'll accept your help. But the war left its mark on me, Anna. You'll have to prepare yourself. What the Leopard Men did is nothing compared to the scars I received in the Great War. If it's too much for you, say so and you can tell someone else what to do."

She nodded, a little wary. "All right, Stewart. Let's start with removing this shirt so I can see the extent of your injuries."

The blood-soaked cloth had dried in spots and tugged his damaged skin. The fire it stoked made Liberian peppers feel like baby's porridge. Anna apologized repeatedly as she worked. He only nodded, his jaw clenched against the pain.

When the shirt was off, Anna silently surveyed the

multitude of puckered, shiny red scars Stewart knew were emblazoned down the side of his chest and on his right shoulder, a horror no Leopard Man had ever conceived of inflicting. Then in a soft voice she said, "Oh, Stewart. What agony you must have endured from these burns. I can't begin to imagine."

Behind her, Jayplo called out and entered the room with the basket. She gasped when she glanced at his injuries, old and new. Anna spoke to her in Pahn, and Jayplo's answer left Anna nodding agreement. Then Jayplo went to work setting out the medical contents of the basket.

"What did she say, Anna?"

"I told her how you got the scars. She is horrified that this is what happens when the white bush goes to war."

"Can she bear to look long enough to help you? Can you…?" He looked away.

"Of course, neither of us is… Stewart, look at me."

He did and she continued, voice strained with incredulity. "Were you worried the sight was so horrible that I couldn't bear to look?"

He nodded.

"Stewart, I've been in the jungle for some time now. Accidents, animal attacks—believe me, I've seen a lot. Yes, it's hard to see, but because it represents what you had to endure. I'm disappointed that you thought I couldn't handle something like this."

"Well, for all I knew you would faint at the sight."

"Why on earth would I do something so impractical?"

"The last woman who saw my burned chest needed smelling salts to revive her. She sent a messenger within the hour and ended our engagement."

"Well, she obviously lacked character." She slapped a hand to her mouth. "Oh, Lord, forgive me. I shouldn't judge the woman. But, dear me, who breaks an engagement over an injury? I am so sorry for what additional pain that must have caused you."

He smiled in spite of the pain. Anna's reaction was a balm to an old wound. He told her the rest. "I got over losing her a lot more easily than what followed. The worst blow came after I was discharged from the hospital. Her father had waited to rescind his partnership offer so he wouldn't look bad firing a hospitalized veteran. I lost my future wife, my job and the ability to provide for my mother's retirement because Julianne couldn't bear the sight of me."

"Stewart, I hope you don't judge all women by her example. I promise, I only faint in the presence of chloroform. And I've only broken an engagement over issues of faith...uh, not that engagements apply between us."

He rescued her from talk of engagements. "Then I guess you're qualified to help. Let's get this over with."

Anna spoke to Jayplo and she brought a lantern for additional light. After the first cleaning with water, Anna made a carbolic solution and soaked gauze in it. "This is going to hurt. Probably a lot."

"At least you're more honest about it than the doctors. They describe the most severe pain as 'uncomfortable.'"

When she finished, she said, "I think only two of these furrows require stitching."

He groaned.

"Oh, please tell me a brave, strong man like you isn't afraid of a few stitches."

"I'm just remembering our conversation about needlework. Dare I hope that despite not liking it, you became skilled?"

"You can always hope." Anna opened a suture kit and got to work. "I doubt my work is up to Dr. Mary's standards, but perhaps it's some consolation that you'll have an interesting tale to tell and the scars to back it up."

The only hope he had was that she would finish soon. He felt like a seat cushion undergoing repair. "I had scars before you started."

She tied off the last stitch and placed her needle in a small basin with more carbolic. "Well, scars from cannibal Leopard Men will make a much better tale at dinner parties for impressionable young women."

He snorted. "I doubt my tale will have the ladies lining up for matrimonial offers."

She stored the unused gauze and suture materials in her basket. Jayplo cleaned up, took Stewart's ruined shirt and left. Anna said, "Oh, I don't know. War wounds are sadly common now. This story will be unique. For all you know, you could gain the attention of your future wife based on this attack alone." She picked up her basket to leave.

"And promptly lose her once she learns of my more extensive disfigurement. You don't have to try to make me feel good. With these scars, no woman will ever marry me."

Anna gripped her basket tightly lest she bean an already injured man over the head with it for speaking such nonsense. He had a serious case of self-pity hidden along with the scars. "I think you'll find the bigger impediment to finding a wife to be feeling sorry for yourself. As long as you stay hidden behind broadcloth, how does any woman have a chance to prove that one woman reacting badly doesn't mean we all will? From everything I know of you, I never would have thought you would act the coward where vanity is concerned."

"Anna, you've been beautiful and admired for your

appearance all your life. How can you possibly understand?"

She put her basket down for the moment and sat beside him. "It's true. I've never dealt with something like you have, but one young man in my home church returned with mustard burns across one side of his face and down his neck. You've had the luxury of hiding yours out of sight."

"Luxury?"

"Yes, Stewart, luxury. I suspect concealing the damage keeps you from having to deal with others' reactions. I watched my church friend. His courage, his ability to win people over to seeing past his ruined face, it was a study in God's grace."

"Then your friend is the exception or simply putting on a false image for the world."

"I don't think so. He spoke of the depression and fear he wrestled with before he finally braved the public eye. It's not easy dealing with a face that scares small children or causes adults to turn away. Not until he began to focus on how God saw him did he find the strength to risk the ridicule and rejection."

"So he comforted himself with religion. We all have our methods of coping."

"Like risking infection to keep hiding yours?" She spoke softly to pull the sting out of her words. "Stewart, to anyone who knows and cares about you, the scars won't matter. If you turn your heart over to God, He can heal this pain and the others you carry. He'll give you a new perspective on life."

"I wish I could believe that. Or that somehow God could magically make me not care." He shook his head. "But I did pray once, and God didn't bother to save me or the men around me."

There was the mystery of Stewart's missing faith. Besides his difficult childhood, he really believed God had failed him during the war as much as he believed no woman able to love him for himself. Behind the stoic features, she caught a fleeting glimpse of raw pain.

"Tell me, Anna, why should I expect Divine intervention now?" He issued a challenge in his tone.

"Stewart, you're looking for proof of God's existence or his love in the wrong place. Yes, sometimes things happen that are clearly Divine intervention, but other times we reap the consequences of our or another's sinful choices. From Adam and Eve on down, God has never interfered with man's free will to choose what is evil versus what is good. And we all pay the consequences of that. It's not about whether bad and unjust things happen, but how we choose to react when they do."

"And what consequences have you paid, Anna? I know you had a difficult childhood, too, and—" he reached out and brushed her cheek "—you bear this mark of your father's rage. But all that's behind you now. Living with something, knowing you can do nothing to change it—it's not the same, and faith is just an easy answer."

"My situation may not compare to yours, but I deal with the other side of the appearance coin. While you worry about your scars repulsing people, I have to deal with men who want me only because of the way I look. Since I was fifteen, I've been bombarded with proposals and insincere attentions. None of those men loved me. My appearance was the attraction. Some, like my fiancé, only desired to possess me to show off to others." She shuddered.

He grimaced from the pain caused by turning to look more directly at her. "I guess shallow people exist in both genders." He shook his head. "You. As a possession. No one who really knew you would think of you as ornamental. No…wait…that didn't come out right."

She smiled in spite of the serious nature of their talk. And then she waited to see how he'd manage to extricate himself from what he'd said.

His words rushed out. "Not that you're not beautiful. It's just that you, Anna Baldwin, have more depth than any woman I've ever met. When I first took in the sight of you on that sofa, and for some time after, I saw only the surface. And who wouldn't? Wars have been fought over women who looked like you. Now that I know you, I see an intelligent woman of strong convictions, a woman who sacrifices and cares for others, a woman who rose far above society's expectations for her. Now I see your beauty and so much more."

He simply took her breath away. Stewart Hastings accomplished what no man in her life had ever done before. He saw her, not her face. "That's the nicest thing any man has ever said to me." Inside, her heart crumbled as she realized she'd finally found a man who could look past her appearance and see her for herself. Why did it have to be one who stood in opposition to everything she believed?

Chapter Twelve

Stewart tried not to scratch the scabs he had left, but the healing process was driving him mad. Trenching and panning in this heat didn't help. He took a break and went to inventory his supplies, a small shadow named Taba close by his side. The young man was a hard worker, striving to keep up with everything Stewart did and learn each step of the process.

Taba lifted the cover on the dwindling cache. Stewart calculated the remaining few tins allowed him two more days before he needed to start the trek back to the village, unless he wanted to make do with only rice.

Taba asked, "Nana Stewart wants the men to hunt?"

"No, Taba. We've camped here long enough. The small game has left the area. Better to return and get more of our supplies from the village." Now that he took more men with him to deter any trouble with the Leopard Men, staying in one area so long made filling the cook pot more of a challenge.

Taba nodded, breaking into a smile. "I can see if my new brother or sister has come. And you can see Mammy Anna."

Precisely the problem. His feelings for her left him

too conflicted. Easier to keep his distance until he left for the coast. He had time for one more short expedition. But that didn't mean Taba had to go. "Taba, would you like to stay back in the village this time? This is your last chance to see your family and friends for a long time."

Taba's face grew serious. "But, Nana Stewart, I am your helper."

"You do a good job, but I can spare you for this last visit with your family. Thanks to you, the men know what I need."

The boy beamed. "Yes, I would stay and say goodbye to my family if Nana Stewart says."

Stewart patted Taba on the back. "Good man. Family is important."

Taba smiled in a semblance of innocence. "Yes, family is important. Mammy Anna would make a good family for Nana Stewart."

"Mammy Anna will make a good family, but not for me, you little matchmaker."

"What is 'matchmaker'?"

"Someone who tries to put a man and woman together to marry."

"But, Nana Stewart, Mammy Anna is worth many pillars of salt, many goats, much cloth. Why do you not want to marry her?"

The truth was always best. "Mammy Anna desires a husband who believes in her God, and I do not."

"All men of the white bush do not believe in the One God?"

"No, Taba. Not all."

The boy stood straighter. "Then maybe Taba will have to travel there one day and tell them to believe. Like Mammy Anna tells us here."

Stewart put aside his own beliefs when considering how to answer. He couldn't bring himself to say anything that might crush the shining sincerity of the child in front of him. "Do well in school, Taba, and you just might get your wish."

Taba nodded sagely. "I will get book and travel there someday."

"Get book?"

"Yes, at Newaka I will get book."

Stewart thought a moment. "Oh, you mean learn."

"Yes, I will do this and then go to the white bush to tell about Jesus. But first I pray that I live to go get book."

He said it as if it was such a casual concern. How did such a young boy accept that his fate might be death? What drove him to go against not only generations of belief, but the threats of the devilmen? Stewart had seen grown men in the trenches who lacked the stalwartness evidenced in Taba. How was that possible?

This child wouldn't die while Stewart drew breath. "Mammy Anna and I will get you safely to school. But we're returning to your village in the morning, so let's finish our work."

"I will tell the others." Taba stopped for one last comment. "Nana Stewart, I pray each night for the devilmen to see the truth. Now Taba will pray for you to know the God I know."

Stewart felt his unbelief wobble in the face of the child's fervent promise. Once, as a boy, he'd almost walked down the church aisle after feeling that same tug at his heart. Then he'd looked around at all the people sitting in the pews. Their lives didn't look any better than his, so how could God really be waiting to meet him at the altar? Nothing had changed for them. But something must have for Taba.

What was Stewart missing if this child could pray for those who wished to kill him? Where did Taba find the strength to hold his beliefs in the face of such evil?

* * *

Anna woke to the sound of talking drums. Even the roosters were still abed, so something was afoot. She completed her morning routine quickly, grabbed a shawl against the cool of the morning air and emerged from her hut as the first fingers of sunlight pushed away the deepest shade of lingering darkness. She headed for the drum station to see what messages had been received and relayed. She questioned two yawning women pulverizing grain for the thin, gruel-like *uji* sometimes served for breakfast. The women shrugged, unknowing.

If she didn't detour a bit, the path would take her right past Stewart's hut. Taba had visited her on his return yesterday, but not Stewart. Should she check on him? Did he not want to see her? Perhaps the emotions he'd hinted at when he'd finally revealed the presence of those mustard scars now embarrassed him. They'd talked of everything else on such a deep and open level, but not about him caring too much for her to risk her reaction in the first place.

Maybe avoidance was the best answer. The Bible said to flee temptation, and she was sorely tempted to become further attached to this man. He'd overcome so much, but stayed closed off to God. She prayed for a way to reach Stewart's heart, to share God's healing love in the short time left and for her Heavenly Father to help guard her heart from loving Stewart.

She remembered Dr. Mary's teasing speculation back in Monrovia that maybe her rescuer would turn out to be a godly husband for Anna. But with Stewart an avowed unbeliever, even Dr. Mary would counsel Anna to steer clear.

Resolved, Anna stepped up her pace and walked on without stopping. Yes, avoidance might be the best policy. She took up humming her favorite hymn, "From

Greenland's Icy Mountains," to keep her thoughts firmly on the mission work God had called her to do.

When she arrived near the stationary drums, she heard a familiar "Mammy Anna."

Taba waved from among a group of Stewart's helpers near the gate. Stewart was obviously heading right back out to prospect. She smiled, as much at the enthusiastic child as at her own wasted debate on avoiding Stewart.

Taba came running, followed by Stewart at a slower pace. She hugged Taba and asked, "Heading back out so soon?"

Stewart answered, "One last exploration before I leave for good. It's obvious there's some gold in those mountains, but I'd like to get a large enough yield in the panning to better prove my suspicions of just how much is there. That would be really good news to take back. Oh, and speaking of which, Taba, why don't you tell Mammy Anna about the news you just brought me?"

Taba's chest puffed out and his face took on a serious demeanor. "I have a new sister, born last night. I am the older brother now. I will pray for her every day that she may come to know the One God." A shroud of sadness appeared, overshadowing his blush of pride at becoming a big brother.

Anna asked, "Taba, what's wrong?"

Taba blinked rapidly and looked to the ground. Anna caught the glint of unshed tears in his eyes. His voice couldn't conceal his pain. "Nana Stewart said…" Anna politely pretended not to notice the hiccup in Taba's voice as he fought for control. "I had thought to stay a few days with my family. It is not to be. My father says the devil-men look more to cause trouble before I go to mission school. My father says I must stay with Nana Stewart. For all my family to stay safe."

Wordlessly, Anna hugged the boy to her again, meeting Stewart's gaze at the same time. The same regret reflected in Stewart's eyes as she felt. They both hurt for the little boy who wouldn't be able to see his sister's early years. Anna released Taba and looked directly into his eyes. "Taba, this is a hard thing. I will pray for you, that God will comfort you and watch over your family."

Taba nodded. Stewart cleared his throat, trying in vain to hide his own emotion, and told Taba, "Yes, well, we'd better head out. The men at the gate look ready to leave."

The gate! She'd forgotten her original task. "Before you leave, wait while I ask what news comes from the drums in case it might affect your plans."

"As long as it's quick. I don't want to waste daylight on my last expedition."

Anna hastened toward the young man near the drums, glad to have her back to Stewart. Hearing about his departure from his lips made his coming absence much more real.

She would miss Stewart, but too many more days in his presence and it would take more than resolve and humming hymns to keep her mind off him.

The drummer's words whisked her back to reality. Anna returned to Stewart and Taba. "Walk with me, Stewart."

He took the hint from her tone and sent Taba to stand with the waiting porters. "Bad news?"

"The Leopard Society is escalating. Three attacks in villages east of here in a very short space of time."

"Please don't worry. You know I won't let anything happen to that boy. You just stay safe within these walls."

"The problem brewing might be bigger than these walls can contain. From listening to some of the evening palavers, I know that Nana Mala has renewed his efforts to become a Paramount Chief. If these new deaths mean the Leopard Society is trying to gain more power, perhaps hoping to thwart Nana Mala's efforts, we could be in for some serious unrest in this area. Perhaps even intertribal wars over the politics."

His eyes narrowed. "And what will you do in that case?"

"I will ask God to give me wisdom, and pray for safety." She knew well the protectiveness he felt and moved to cut off the impending argument she could see he was already forming. "Your men are looking a little impatient."

He heaved a short sigh. "Hint taken. I won't lecture you on your safety. But you've seen my scars, proof positive that you'll need something more practical than prayer to save you in times of danger." He tipped his pith helmet awkwardly, turned on his heel and left her with a positive proof, only not the one he intended.

No, the stark reminder of his unbelief only showed how foolish she was to harbor any romantic feelings toward him, no matter how good a man he seemed. Her decisions would always be made through prayer.

Stewart paced behind his tired men. Five days and several more finds of consistent small nuggets mixed in with smaller flakes. But even more telling were the other indicator minerals he'd found: mica, topaz and magnetite. With these present in addition to the others they'd already found, there was surely more gold in those mountains than he'd yet located. The location of larger deposits hidden in this land taunted him with hints of their existence while eluding his every twist, turn and tumble. But his time was up and what he'd found was enough for American Mining to assay and make their decision. Besides, he'd gained an invaluable understanding of the area his bosses lacked. They thought it was all about the presence of gold, but factoring into the financial risk was the unpredictability of Nana Mala and the political unrest resulting from his desire to rule the villages around him. And what would the board of American Mining think when they heard about the slave labor being taken from the villages in lieu of tax money? Some investigation in the capital was needed to determine the impact on available employable labor in case the local troops decided to take workers from the Pahn, an event the Pahn would turn into a fight.

And what about Anna if that risk came to pass? She told him missionaries on the Cavalla fled during the uprising. Surely she'd leave if the dangers grew too great. Or if she failed to find funding past their agreement. If her ministry opportunities failed, her life would need a new direction. Could he be her new direction?

Until Anna he never would have considered living with a religious wife. Now he'd do almost anything if it meant she remained in his life. Where else would he find a woman like Anna? He'd attended church before. He could do it again, anything to make her happy.

Anything except true belief.

He stopped when he ran into that wall of truth. Taba propelled past him in lockstep with the porters in front. Stewart was buying into a delusion bigger than the existence of God. These daydreams would never work. He marveled at his desperation to find some way to be with her, one so strong he'd considered living a lie. This had to stop.

He adjusted the burden of his pack and set about catching up with Taba. Once they returned, he'd have only a day or two before he needed to leave the Pahn and get back to file his report. Right now it couldn't be too soon. The best thing for him was to pack his gear one last time, walk away and never look back.

* * *

Sitting alone in the school working on tomorrow's lessons, Anna fought the distraction that had plagued her all day—the chief's latest behavior. His angry outburst last night when she tried to take her turn in the communal storytelling signaled a change in his attitude.

Normally she would entertain large groups by the fire once a week, dramatically telling one of the more heroic Bible stories. They loved the battles that Israel fought for the promised land, and the chief delighted in finding as many similarities of Bible heroes to himself as possible. But once she switched to anything more directly evangelistic, the chief always cleverly dodged the issues she raised.

Was having a missionary in his village only about the prestige in other villages' eyes, the power he'd hoped it would bring? Maybe her presence was as much a good-luck fetish as Stewart's after saving the village from the ants.

She sighed and put away her planning. She'd held high hopes for Nana Mala's conversion. What would it take to reach him? Or was she destined only to plant seeds for the future?

Anytime now she expected word of Stewart's return. This close to dusk and he should have already been back. Maybe they'd arrived and no one had thought to tell her yet.

Anna jumped at Jayplo's voice behind her. "Mammy Anna, is Donyen with you? My sister is seeking her and asked me to check."

"No, she left right after school with Togar."

Jayplo shook her head. "My sister worries. Donyen is never this late. She is usually an obedient child and brings no worry to my sister."

Anna stood. "Jayplo, she's likely lost in play. I'm finished here, so let's go find her and put her mother's mind at ease. Perhaps she is at Togar's home."

Together they walked the short distance to where Togar's family resided. There they found Togar, who broke into a big smile. "Mammy Anna!"

She smiled in return. "Hello, Togar. We are looking for Donyen. She has not returned home. Have you seen her?"

"Yes, Mammy Anna. She left only a little while ago."

Jayplo asked, "Togar, do you know where she went?"

He nodded. "Donyen had a special job. She went to draw water for someone important."

Anna said, "To draw water? Who asks a small girl to draw water for them this close to night?"

The boy shrugged. "She only said she must keep the secret."

Anna glanced toward Jayplo. Her expression indicated she found this as odd as Anna did.

Togar asked, "Is something wrong, Mammy Anna?"

Anna reassured him, "No, Togar. We'll go check on Donyen and make sure she gets back before the gates close."

Once out of Togar's hearing, Jayplo asked, "What does this mean?"

"I don't know. I don't like this secret business, but there could be a simple explanation. Before we roust the village to find her, let's check the stream."

They passed through the front gate. Anna picked up her pace and Jayplo stayed right behind her. Donyen knew better than to be outside the stockade alone this close to sunset. Her ears would burn from the scolding her mother would give her later. Anna prayed they would find the child unharmed and get to the bottom of this secret business.

Secret… Oh, no. The last secret Donyen had… Leopard Men! Donyen had seen them once before, but why had the child been at the stream by herself that time? Anna broke into a run.

A startled Jayplo caught up with her and asked, "Mammy Anna, why are we running?"

Anna took the fork in the path leading to the spot where the village women usually drew water. "Not sure. I hope I'm wrong."

The trail opened to a clearing at the water's edge. Donyen stood by the water, unharmed and struggling with a jar never intended for her tiny frame.

Anna stopped short and bent at the waist, trying to catch her breath. When they got back to the compound, whatever lazy villager had sent Donyen to do her job would hear from Anna if Jayplo didn't get to them first.

Jayplo's voice startled the child. "Donyen, what are you doing out this late by yourself? Your mother knows not where you are and worries."

Donyen looked puzzled. "But, Jayplo, Nana Mala ordered me to draw extra water for your household." Donyen's face looked stricken. "Oh, no. Now I have told the secret."

Jayplo said, "My husband? The water is my job. Why? He knows the danger."

Donyen cringed and looked to Anna for support. "Mammy Anna, he said it would be safe. I told him about the Leopard Men last time, but he said they were gone." Her head hung. "I did not mean to disobey my mother."

Jayplo took the water, and Anna pulled Donyen into a hug. Over the child's shoulder, she cast a quizzical look at Jayplo, who shook her head, indicating her own confusion.

Anna released Donyen. "Don't worry, little one. Your mother will understand. But if anyone asks again, get your mother or aunt to go with you."

Donyen smiled. "Yes, Mammy Anna."

The bushes rustled.

Leopard Men, every inch as Stewart had described. Painted masks, headdresses, yellow clay covering any skin that showed outside their leopard-skin clothing. Anna's inventory stopped at the iron claws, having seen firsthand what they were capable of doing. Only with great effort did she lift her gaze from them to the masks.

Four faces of death stared back at her.

Lord, deliver us from evil.

Anna spoke to Donyen and Jayplo in English. "Get behind me. Be ready to run when I say." She watched for any sign the Leopard Men had understood what she'd said. None. A small advantage, but all she had.

The Leopard Man in front tensed.

Anna whispered, "Run."

Surprise gave them a few seconds' head start. She heard the shout in Pahn behind her. "Get the sacrifice."

Pahn. He was speaking Pahn. No other tribe... These were men from the village.

One of them caught up to Anna but made no move to grab her. She threw herself in his path before he could pass and get to Donyen and Jayplo. The one immediately behind him stumbled over both of them, regained his footing and ran on. The third never broke stride. She prayed Jayplo and Donyen would get to safety.

The one she tackled rolled her to the side with a punishing swipe of claws to her right arm before he continued after the others. Blood soaked her sleeve. She struggled to stand. The fourth man, the one she'd pegged as the leader, advanced on her in a leisurely fashion. An iron claw encircled her already bleeding arm and hauled her upright.

A moan of pain escaped her lips. *Father, if I am to*

meet You face-to-face today, let my death count for something here. Keep Jayplo and Donyen from harm.

Peace flooded her. She looked into the eyes staring out of the mask. He raised his other arm to strike. Pahn words sprang to her lips, and she spoke them in faith to God's prompting. "The One True God loves you. Turn now from your wicked ways and serve Him."

His arm remained still, but the one gripping her didn't slacken. His eyes narrowed. She pressed on. His arm slowly lowered. Had God's words reached his heart?

He bent his face closer to hers. She smelt his fetid breath. One single finger touched its claw high on the outside of her left cheek. For a suspended moment of time, they both stared at each other. Then with deliberate care, the iron tip pierced her skin and slowly dragged downward as her captor began to cackle. In the midst of the pain, she realized he'd made his choice, and it wasn't repentance.

Stewart shrugged his gear off his shoulder, retaining his rifle. He supervised as porters stacked their loads against the interior wall near the gate for his morning departure. No point moving things twice. He'd learned early on that the curious villagers were scrupulously honest and would leave his possessions unmolested.

Taba's eyelids struggled to stay open as he waited on his parents. Looked as if the long trip had finally caught up to him. Taba would sleep well tonight.

Stewart needed rest, too, but first he would let Anna know he was back. He released Taba to his waiting parents just as Donyen, Anna's young student with the Leopard Men story, entered the compound yelling hysterically. What was such a young one doing outside the compound unaccompanied? The Pahn parents he'd observed diligently cared for their children. Poor little thing, crying for her mother, no doubt.

Gardiah parted the circling adults. A few sniffles and she responded to the warrior's firm, gentle tone. Her clear little voice rang out. She repeated the one word he knew in several dialects. "Leopard, leopard, leopard."

Donyen grabbed Gardiah's hand, attempting to drag him outside the gate. Her pitch shrilled and combined words Stewart also recognized, each delivering a hammer blow to his heart.

"Mammy Anna. Mammy Anna and leopards."

Maniacal laughter echoed within the mask of the man in front of her. She straightened and said, "I forgive you."

A blow sent her to the ground. Today might be the day she would stand in front of her Father in Heaven, but at least nothing this man did would change her final destiny. A loud crack rent the air and a heavy weight landed across her leg. Strong arms lifted her, and she found herself crushed in Stewart's embrace. He shifted her to one side and freed his rifle for use. She cut her gaze to the form on the ground struggling to his feet, clutching a bloody shoulder.

Stewart's eyes never left the threat in front of him as he whispered in her ear, "Hold on, Anna, more help is coming."

Hold on? The strength of his grip pinned her in place. Taking a deep breath was her biggest problem. "Donyen and Jayplo?"

"The child made it to the village and alerted us. Jayplo was injured, but delayed the other Leopard Men long enough for Donyen to get away."

The ordeal was over, but mild tremors testified to the strain and she grew cold. "Why am I shaking?"

Stewart spared her a quick glance. "You're in shock.

Hang on a bit longer. Gardiah and his men are dealing with the others. They'll be here soon. Anna. Your arm… your face."

His grip loosened and she lifted her uninjured hand to explore her cheek. A single touch sparked a wave of sharp pain. Her fingers came away covered with blood. "How bad is it?"

"He made sure you would always bear his mark. For that alone, I regret my aim." His muscles tensed. "Tell him I want him down on his knees. If he tries anything…"

"Don't kill him, please." Was that her voice? Hardly commanding. She translated Stewart's order to the captive, who complied as a dozen warriors ran into the clearing, Gardiah leading the way. His face hardened at the sight of her.

Gardiah strode toward their captive, jerked the mask away and revealed a glowering Nana Mala. Anna's world came sharply back into focus. The chief?

For a brief span, father and son stared in silence. Nana Mala started to speak, but Gardiah dropped the mask on the ground and turned his back. In a firm voice, Gardiah gave orders and his men led his father as a captive back to the village.

Anger dominated Stewart's reaction to the revelation. "This is who you would give your life to save? Even you should see now there's no changing a man so depraved."

A bone-deep weariness enveloped her. She wanted to answer Stewart, but lacked the strength. The temptation to agree with him loomed in front of her. Nana Mala had plotted a child's murder. He'd tried to kill her when she got in the way, and sent men after his own wife.

Father, have I failed? Has Nana Mala gone too far down the path of evil? I cannot believe anyone is beyond Your redemption, but the choice he made is clear. Have

I prayed and worked here in vain? Lord, I don't know what to think. I need You to show me.

"Anna?"

Stewart's concern brought her back to the moment.

"Yes?"

"What will happen to the chief?"

She roused what energy remained to her to answer. "He's no longer a threat to anyone. He's subject to the will of his people. They will likely punish him and hope word doesn't spread of him being a Leopard Man. Otherwise it could bring the army down on the whole village. The government has been known to hang men for his crime."

"So one of the things he wanted to prevent, he's brought upon himself? What irony." Stewart hung his rifle from his shoulder, placed her uninjured arm around his neck and swept her off her feet.

She started to protest, but it sounded more like a hiss as the shock wore off and the pain blasted her. She felt safe in Stewart's strong arms. God had used Stewart a second time to save her life. Only moments ago, she'd believed her life had come to an end. Was she an ungrateful wretch to want more?

Because right now she wanted something she couldn't have: to remain held in time, in this moment, with Stewart this close to her. To face the future God had given back to her, only with this man at her side the rest of her days. She laid her head against his chest. She'd have to settle for just this much, since they would never be so close again.

Chapter Thirteen

Waiting any longer to get Anna and Taba to safety was not an option anymore, though Stewart could see the precautions taken to secure the former chief. Nana Mala slumped on the ground in an unshaded area of the village's central common space. He was secured in a primitive version of stocks, one ankle firmly wedged in an opening between two halves of a log that had been riveted together. Chains at each end of the log attached to an iron collar around his neck. From the collar, another length of chain joined a post.

For three days Stewart kept one eye on Anna's recovery and the other on the power struggle between the council, Gardiah and the devilmen. Taba did rudimentary translations, but as a twelve-year-old boy he lacked understanding of the nuances of politics.

Nothing good would come if the devilmen gained control in the village or if the council released Nana Mala from his imprisonment. Either way, Anna would be in jeopardy and the contract for Taba could be nullified. Maybe he should have carried Anna out of here while she was still too weak to protest. As it stood, he'd have to make her see reason before the vote was taken tomorrow night.

He was halfway to her hut before he unclenched his fists. The sight of Nana Mala provoked a deep anger within Stewart, bringing up every black memory of his father's abuse of his mother. When he'd seen Anna and thought he was too late… He'd obeyed her soft plea not to kill the man only to prevent her further trauma, not because he believed in offering the other cheek. Evil like Nana Mala counted on the cheek-turning of others.

Anna's soft heart would be her undoing. She needed someone to watch out for her. Meddling in generations of beliefs with powerless spiritual tales only put her life at unnecessary risk.

And the risk was growing. Shuttered looks dominated the face of every villager. If they were afraid for themselves, what chance did an outsider like Anna have once things reached a pinnacle and exploded?

None.

He found the man Gardiah assigned for Anna's protection standing vigilant outside her hut. A precaution in case there were any unrevealed Leopard Men within the village. Stewart nodded to the man blocking the door. "Anna, may I come in?"

She called to her guard in Pahn and the man stepped aside.

Anna sat on a stool, wearing a neat white shirtwaist and brown skirt, her hair back in a modest bun. Only the long, crimson wound on her cheek contradicted the normal appearance she tried to present.

"Shouldn't you still be resting?"

She stood from her seat. "Three days of you telling me not to worry when I ask what is going on in the village leaves me no choice but to find out for myself. Even

Jayplo refuses my questions. Besides, the longer I lay abed, the longer you'll delay your departure out of concern for me. I'll not cost you that bonus for your mother. You'll need long marches as it is to get to the coast on time and file your report."

"Sit back down, Anna. The village is no longer safe for you to just go strolling around. We need to talk."

Her brow furrowed. "What's going on?"

He motioned to the stool and she sat. He chose his words carefully to impress the seriousness of the situation on her. "The unmasking of Nana Mala as a Leopard Man sparked major unrest. A volatile power struggle ensued. One faction supports Gardiah, another the devilmen's candidate. Although I don't understand why Gardiah can't just take power."

Anna explained, "Heredity is important, but village laws don't give Gardiah the position without approval. The council considers their ancestors' wishes in choosing the next chief. Power is transferred based on superstition as much as parentage. Likely one of the devilmen has reported seeing a 'sign' of some kind from the village's ancestral spirits that the true leader is someone else."

"Whichever way the decision goes, it is no longer safe here. I've made arrangements for a caravan out tomorrow."

She smiled. "You made arrangements? Just promise me not to rely on maps this time."

"Anna, I need you to take this situation seriously."

She sobered. "I do, Stewart. I understand all the implications."

Did she? "Then you also understand that we all need to get out of Pahn territory before things worsen. Since you're still recovering, I arranged for a hammock chair to be made for you. It was finished about an hour ago.

It's temporary until you're stronger." He braced for her protest.

None came. Just a soft insistence. "I can't leave here. God hasn't released me. Not yet."

"You disappoint me, Anna. I'd hoped this incident would bring you to your senses to the danger here. Don't make me resort to throwing you over my shoulder and carrying you all the way to Newaka. I can't let you stay here."

One delicate eyebrow rose. "I lived here long before you arrived, Stewart. I won't be forced to abandon what God has called me to do. You should know that about me by now."

This wasn't going as he'd hoped. Oh, he'd throw her over his shoulder if he thought he could succeed, but Gardiah would no doubt interfere. "Didn't coming so close to death give you perspective on the actual way the world works?"

The second eyebrow joined the first. "The *actual* way the world works?"

In his mind, he heard a sound like quicksand made when you tried to pull your foot back out of its first grasp. He ignored it and barreled ahead. "What happened with the Leopard Men should show you that a rifle in hand is worth far more than your prayers. I admire your dedication to your faith, but can't you see it lacks real power?"

Her silence prodded him on. She *had* to grasp the futility of the problem or she'd keep putting herself in these situations. Next time he wouldn't be there to save her. "Tell me how your presence here and almost dying benefited these people. Your interference with the order of things here has only made things worse for them."

"Stewart..."

"No, let me finish. Taba embraced your faith and is now at risk from his conversion. Jayplo, I've figured out, hides her beliefs out of fear. Will she end up as the next target of the devilmen? Your blind dedication to a nonexistent God fed right into Nana Mala's ambitions. He hoped your presence would give him power from your God."

Truth was painful, a fact he well knew from the trenches. He hated the stricken look on her face. But she needed to wake up to the reality, even though he wanted to gather her in his arms and take back each hurtful syllable. Had he been too harsh?

For one terrible moment Anna considered the truth in what Stewart spoke. Her cheek throbbed as she weighed his words. New converts were often ridiculed, hurt or even killed by their own people for going against their old beliefs. But were Taba or Jayplo worse off?

Not in the sense they'd come to know God and found the peace and strength that only came from Him. Certainly not in the sense they'd been freed from superstition and fear. Definitely not in the sense they'd gained eternal life.

A renewed certainty flooded her. Without knowing God for himself, Stewart could only perceive a partial truth. Not God's truth. For someone who'd never experienced the reality of God, this would appear to be an empty effort.

But why was he so angry? Usually his humor prevailed. The intensity throughout his speech, the obvious fear for her safety, the circles under his eyes, the lack of his morning shave... All clues she'd almost overlooked.

Only someone who truly cared for her would react so deeply.

Oh, Stewart.

She longed to reach out and stroke the stubbly cheek, to soothe the pulsing tic in his jaw and to tell him his feelings were not unrequited. But to what end? His arguments only reminded her of the extent that faith was an uncrossable divide.

Somehow she had to trust God to give her strength to do what else was needed in this place and to help her deal with the man who sat in front of her.

"Stewart, we will never see eye to eye on this, the most important truth in my life. God is indeed real and serving Him worth any sacrifice. Whether it be a world at war, one tribe's infighting or a father's inhumanity to his own family, God does not always deliver us from another man's free will to act…." She shook her head for emphasis. "And He never promised a life in Him would be one of ease. But since accepting Him into my heart and receiving His forgiveness, I've found that knowing His love is worth every trial here on earth. I won't needlessly throw my life away, but if it is required, I will willingly give it."

He looked at her with great sorrow. "I had hoped…" His shoulders slumped. An empty silence enveloped them.

"Hoped what, Stewart?"

He straightened, a stoic appearance firmly in place. "What I'd hoped doesn't matter."

Her heart pinged at the tone of his voice. Instinctively, recklessly, she reached out her hand in an attempt to touch his shoulder and offer some comfort.

He grasped her hand midgesture and held it gently suspended in the air. He shook his head and said softly,

"Please, don't. If this turn of events hasn't dissuaded you from your beliefs, I'd hoped in vain." He squeezed her hand. "You have a tender heart, Anna Baldwin, and I've grown to love you for that and so much more. I'd hoped for some kind of future with you, but I see I can't even persuade you to take actions that would ensure you even have a future. Right now your comfort will only make things worse."

Her chest ached with grief. It must be so difficult for him to understand her choices without knowing God's love himself. And he'd been brave beyond measure to speak of his feelings. He deserved her honest disclosure. "I can't bear the pain I've caused you and feel it is in some measure my fault. You see, I…I've allowed my own heart to hold a hope, as well.

"I knew the Scriptures' admonitions against being unequally yoked, but my feelings prevailed despite my prayers." She paused to gather her courage. "I have known I loved you for some time now. Perhaps my failure to conquer this feeling allowed you this hope. This is my burden to bear, too."

He placed his other hand over the one he already held. A spark flared in his eyes. "But if we both love each other, is there not some way…?"

She shook her head and extinguished the spark. "God's Word is clear. Were we to marry, we might find some happiness in love's first bloom, but the barrier of faith wouldn't allow the garden of our marriage to truly be fruitful. Eventually, I would wither on the vine, the guilt of knowing I had not put God's Will first in my life eroding my soul."

"Then I must not pursue this any further, though I still urge you to leave here for your safety. I prefer the vibrant

Anna before me to my own selfish desires. I refuse to become like all the other men in your life."

"Stewart, you are nothing like any man in my past."

"And I won't be, Anna. Your father, your fiancé and Nana Mala—all significant men in your life who have only wanted to use you for their own gain. Even if I found some way to convince you to marry me, I would be another in this line of selfish men. I love you too much to be one of them."

"I…I don't know what to say."

"My biggest fear for you now is you won't live long enough to find happiness with someone who shares your faith and truly loves you." He pulled her hand to his lips and placed a tender kiss before she realized his intentions. She pulled it back as she knew she must.

"I beg your forgiveness for taking one selfish moment—one memory to cherish. Is there nothing I can say to change your mind about leaving?"

Her hand burned where his lips had touched. Not trusting her voice, she merely shook her head.

"Then I'll go. Don't leave your hut without the guard accompanying you. If you change your mind or need assistance before Taba and I leave in the morning, please send for me."

He left behind an empty solitude. She peered out the doorway and watched his purposeful stride, his rigid posture.

When he vanished from her sight, she turned back and went to her knees.

Father, I know You are capable of performing mighty works in this place, of reaching the hearts of these people for You. I plead with You that even in the midst of this turmoil, You will show me how to reach these people for You. Turn their hearts, oh, Lord….

What about her own heart? When Stewart spoke of the pattern of the men in her life, his mention of her father stirred something deep within her. She'd spoken about giving up her life for the Gospel but had refused to give up something less, her anger toward her father. Unforgiveness was the beam in her own eye; was it keeping her from seeing how to assist others in taking out the tiny mote in their own?

Oh, Lord, I've not lived up to the example You gave me when You forgave those that hurt and rejected You. Heavenly Father, forgive me. Give me strength to release this hurt and to forgive my father.

A new lightness ran through her heart. God forgave her. That same forgiveness flowed through her to her father and all the others who'd hurt her through their own selfish acts. She was released from a prison of her own making.

But another remained an actual prisoner, to his superstitious beliefs most of all. The answer to her earlier prayer became clear and so did the fact that God was releasing her from this place. She would leave with Stewart in the morning, but first she had one last task in front of her. She prayed for the strength and wisdom to speak from her heart to the man who'd tried to kill her.

Stewart finished an early supper of village rice he'd supplemented with a tin of salmon steaks. Nothing remained to do except to stow a few personal items. He rubbed one hand over his rough chin and decided not to worry about his overdue shave. Why bother? He scoured his plate with sand and rinsed it in a water basin before rehanging it on one of the pegs. He wouldn't dishonor his mother's lifetime of service by leaving a mess for the women who'd extended him hospitality.

"Nana Stewart?" Taba stood outside his door.

"Come in, Taba." The boy was early. The evening council wouldn't start for another hour or more by the sun's reckoning.

Taba stepped inside, his innocent face betraying his worry. Even the children weren't immune to how the wrangling for power salted the village with fear.

"Taba, have you brought all your things? We leave before the sun is up, and I want the packs divided and ready to carry."

Taba's worry dissolved to laughter. "Nana Stewart, you make a joke. I can carry my water skin, a bow from my older brother and a blanket."

Stewart laughed with him, having forgotten one of the differences in their two worlds. "I guess I am funny. So tell me, why have you come so early? This is your last night with your family."

"I thought you would wish to join the gathering with the others."

"Is the evening palaver starting early?" Had they come to a decision? Unless Gardiah prevailed… Stewart's hope for getting any of them out of here alive plummeted.

"No, Nana Stewart. Mammy Anna goes to talk to Nana Mala. Everyone gathers to hear what she will say."

No, she couldn't. The whole village would turn out for that. One guard wasn't nearly adequate. Stewart grabbed his rifle and motioned for Taba to follow. "Let's go before your Mammy Anna gets herself in trouble I can't fix."

Stewart broke into a run. Didn't she understand that now was not the time to provoke anything? Why couldn't she just stay out of trouble this one last night? She may claim to understand the danger, but it appeared the woman had an actual death wish.

Chapter Fourteen

"Soon, Mammy Anna? Will we be there soon?" Taba practically danced on the top of a fallen tree blocking their path. He'd asked her three times since their noon meal.

"Yes, Taba. Soon. You run ahead to the front of the line with Nana Stewart. Let me know when you see the shine of the tin roofs."

Taba took off running. She climbed over the tree, pulling her skirts over the tops of her boots with one hand and balancing with the placement of the other. Her aching muscles spoke of far too much time in a hammock chair on this trip.

At first she'd chafed against the need to be carried. But after several days, the hammock became a refuge of sorts as the finality of their departure and what it meant for her future weighed on her. Only the embarrassing thought of having Karl and Hannah Jansen see her carried into their mission at Newaka roused her to her old self.

She had no real cause for sadness, not after several more in the village came to the Lord after she'd prayed with Nana Mala. Although in chains for his crime, the chief was free at last.

Heavenly Father, who am I to question Your timing? Still, it hurts to leave when so many of the people I've grown to love don't yet know Your love. Send another to the harvest, Lord.

She'd sent a message to Nynabo. Pastor Mayweather or Dr. Mary would follow up with her new converts once stability returned to the area. She prayed the bishop would find a permanent replacement for her.

Once she'd abandoned the hammock chair, the exercise lifted her spirits. She couldn't wait to visit with Hannah and Karl again. The time she'd spent with them before moving on to her post with the Pahn seemed forever ago. How fitting to end her mission days where they'd first begun.

The runner she'd sent ahead should have reached Newaka with news of their arrival. Two things she dearly desired would soon be hers: a comfortable bed and a chance to counsel with Hannah about her problem with Stewart. His behavior toward her had lived up to his promise; her own heart was the problem.

A shout from ahead sent bands of monkeys in the canopy screeching. Taba ran toward her, oblivious to the cacophony he'd orchestrated. "Mammy Anna, the shiny tin, the wooden buildings… I saw… We are here!"

"Stop and get your breath. Calm yourself before you meet everyone."

Wordlessly, he nodded.

Anna caught the anxious look that followed. "Are you all right?"

His silence answered her. She put her hands on his shoulders, turning him to face her. "What's wrong?"

The answer poured out in Pahn. "Will they like me, Mammy Anna? The teachers, the other students?"

She answered in Pahn. "Of course they will like you. I promise Nana Karl and Mammy Hannah will love you like you are their own son."

He fidgeted. "But the other boys? I am no one here. At home, everyone knows me."

"Taba, God brought you here for your good. When you encounter troubles, turn to Him, but I think you will find the other boys will want to be your friend."

Eager eyes locked on to hers. "They will?"

"Who among them has been an apprentice to a foreign man and responsible to help guide him?"

Taba's smile grew. "Yes! Thank you, Mammy Anna."

"Just don't act like a bluff boy in telling your stories. Do not brag or exaggerate."

He digested her caution. "No, Mammy Anna, I will not be a bluff boy and grow my tales." A grin peeked through again. "But they might think I am one when I say about the Leopard Men and how Nana Stewart saved me."

She laughed. "Save that story for another day. Get to know them first. Now, back to English please. You must practice."

"Yes, Mammy Anna."

"Go ahead now. There is much more to see than the tin roofs of the mission. I will catch up."

He took off running, hollering back as he did, "Thank you, Mammy Anna. Thank you."

Anna picked up her pace. At his age, problems were easy to fix.

Lord, give me peace in whatever You have planned for me. Continue to draw Stewart to Yourself. I pray the seeds You allowed me to plant in his life come to harvest one day, so he will find the same joy I found in You.

Ahead stood the welcoming arches of Newaka Mission Station. A crowd surrounded Stewart and Taba. Only Karl Jansen was a match for Stewart, both towering over the sea of shorter bodies. Anna spotted the padded curves of the aproned Hannah, as she broke from the group and headed straight for Anna.

Peace settled over her. Hannah was the soul of motherly kindness. She would give Anna wise counsel on God's Will for her life. If only she wasn't so desirous of God's Will to include Stewart.

Anna swatted at the thought as if it were a malaria-bearing mosquito. Tomorrow, the next day at the latest, Stewart Hastings would leave for Garraway without her. He had no place in her future. Three steps from Hannah, the finality of leaving her post, of saying goodbye to Stewart, all of it broke Anna's composure. The stout German missionary encircled Anna in her arms and let her quietly cry.

Sleep eluded Stewart. He stood at the porch rail of the Newaka mission house and stared up at the inky-black sky while others inside dreamed. In the distance, he heard the restless monkeys and the now-familiar lemur call, a close imitation of a crying baby.

He looked upward. The full force of the constellations returned his searching stare. There was Orion the Hunter and Andromeda. He knew some believed stars controlled their fate, but he never believed that any more than he'd believed the God of the Bible to be more than a consoling fiction.

Oh, like every other desperate man in the trenches unprepared for the German mustard gas, he'd latched on to hope and cried out to the God he'd heard preached about throughout his childhood. When the screams of pain rolled down the trench until his own voice blended with them, God was the only one silent. The gas burned his skin and consumed any hope for deliverance. He'd finally had his proof. He'd tested God and found Him powerless. He'd known then that God was a hollow hope.

Now he knew that he couldn't have been more wrong. He slammed his fist against the rail and quickly regretted his action. What if he woke someone? Or Anna?

What happened between Anna and Nana Mala that last night shook Stewart to his core. How was she able to forgive such evil? Stewart could no more have done such a thing than he could forgive the men who'd sent the gas into the sky in France.

But forgive him she had. Without reservation, without judgment and with strength Stewart had never known possible. Watching her pray with the man who'd tried to kill her, Stewart had grasped how little he'd understood of the faith he'd derided, of God and of his own heart.

He sat in one of the porch rockers and ignored the heaviness of his eyelids. Every night since they'd left the village, those moments right before sleep claimed him brought the same visions. Anna kneeling in front of Nana Mala, treating his wounded shoulder and the sores from the chains, holding the hands that wielded iron claws and marked her forever. She'd prayed with such authority, peace evident within her. Maybe it was Stewart's imagination, but as Nana Mala prayed in response, evil slithered away as if it was a tangible thing. Translation was unnecessary. The power of what happened didn't dwell in specific words. Nana Mala remained in shackles, but a different man looked out from behind those eyes.

Stewart's failing eyelids opened at the sound of someone coming onto the path behind the house. *Not Anna, please.* A swinging lantern cast its light on Stewart's host, Karl Jansen. Karl nodded to Stewart, stepped up to the porch and sat in the other rocker. He placed his lantern beside him.

Karl's silence left Stewart uncomfortable. At dinner the missionary exhibited nothing but polite hospitality. Yet every eye contact gave Stewart the ridiculous sensation of having his innermost soul on display.

Between Nana Mala and now Karl, Stewart concluded his imagination needed tempering. There was no reason to be uncomfortable around his host. The schoolchildren boarding in the compound flocked to him, including Taba once he'd overcome an initial shyness. After cannibals and Leopard Men, a liver-spotted, fatherly missionary posed no threat.

Unless, like Stewart, you'd never learned how to act around a father or a fatherly type who didn't speak with his fists.

Karl interrupted Stewart's inner revelation. "Couldn't sleep?"

"No."

"Troubles will do that to a man. This is my favorite place to sort through mine."

Stewart turned. "Whatever Anna told you…"

Karl waved a gnarled hand. "Anna told me nothing. The evidence is clear."

"What evidence?"

"You pointedly avoid her, both of you painfully polite when circumstances force you to interact. Either you two got into a lover's quarrel or something larger stands between you. One thing is for sure, love is at the root. Do you want to tell me about it?"

Stewart was so stunned at Karl's perception that he considered the offer.

"Son, if you don't mind an old man's prodding, I'm here to listen. What can it hurt?"

What indeed? An end to the confusion tearing at him would be welcome. His mind refused to reconcile what he'd believed about God and what he saw happen in the village between Anna and the chief. He was desperate enough to grasp at the proverbial straw sitting beside him.

Later, he couldn't say how long their talk lasted or the duration of the prayer that followed. Time lost meaning after such a life-changing event.

No wonder Anna found the strength to minister in this place and needed to share the Gospel with others. He wanted to shout to the rooftops—thatched, tin, shingled, all of them—how he'd experienced the reality of God for himself. Only Karl's twinkle-eyed admonition to wait for morning as he'd left for his own bed kept Stewart from finding Anna, dragging her out of bed and telling her the news.

He remained on the porch, contemplating how his life had found a dividing place, a before and an after. Nothing would ever be the same. He thanked God for Karl Jansen, a man who'd waded into the morass of Stewart's unbelief and gently guided him to the answers.

Karl finished what began with Anna. Her life's example had prepared Stewart for this moment. He owed her so much, the least of which was an apology. After she was attacked, when he'd recognized she was at her most vulnerable, Stewart had launched his own offensive. He'd torn at her faith, accused her of only bringing trouble to people's lives through her preaching.

How did he begin to apologize? He remembered the first time he'd needed to apologize to Anna on board ship. *How hard could it be to apologize to one little missionary woman?* Even harder now. He tried several ways in his head, but words seemed inadequate. Maybe he should pray.

God...Heavenly Father. I've heard others speak to You, but I lack their eloquence. All I know is to ask for Your help. I need to make things right with Anna. The bishop was right when he said we were a match made in Heaven. Without her, I wouldn't have learned how wrong I was about You. I need the words to tell her that and how much I love her. I fear I'll make a mess of things. I know I already have.

Stewart paused, his thoughts running amok. *What's to tell her the change in me is real? She said she had feelings for me, but...* A gentle tapping at his spirit slowed his runaway fears and replaced them with peace.

Heavenly Father, I guess a little trust is in order. As Anna is so fond of saying, after all You've done to get me to this place, I have to believe You can complete the rest. Let her see the change in my heart. And, God, give me the right words as I ask her to be my wife.

Anna sat idle at Hannah's kitchen table while her hostess went to gather eggs for breakfast. Every offer of help had been promptly refused and her insistence silenced when Hannah pulled an envelope out of her pocket before going to face off with the chickens. Of all the surprises life in the jungle presented to date, this one was the most unexpected.

A telegram from her father. It had arrived at the mission headquarters in Monrovia three weeks ago and made its way down the coast with letters and supplies bound for the interior. Afraid the message would cross paths and miss Anna entirely, Hannah had held it back from the last supply run to Nynabo. Anna thanked the Lord for Hannah's foresight.

The clipped words of the telegram had her gripping the paper's edges. Despite having memorized the contents, she reread the message again.

> Come home. I'm dying. Need to make things right with God and you. Money for passage paid to Elder-Dempster company agent. Time is short. Hurry.

Her stomach clenched at the news. The smell of Hannah's fresh bread no longer tempted her appetite. Her father was dying. Mortality accomplished what nothing else had ever managed: turned his heart toward the God he'd ignored and the daughter he'd repudiated.

What if she was already too late? No, she couldn't be. Her father wouldn't send a telegram unless there was time. Would he?

Fat tears rolled down her face, splashing the paper. She wiped them off, folded the message and put it in her pocket. Between passage back to Monrovia and the transatlantic steamer-trip home, she wouldn't arrive in the States for at least three weeks. She'd have to leave immediately.

Hannah entered the kitchen with an apron full of eggs, which she placed in a bowl on the table. "One day those chickens will learn that I know all their hiding places. Maybe then they'll give up and lay in the lovely coop that Karl built… Anna, what's wrong?"

Anna pulled out the telegram and placed it in front of Hannah.

"Oh, my. You poor lamb. What a hard thing. I understand your tears, but dry them and celebrate the goodness of God in this. The father you feared lost to sin forever reached out to the daughter he'd rejected for her faith. I am only sorry it has taken death's knock at his door to bring him to this point."

"Hannah, what if I'm too late? If he dies before I can pray with him…"

"Now, now, child. Do you think our Heavenly Father would allow your father's chance of salvation to be lost because you weren't there? God makes a way for a willing heart. He has others to bring His Word, and not all of them are separated from your father by an ocean."

"You are so wise, Hannah. God knew this situation long before I received word. I need to send a telegram home so I can learn if he still lives, and then one to my church to ask someone to minister to him until I arrive."

"Now who is the wise one? The Word says we have not because we ask not. It may be that your father has told no one else of his illness or this change of heart. And if he still lives, I pray you will have a chance to see him again this side of the grave."

"If not, may God give me grace to content myself that I will see my father again one day."

"Good girl. Now, down to practicalities. The nearest telegraph is in Garraway. I will finish cooking breakfast. I'll not have you leaving on an empty stomach. Meanwhile, you go say your goodbyes to Taba…"

"Taba. Hannah, what will I say? He was so nervous about a new place. I told him I would be here for his first weeks."

Hannah laughed while she cracked eggs and pushed them around in her skillet. "He might be sad for a moment, but based on Karl's reports of chatter from the boys' dormitory into the small hours of the night, Taba will do fine. Go see him and then tell your young man out there overseeing his own preparations for departure that you will be leaving with him."

"Hannah, he's not *my* young man. How can you say that after what I confided in you yesterday? Even now I'm torn to pieces as I realize I must spend two more days in his company. Or worse, depending on the steamer schedules, we might both be returning to the States on the same ship."

Hannah pointed her wooden spoon at Anna. Tiny flecks of partially cooked egg flew off the handle with Hannah's every syllable. "Listen to me, young lady. I meant to speak to you later, and more gently, but now there is no time for soft words. You may believe there's nothing left to do but suffer like some misguided martyr to love, but you are wrong. And don't think I wouldn't have known you loved each other even without your confidences." More yellow and white dotted the kitchen table as Hannah shook her spoon. "Both of you at dinner, two lovesick calves trying not to moo in each other's direction. Where is your faith?"

"Faith in what? The Scriptures are clear on the subject of marrying an unbeliever."

"As they are equally clear on God's ability to reach even the hardest of hearts. Did you not learn anything from your father's telegram? We serve a God who delights in what seems impossible. Why, my own Karl is a perfect example of how God can work."

"Karl wasn't saved when you met him?"

Hannah's gaze landed on the mess she'd made. She put the spoon down and reached for a cloth. "No, but I fell hopelessly in love with him anyway. I was convinced

God put Karl in my life for a reason, even if it made no sense to me at the time."

"What happened?"

"The simple version is God prompted me to wait and pray for Karl. The waiting took two years before Karl came to know our Lord. Forty-two years now I've been blessed to be his wife." Hannah continued wiping the table. "So is Stewart the man God intends for you or not? Why did God put him in your life?"

"I don't know, Hannah. I'm confused."

"God's Word says He is not the author of confusion. God gives peace when He speaks." Hannah pulled her pan off the stove and sat by Anna's side. "Anna, you need to seek God's Will on this before you get on a ship home and make a mistake that can't be easily undone."

"Pray with me, Hannah. I'm ready to hear, no matter what the answer."

Stewart culled out all the packs with food tins. He'd need little on the short trek to Garraway, but given the number of children who boarded here, the food could be put to good use. He wished leaving wasn't such an imperative today, but he couldn't risk missing the report deadline. While he worked, he kept watch on the main house, hoping to see Anna and talk before breakfast.

Not that he yet had any idea what to say. "I'm a Christian, now will you marry me?" was short and fit his time constraints but seemed to lack that special something a woman wanted to hear. How did he properly propose? What if she said no?

He could use another long talk with Karl about now. A relationship with God proved simple once he opened his heart. This love business was complicated.

Children poured out of the chapel on the other side

of the compound. Stewart watched for Taba. He wanted to say goodbye. Where was he?

Ah, in the middle of about six other boys and having fun on their way to breakfast. Stewart would find him later.

"Stewart?"

"Anna!"

"I'm sorry. Did I startle you?"

"I didn't hear you coming. I was watching Taba and his new friends. He seems happy already."

"Stewart, I have a problem."

He looked closer at her. Biting her lower lip. Definitely worried. "How can I help?"

"I must leave for the coast. Today."

She was leaving with him. His heart beat a little faster. "Then I'm your man. Can you be ready after breakfast?"

Tension fled her face. "Yes, thank you. After our trip…our conversation before we left the Pahn, I… Well, I wasn't sure you'd want to spend any more time traveling with me."

"I would do anything for you, Anna. But what changed? I thought you were staying here for a few weeks. I thought I might…"

"Might what?"

Return and plan a wedding with you. If something drastic had changed for her, his plans would be for nothing. "Never mind. Tell me what brought this about."

"A telegram." Her eyes glimmered and tears brimmed.

This didn't look good. "Anna, what's happened?"

She pulled a handkerchief from her skirt pocket and dabbed at her eyes. "My father. He sent a message saying he wants to reconcile with me. He wants to know about God."

"That's good, isn't it? Why the tears?"

"He's dying. I've prayed for his salvation since I first came to know our Lord. Now I hope to see him one more time and share the Gospel with him if he still lives. I need to get to Garraway and send a telegram, then book my passage home."

Was it even fair to ask her to marry him right now with her father dying and all her hopes and dreams pinned on being there for him? Whatever he decided, he still needed to tell her about his conversion.

He took both her hands and gave them a reassuring squeeze. "Before we travel, I need to tell you something. Come sit with me a moment on the Jansens' porch."

He led her to the rockers, turning them so he could face her directly.

Anna sat. "This looks pretty serious, Stewart."

"It is, Anna. To start with, I need to ask your forgiveness. The things I said about what you'd accomplished in the village, about your faith making things worse, I was wrong. Forgive me, please."

She smiled and the compound grew brighter. "I forgive you, Stewart. We first met because you stepped in to protect me, and I don't think you've ever stopped. I know that what you spoke was exactly what you truly believed about my faith, but I also know you never would have said those things out loud except out of desperation to get me to safety."

"I guess you know me better than I know myself, Anna Baldwin. The first time I wasn't able to protect a woman, I was five and watched my father beat my mother senseless over a late dinner. I measured time in the inches I grew after that, waiting to be big enough to put a stop to his fists. And I did."

"You still protect your mother. You came halfway around the world this time to save her again. I know you don't believe in God, Stewart, but He's made you a mighty protector. But without Him in your life, that's also a burden. You can't protect every woman, even your mother, all the time. When you invite God into your life, you'll understand that He is the only true source of protection. Having that understanding will free you to know when to step up and protect and went to stand back and trust."

"I think I'm beginning to understand that now, Anna. Our trip here gave me time to think about what I saw between you and Nana Mala. There was such a love, a strength of forgiveness and acceptance. I tried, but I couldn't explain it away."

"I thought you were just angry at more of my foolishness. You never said anything once I sent word later that I was leaving with you. And you kept such a strict distance on the trip."

"What I saw overwhelmed me. I needed time to consider not only the change in Nana Mala, but what happened in you, Anna. God's love flowed through you to the chief. Every night since then, when I close my eyes before sleep, I see you kneeling in the dirt, bringing him water, your arms around him as you prayed. I asked myself how anyone was capable of so clearly loving and caring for someone who only meant evil for her. I finally realized the truth."

Her voice came out as a desperate whisper. "What truth?"

He took a deep breath and continued, "No one could. Not really. Not unless God loved that man through them." His gaze bore into hers. "Which meant God was real. Not some fairy tale where everything was a happily-ever-after. But real, Anna. A God who showed up in the trenches. Not always to save you from what happened, but to be there and give you strength and anything else you needed to get through it."

"Oh, Stewart."

"There's more. I kept poor Karl up for hours last night. He prayed with me and I gave my heart to God. I have a lot to learn, but my life has been changed forever."

"This is almost too much in one day. First my father, and now God answered my prayers for your salvation. I don't even know what to say."

Stewart slid out of his rocker and knelt in front of Anna. He took her hands in his. "Say you'll marry me, Anna. Say that whatever life brings us we will face serving God together."

Anna threw her arms around Stewart. "I will.

Behind her a small cheer went up. Taba and a dozen cohorts grinned. Stewart whispered, "Our audience caught up with us."

Stewart stood and Anna twisted to see for herself. The children giggled and ran off.

Stewart offered Anna his hand. "I love you, Anna."

"I love you, too, Stewart." She pulled him into the house. "I've got to tell Hannah."

He let himself be led. "I can see how you feel about the Jansens. Did you want Karl to marry us? There would be no time for more than saying our vows before we have to leave. I don't want to rush you. I know how women love a good wedding."

She stopped outside the kitchen. "No, but not because I care about doing something fancy. I just think Bishop Michaels should do the honors since he put us together in the beginning. And while Karl and Hannah will understand, Momma Elliott might not forgive me if she wasn't there."

"Still not much time to plan a wedding. Not if we try to take the first steamer scheduled for the States."

Anna threw her arms around him. "You are all I need, not some fancy event." She stepped back. "Now let's tell the Jansens, because I hear our caravan is leaving very soon."

Chapter Fifteen

"Is something wrong with your breakfast, Miss Anna?" Momma Elliott waited for the verdict.

Anna stopped pushing the food around and put down her fork. "No. Everything is wonderful."

Momma Elliott crossed her arms. "Then why are eggs still on your plate? Do you have bridal jitters?"

Anna caught herself rubbing the thin, raised line on the side of her face. She folded her hands in her lap. "I'm fine."

"Out with it, girl."

"I always pictured my wedding in…well, something more bridal than any of my three skirts or traveling suit. God has done so much for me, and here I am moping about a wedding dress after I told Stewart I didn't need anything fancy."

"Child, there is nothing wrong with wanting to look special on your wedding day." Momma Elliott cleared the plate.

"That's kind of you to say." She gestured toward her face. "I thought I was all right…" She dropped her hands back to her lap. "Well, considering no dress will cover what's on my face, it is a foolish vanity to wish for one."

"You are lovely, my dear, no matter what scars you bear."

"Thank you, Momma Elliott. Talking helps. I shall content myself with my traveling suit. It is the least threadbare of all the garments I own."

"Oh, no, my girl. We'll get you a dress."

Anna shook her head. "Even if God dropped the fabric in my lap, there's no time to make something."

"Wait here a moment." Momma Elliott left the room and returned with paper and a fountain pen. "Not make. Borrow."

"Borrow?"

She sat and wrote. "Are you a parrot, child? Yes, borrow. One of the abandoned rubber plantations was purchased last year. After some unfortunate problems with his manager, the new owner has come in person to set the operation right. And he has his niece in tow, a Miss Reynolds, a young woman about your age. I met her at church."

"She attended your church?"

Momma Elliott stopped writing and cackled from deep within her belly. "Walked in the front door right after the chorus of the first hymn. One look at the cut of her clothes and the color of her skin and everyone waited for her to turn around and walk back out. She's been to every meeting since and sits with me."

"Impressive. And you think she might loan me a dress?"

Momma Elliott finished writing, folded the paper and handed it to Anna. "Not just any dress, an actual wedding dress. Miss Reynolds is a generous spirit whose maid accidentally included the trunk with her wedding dress with the others being sent ahead to the steamer."

"But you said she was Miss Reynolds. Will she mind another woman wearing it before she does?"

"No child, she's not here to marry. I'll let her tell you the story behind the dress if she so desires. But for now, trust me. She'll be happy to put that dress to good use. Now take this note to the American Legation, where they are staying temporarily, and ask for her."

Anna jumped up and hugged her until Momma Elliott disengaged her arms and insisted, "Now, get on with you. She's taller than you, so we'll need time to put in a hem."

Anna took two steps and stopped. "Are you sure she will welcome a visitor at this early hour?"

"Child, you're getting married this afternoon. She'll understand."

Anna put on a light wrap and her hat and gloves. She reached the front door and grabbed an umbrella from the brass stand. She opened the door and called out, "Tell Stewart where I've gone if he rises before I return." She stepped onto the porch. The dry season producсd little rain. Did she need an umbrella? If she carried the dress back herself, her hands would be full.

No, a woman in Miss Reynolds's position would send it back with her via a servant. The umbrella might not see the first drop of rain, but it still had its uses, if only to discourage any of the roaming livestock that grazed the turf-covered streets of Monrovia.

She went down the porch steps and headed in the direction of Broad Street. The first sliver of sun had arrived and lightened the night to an early-morning gray. Even so, she had a few brief seconds of warning as two Kru men rushed out from between the buildings.

Not again.

She turned and ran toward the boardinghouse. Fingers brushed her arm. Stewart slept in a back room. She screamed anyway, hoping for help from any quarter. The fingers gained purchase on one arm and jerked her to a halt. She swung her umbrella with her free hand until it connected with the man's head and produced a satisfying smack, followed closely by his howl of pain.

She took a breath to scream again. The second man clamped a hand over her mouth and the first wrenched the umbrella from her. Both proceeded to drag her toward a narrow alley.

She struggled to go anywhere but where they wanted. If she could just get one of her arms free, they'd find out how dangerous a woman with a hat pin could be.

Assailant One ordered the other to subdue her. Out of his pants pocket came an unwelcome white cloth. She took a deep breath in through her nose before the hand against her mouth relaxed, and she screamed a staccato sound, quickly sucking in more wholesome air before the drugging cloth was in place.

Someone had to have heard.

She held her breath and sank an elbow into soft flesh behind her, all the while trying to twist her face away from the anesthetic covering. An answering grunt of pain, and the chloroform-laden fabric slipped from her face. She sucked in saving air before the cloying drug was replaced again.

This time both men held her tightly. She struggled not to breathe. Tiny black pinpoints appeared in her sight and her lungs burned with need.

Tears filled her eyes, blurring everything. She couldn't hold out. Her vain desire to look beautiful on her wedding day had cost her the chance to walk down the aisle at all.

The smell of fresh biscuits woke Stewart. For a moment he lay still, enjoying the aroma and contemplating the day ahead. He'd finished filing a timely report detailing the limited amounts of gold he'd found, the area's iron-ore deposits and the instability and warlike nature of the groups in the area. Work was behind him for the moment, and all his focus centered on marrying Anna later today. Anticipation propelled him out of his warm bedding.

He dressed and shaved quickly, then pulled the bay rum out of his kit and patted it on. His Winchester hung by the door, but carrying it to the altar might turn a few heads. He slipped his knife into the scabbard, making sure his dress jacket hid the weapon. Even without Leopard Men, Monrovia had proved to have its own dangers.

Satisfied, he opened the door. The hinges needed a serious oiling.

Not the hinges. A high-pitched scream he recognized at once.

He grabbed the rifle and ran down the hall.

A very agitated Momma Elliott had almost reached the front door. "Hurry, Mr. Hastings, they have Anna."

He threw open the door and heard an angry howl. "Stay here. Or go for the constables. I can't protect two women at once." He ran out and spotted a gentleman in his bedclothes standing just outside the doorway of a residence halfway to Broad Street. The man saw him and shrugged, then pointed to a spot midway between their positions. Anna must have been dragged into one of the narrow passages between houses, or even inside one.

Where are you, Anna? Lord, help me find her. I can't lose her now.

A short scream gave Stewart direction. He ran to the far edge of the house he'd identified and peered around the corner. In the narrow pathway, a native in blue calico pants and a white flannel singlet stood with his back to Stewart, blocking a full view of Anna and a second man. Had to be the same guys.

Stewart fired a round into the air. Both men froze.

"Step away from her now before I decide that letting you live is too much trouble this time." They released her and took a step to the side. Stewart kept his rifle on them and moved toward a red-faced Anna, who was bent over and desperately sucking in air. Stewart held out his free hand and motioned for her. "Anna, I need you to come over here and get behind me."

She ran to his side.

He tried to maneuver her behind him, but met with resistance. "I'd feel safer with you behind me. Just in case these two get any foolish ideas."

Her voice trembled. "When will you learn, Stewart? That request didn't work for you last time."

"Last time you were unconscious."

"No, I mean when Nana Mala threatened you. I wouldn't hide behind you then and I won't now. Behind you is not where I belong."

He reached out and pulled her close. "How about by my side?" He whispered, "Forever."

Momma Elliott called his name.

He answered, "Over here." The two men he held at gunpoint glared.

She came up behind him. "I've got the constables."

He spared a quick glance. Three uniformed men stood behind her.

The warrior grandma he'd come to love edged around him, ahead of the constables.

"Careful, Momma Elliott. These two are dangerous."

While the constables secured them, she launched into a tirade. Beyond Gradoo's name, Stewart understood only her rebuking tone. Both men hung their heads at her words.

Stewart spoke low and asked Anna, "What is she saying?"

Anna stayed pressed to his side. She answered, "Imagine the worst scolding you ever received and then imagine much, much more. Wait…this is interesting. She's asking them why they'd do such a thing. She's reminding them that they might hang if they don't speak up."

The one called Gradoo lifted his head and mumbled. Momma Elliott barked at him. He answered, but this time more distinctly. Or at least it probably was if you spoke Kru.

Anna pulled away from Stewart at Gradoo's answer.

"Anna, what did he say?"

Anna looked at Gradoo, back at Stewart and at Gradoo again. Her color went ashen. "He says he was paid to capture me. A rich white man promised him a lot of money and told him I'd be coming out of the jungle soon." She blinked rapidly. "Stewart, the telegram from my father. Could he be here instead? A white man, a telegram hitting just the right notes to get me to leave the jungle… Was this all a part of some scheme of his?"

Stewart could see the hurt roll off her. "Anna, I'm sorry."

The constables marched the prisoners away and Momma Elliott shook her head, saying, "This is a terrible thing. I am not sure I can keep them from hanging. Especially since they can't name the man who paid them or identify where he's staying. They will carry all the consequences."

"So Anna is still in danger."

Momma Elliott nodded. "We need to keep her safe, preferably out of sight."

Anna's velvet-soft voice carried iron determination. "No. This is our wedding day and I intend to stand in front of Bishop Michaels today, danger or no danger, dress or no dress, by your side, Stewart. I refuse to allow my father to spoil this for us."

Stewart was torn. He stroked her cheek gently with his hand. "Anna, there is nothing more in this world that I want than to watch my beautiful bride walk down the aisle. Your safety…"

Momma Elliott interrupted, "Then again, Mr. Hastings, maybe marriage is the best form of safety. Her father doesn't want her dead, or those two wouldn't be trying to kidnap her. What better way to protect her than through marriage? Her father will lose any legal standing in her life, no matter what he has in mind."

The weight on Stewart lifted. "Momma Elliott, what would we do without you?"

She looked back at him, cocked her head and said, "Be late for your wedding, for one thing. You two need to hurry if we're going to be at the chapel by two. Escort Anna to the Legation House so she can pick up her wedding dress and I can alter the fit. Now, I have a cake to put in the oven. Get on with you." She walked away like a woman on a mission.

Stewart waited till she was out of sight and glanced at Anna. "I guess those were our marching orders. But there's something I must do first."

She looked up at him. Stewart pulled Anna into his arms and stared into the depths of her brown eyes. He bent down and skimmed her lips with a gentle restraint. Her soft mouth pressed into his in response, and he tenderly kissed her again, enthralled at the fullness of love she brought to his life.

He pulled back, banking the fires of his love till the

bishop made them one. "So I hear we have a wedding dress to acquire?"

She grinned. "Imagine the scolding we'll get if we keep Momma Elliott waiting because we were kissing in the streets."

He took her by the arm. "One reprimand a day is enough. Let's go."

They headed down Broad Street, past the harbor landing and the government buildings and on to the American Legation. Stewart put aside the distraction of the kiss and turned to the job at hand. Let Anna dream of lace and frippery while he kept a wary eye on the people they passed. Until they were married and her father behind bars, Anna was still in danger.

Anna stood in her silk chemise, stockings and bridal slippers with her arms held high while Momma Elliott and Miss Cady Reynolds slid the elaborate satin-and-lace dress over her head and into place.

She reveled in the feeling of femininity the fabric imparted. Initially, she'd cried off borrowing the dress when she'd recognized the magnificent gown as a couture piece, far too costly to risk spoiling. Cady argued that she'd worn the gown once, but it was obviously meant to bring happiness to someone besides herself. Her insistence that it would mean everything to her to watch someone truly in love wear it down the aisle finally swayed Anna to agree. Silently, Anna prayed for Cady and asked the Lord to bless her generous new friend with a love to match Anna's for Stewart.

She corralled her impatience while each tiny satin-covered button down the back was worked into its buttonhole. Then they started on her hair. Forty hairpin stabs later and they moved on to their next project.

Cady brought out the latest trend from home, Max Factor Society Make-Up. Anna objected until she saw the finished result, her scar concealed so skillfully that she'd been granted a few special moments to forget the glaring mark. Not until the cloche-style, seed-pearl veil was in place did Momma Elliott and Cady both step back to survey the result of their efforts and announce their work to be complete.

They slipped out and left her to herself, promising to ask the organist to give Anna the space of two preliminary hymns, and their last chords would be her cue to enter the sanctuary. Anna breathed in the silence and thanked God, asking Him to bless her with a heart to serve Him and her husband. She called for God's blessings on Stewart and the children they would have. Finally, hearing the second hymn hit its midpoint, she prayed for calm nerves as she walked down the aisle to her groom.

With one last peek in the mirror to marvel at Momma Elliott and Cady's work, Anna picked up the bouquet of yellow allamandas and roses that Momma Elliott had prepared from her own garden. She ignored the slight quickening of her heart, took a deep breath and opened the door to go to her waiting groom.

And found a figure from her past standing firmly in the way of her future.

Stewart slid a finger under the collar of his shirt for relief from the afternoon heat. The bishop stood patiently at his side, Bible in hand. Guests from the local mission college were long since seated in the pews and the processional music had begun, but Anna hadn't appeared. Momma Elliott and Miss Reynolds took turns glancing back at the sanctuary entrance.

The last time a woman decided not to marry him, she'd sent a messenger. For one black moment he wondered if he'd made it all the way to the church this time only to leave alone.

He thought back to their kiss, the look of love before their lips ever touched, and every doubt fled. He was left with only one other possibility. Something was terribly wrong.

He leaned in and whispered his concerns to Bishop Michaels before slipping out the vestry door. Anna's father—if it was he who'd hired the kidnappers—was still unaccounted for by the constables. Stewart prayed along the way. *Dear Lord, keep her safe. I can't lose her, not now. If she is in danger, Lord, protect her and let me get there to save her one more time.* Stewart picked up his rifle where he'd left it after admonitions not to carry the weapon into the ceremony. He wondered what the bishop would have said if he'd seen the knife concealed under Stewart's frock coat.

When he reached the door to the vestibule that opened across from Anna's dressing room, he forced himself to stop. If she was in trouble, a little reconnaissance was needed. And if she was simply late, he could turn around and save himself the embarrassment of having her know he'd panicked. In hindsight, he should have stood outside her door the entire time, fully armed, and escorted her down the aisle—then she'd be safe. He arrived at the door to the vestibule at the same time he arrived at an inescapable conclusion. He couldn't keep her safe, not all the time. And a burden lifted as he turned the assignment over to God, trusting that He was the One who would always be with Anna.

He inched open the heavy wooden door and gained a clear view of the back of a man standing in front of

Anna. Medium height, straw-brimmed hat and wearing a tropical white suit several cuts above the everyday cotton drill.

Who was she talking to? Invited guests remained in the sanctuary, and none of them owned clothes of such caliber. He opened the door farther. *Lord, don't let it squeak.* He put aside his urge to go directly to her side and slid out into the vestibule. He stepped to where he could see Anna's face. A malevolent male voice spoke to her in tones that raised the tiny hairs on the back of Stewart's neck.

"Surprised, my dear? You shouldn't be. I told you once before how I always get what I want. Did you think an ocean between us enough to dissuade me?"

Her father? So not at home dying, after all. He stood inches from Anna, but would he hurt her?

Anna spoke in incredulous tones. "Reginald, there is nothing you can do to change my mind. I am about to be married to someone else."

Reginald? This wasn't Anna's father....

"You will marry no one but me, Annabelle. My wealth buys a lot in life. Your parents understood that when they brokered a deal for you."

The fiancé Anna rejected. Reginald Hightower.

The man continued in a polite after-dinner parlor tone. "And so does the freighter captain waiting offshore to marry us."

Time to show himself and get the deluded doctor away from Anna. She wasn't going anywhere but down the aisle with Stewart.

Anna's eyes widened when he came into her view. He put a finger to his lips and shook his head. No point in alerting the guy and complicating things.

Her pitch increased. "You can point that pistol at me all you want, Reginald. I won't cooperate with you."

Stewart froze. The man had a gun. He had to get that gun aimed away from Anna before the constables he asked Bishop Michaels to summon rushed in and got her killed. He mimed to Anna to move away. Stewart closed the distance between him and his target.

Anna kept Reginald distracted. "Why on earth would you want to marry a woman who doesn't love you?"

Reginald's veneer of politeness fell away. "I am the best society has to offer. I *will* have the most beautiful woman on my arm, a dutiful wife to show the world. Love is for fools. As my wife, Annabelle, you will be taught the respect due me and take your proper place by my side." He stepped forward and grabbed her chin, twisting her head to one side. "What's this? You've painted your face?"

When he released his hold, she said, "The makeup covers a new scar. I was attacked in the jungle by a member of the Leopard Society."

Reginald moved his gun to his left hand, pulled out a handkerchief with his right and rubbed at the makeup. Motley red splotches appeared on the back of his neck after he succeeded. "Bad enough that your fool of a father first marred your cheek, but this…this…" He stepped back. "We will need to employ a skilled ladies' maid to conceal the mark when we attend social functions. It won't do to have people think the wife of one of the most esteemed surgeons in town paints her face like some common theater performer."

Surgeon? If the man was a surgeon, the use of chloroform made sense. Reginald's handkerchief fluttered to the ground. His confidence in his own success would be his undoing. He continued to hold the gun in his left hand. The man was lucky that the deadliest weapon available to Anna right now was her bouquet. If he'd seen her take on those Kru men he'd sent, he wouldn't be so relaxed.

Now to put an end to this madman's plans.

Stewart saw the look on Anna's face as Reginald outlined his scheme. *No, don't challenge him.* Stewart shook his head at Anna. She ignored him.

"You are deceived in many ways, Reginald, and I pray for your salvation."

Recognizing the distraction she was creating, Stewart moved in behind Reginald.

Anna continued delivering chapter and verse to the madman. "Make no mistake—I will never be at your side, upholding some fictional appearance. I trust God to deliver me from your scheming, but even if He doesn't, He is still the only One I will ever serve. Not you. Not ever."

Reginald sputtered and his gun arm waved to the tune of his rage.

If Stewart could just catch that arm in the right position away from Anna…

"I thought your little show of holiness in your parents' parlor would have crumbled after the reality of living with jungle heathens. I see I was wrong." Reginald's voice turned icy. "No matter. I am an adaptable man. It strikes me that I will make a wonderful example of a grieving widowed surgeon whose new wife was lost at sea. Come along, Anna." He waved the gun to point toward the church entrance.

Stewart seized the moment, grabbed the hand with the gun and threw Reginald to the ground. Stewart wrenched the gun away and planted a knee in his captive's back.

Anna said, "I'll find something to bind…"

The front doors opened and six constables burst in, a worried Bishop Michaels behind them.

Reginald, shouting about who he was and how they had no right to put their hands on him, was soon dragged off to jail.

Anna laced her arm through Stewart's. "I never realized his mind was so unsound." She leaned her head on Stewart's shoulder and looked up at him. "At least we can go forward now. No more kidnap attempts, no Leopard Men, nothing but what God has planned for our lives."

Stewart pulled away just far enough to hold Anna at arm's length and drink in the sight of her in that borrowed dress with all its satin and lace. "Reginald was wrong, you know."

"About what?"

He cupped her scarred cheek in his hand. "You need no concealment. You are beautiful to me. The mark you bear will forever remind me of your courage and strength."

He leaned down to share a kiss just as Momma Elliott came out from the sanctuary and gave them both a pointed look. "The bishop is ready again and waiting. I believe we still have a wedding to attend." She turned and walked back.

Once the sanctuary door closed, Stewart pulled Anna into his arms, looked down at her and said, "You know, while I was coming for you, God showed me what you meant when you talked about the limits of my ability to protect those I love. I do trust Him, Anna. I'll come running with my rifle when the situation warrants, but I know that God will never let you out of His sight. I believe that now."

Anna beamed. "I'm so happy you see that truth."

She took his hand and pulled him toward the sanctuary. "Come on, we'll walk down the aisle together."

Stewart took Anna's arm in his and they went to join the bishop at the altar. Strains of the processional music began when they were already partway to the altar. They took their places and the bishop began, "Dearly Beloved..."

Stewart fingered the surprise in his pocket that he had for Anna. After their vows, Bishop Michaels called for the rings. Stewart pulled out the garnet he'd been hand-polishing ever since Anna had agreed to marry him. Getting it set had been the tricky part, but it was worth every bit of trouble for the look of surprise and wonder in those big brown eyes as he slid it onto her delicate hand. Later he'd tell her why he'd chosen something from this wild, untamed land to be on her finger always. It was meant as a reminder to them both of where and how their love had truly become a match made in Heaven. Stewart could only marvel as he bent to claim a kiss from his new wife how he'd come to this country for one treasure and was leaving with the greatest treasures of all.

Epilogue

Anna stood by her new husband at the ship's railing, watching the retreating shoreline of Liberia. She squeezed Stewart's hand for reassurance.

Stewart wrapped his arm around her. "We'll be leaving the States again before you can blink."

"I know. Between the speaking engagements the Mission Board lined up and getting your mother set up in her new home with a housekeeper, I think we'll be busy right up till your next mining assignment."

"Are you going to be disappointed if they send me somewhere besides Liberia? If American Mining abandons the idea of buying that mining concession, my next assignment could be anywhere in the world."

She looked up. "Liberia will always be special, but wherever you go is now my home. I can minister anywhere."

He leaned in for a tender kiss. As their lips met, she reeled with joy.

He ended the kiss and she saw the amused faces of the other passengers. Heat flooded her cheeks. "Stewart, we're in public view."

He laughed. "You're my wife. I plan to make a habit

of kissing you. In fact, I formally rescind any previous promise to not spin the missionary like a top and add that I will kiss her when I please, provided you agree, of course."

She laughed. "Perhaps in less public situations?"

"Are you feeling shy? I'm pretty sure everyone on board already heard the story of our wedding. If not, they will by the evening gathering in the Saloon. A good tale travels fast on board ship."

"Oh, my. I hadn't thought about everyone knowing our story."

"Don't be embarrassed, darling. When people ask, think of it as an opportunity to tell about God's goodness in our lives."

She nodded. "When did you get so smart about sharing the Gospel?"

"I watched a beautiful missionary and learned from her. To think I came here with one form of riches on my mind but left with so much more."

"For me, as well. I'm leaving with a new husband, a mother-in-law and the hope of my own family coming to Christ."

"I'm just glad I get this time with you all to myself before we arrive."

Anna rested her head against him. "Me, too. The time will also help me prepare to see my parents again."

He gave a gentle squeeze. "I'll be right there by your side."

Anna pulled away. "From his latest telegram, I am cautiously optimistic his change of heart is sincere. His shock at Reginald's attempt to kidnap and kill me rang true in his reply."

"I agree. But it wasn't until the authorities back in Connecticut confirmed a few things that I finally believed your father wasn't involved." Stewart pulled her away from the railing. "I'm glad you've been able to forgive him and put the past behind you. And speaking of putting the past behind you, we're at the wrong end of the ship, my darling."

"What are you talking about?"

"I think we need to move to the ship's bow."

She followed him, waiting to hear why.

When they stood at the bow, he said, "The time for looking back is over. Our future, Mrs. Hastings, lies ahead of us."

* * * * *

Dear Reader,

I'm often asked by former mission workers how I "get it right," when I've never traveled to Liberia and never served on a long mission trip. I must confess—I am a total research nut. I get lost in reading personal journals, letters and books written by former missionaries. I know I don't get everything right, but research, scores of volumes and hours, is how I create the settings and the characters between my pages—characters like Anna and Stewart in this book, or Mary and William in *The Doctor's Mission.* The happily-ever-afters, however, aren't from research books but from thirty-six years of experience with my own romance hero, a man I'd follow into the deepest jungle anywhere.

I love hearing from readers. Here's how to connect with me: www.debbiekaufman.com, www.facebook.com/debbiekaufmanfanpage, www.twitter.com/debbie_kaufman or debbiekaufmanauthor@gmail.com. You can also write to me at P.O. Box 444, Griffin, GA 30224.

Blessings,
Debbie Kaufman

Questions for Discussion

1. After Anna hears the bad news that she lost her financial support and then is the victim of an attack, she still wakes with a certainty that God is in control and has a plan for her life. Is that a realistic attitude? Have you ever faced a situation where it seemed that everything you'd planned for was about to be lost? If so, what was your reaction and how did it work out?

2. In the first chapter we learn that Anna defied her parents' wishes in order to fulfill her calling to serve God as a foreign missionary. When you consider God's commandment to honor our parents, do you think Anna's decision was a godly one? Can we honor our parents and still take actions that defy their wishes?

3. The bishop states his belief that it was "God's providence" that Stewart came to Monrovia when he did. What do you believe about God's providence versus chance and circumstances? Have you ever had a situation where you believe it was God's providential provision that saved the day?

4. When Stewart suffered a mustard-gas attack in the trenches of the war, he looked for God to deliver him. When Divine intervention didn't change the situation, he concluded that God didn't exist. How do we account for the existence of a loving God in a world where terrible things happen? Has your own

faith ever been challenged? Where do you believe God was in that situation?

5. One of Anna's objections to guiding Stewart to the Pahn village is the fear that mixing God's business with man's business will interfere with the effectiveness of the Gospel. In what circumstances, if any, do you think that the two can be mixed? Do you have any examples of when it worked or didn't work?

6. Both Stewart and Anna have dire needs for money; Stewart to care for his mother and Anna to save an endangered child and continue her mission work. Yet, at the rope bridge crossing, Anna cautions Stewart about the dangers of wealth. Why does she do this? Is money itself a source of evil? How can wealth change us?

7. On their journey, Anna reveals to Stewart that she was not only punished for her defiance of her father's marriage plans, but also held prisoner in her home so she would not be able to go to the mission field. Have you ever faced persecution for your faith? How does Anna's explanation that "in God, we receive the strength to walk through life's trials, whether we are delivered from them or not" match your experience or beliefs?

8. Anna struggles with the beauty that God gave her and feels her appearance will only cause men to want her for the wrong reasons. How hard is it to look past someone's outward appearance and see

who they really are? Have you ever judged someone by their appearance only to find out they were very different from what you expected?

9. After Anna's attack by the Leopard Men, Stewart lays out a logical argument to back up his plea for Anna to leave the village for her own safety. Anna answers him by saying she won't needlessly sacrifice her life, but is prepared to die for her faith if necessary. How do you feel about that attitude? Is dying for one's faith ever necessary? Can you think of a situation in which you would be prepared to make that sacrifice?

10. When Anna and Stewart are finally honest with each other about their feelings and then acknowledge why faith makes a relationship between them impossible, do you think they are right or wrong? Why doesn't "love conquer all" in this situation?

11. Stewart speaks plainly to Anna, showing her the destructive pattern in her life of men who use her for their own gain. Anna is forced to confront her own unforgiveness toward her father before she can even begin to address what the chief did to her. How does this fit with your view of missionaries or others who hold a visible role in spreading the Gospel? Can we serve God and still harbor our own issues? How does forgiving her father change things for Anna? For Stewart? How can forgiving others change things for us?

12. As he kisses his new bride, Stewart realizes that he came to Liberia seeking one type of treasure and yet is leaving with "the greatest treasures of all." What are his greatest treasures? What are yours?

COMING NEXT MONTH FROM
Love Inspired® Historical

Available February 4, 2014

HEARTLAND COURTSHIP
Wilderness Brides
Lyn Cote

Former soldier Brennan Merriday will help Rachel Woosley with her homestead—but only until he has enough money to leave town. Can Rachel convince him that he has a home—and family—in the heartland?

THE MARSHAL'S READY-MADE FAMILY
Sherri Shackelford

Discovering he's the sole guardian of his orphaned niece has thrown Marshal Garrett Cain's world out of balance. Luckily feisty JoBeth McCoy has the perfect solution: marriage.

HEARTS REKINDLED
Patty Smith Hall

Army air corps informant Merrilee Davenport will do anything to ensure her daughter's safety—even spy on her former husband. When a crisis forces them to work together, will secrets drive them apart again?

HER ROMAN PROTECTOR
Milinda Jay

To rescue her baby, noblewoman Annia will search the treacherous back alleys of Rome. A fierce Roman legionary holds the key, but she must trust him with her life—and her heart.

SPECIAL EXCERPT FROM

When the family he's been searching for finally returns, Blake Cooper's not sure if he can ever forgive *or* forget.

Read on for a preview of
THE COWBOY'S REUNITED FAMILY
by Brenda Minton, Book #7 in the
COOPER CREEK *series.*

"I can't undo what I did." She leaned back against the wall and with her fingers pinched the bridge of her nose. Soft blond hair framed her face.

"No, you can't." He guessed he didn't need to tell her what an understatement that was. She'd robbed him. She'd robbed Lindsey. Come to think of it, she'd robbed his entire family. Lindsey's family.

Jana's shoulder started to shake. Her body sagged against the wall and her knees buckled. He grabbed her, holding her close as she sobbed into his shoulder. She still fit perfectly and he didn't want that. He didn't want to remember how it had been when they were young. He didn't want her scent to be familiar or her touch to be the touch he missed.

It all came back to him, holding her. He pushed it away by remembering coming home to an empty house and a note.

He held her until her sobs became quieter, her body ceased shaking. He held her and he tried hard not to think about the years he'd spent searching, wishing things could have been different for them, wishing she'd come back.

"Mrs. Cooper?"

He realized he was still holding Jana, his hands stroking her hair, comforting her. His hands dropped to his sides and she stepped back, visibly trying to regain her composure. She managed a shaky smile.

"She'll be fine," he assured the woman in the white lab coat, who was walking toward them, her gaze lingering on Jana.

"I'm Nurse Bonnie Palmer. If you could join me in the conference room, we'll discuss what needs to happen next for your daughter."

Jana shook her head. "I'm going to stay with Lindsey."

Blake gave her a strong look and pushed back a truckload of suspicion. She wasn't going anywhere with Lindsey. Not now. He knew that and he'd fight through the doubts about Jana and her motives. He'd do what he had to do to make sure Lindsey got the care she needed.

He'd deal with his ex-wife later.

He's committed to helping his daughter, but can Blake Cooper ever trust the wife who broke his heart?

Pick up THE COWBOY'S REUNITED FAMILY to find out. Available February 2014 wherever Love Inspired® Books are sold.

LIEXP0114

Love Inspired™®

Love the Love Inspired book you just read?

Your opinion matters.

Review this book on your favorite book site, review site, blog or your own social media properties and share your opinion with other readers!